STORIES FROM AN OLD TOWN

GRACE, GRIEF, AND GOSSIP IN A RURAL MINNESOTA TOWN

To Henry and Mary -
I hope you enjoy these stories, set in old Mt. Lake, the home of my grandparents Johann and Helena Jungas. The photo on the cover shows the front of his hardware store and windows of their home above it.
Phyllis Martens

PHYLLIS MARTENS

outskirtspress
DENVER, COLORADO

Stories from an Old Town
Grace, Grief, and Gossip in a Rural Minnesota Town

v3.0 r1.0

Outskirts Press, Inc.
http://www.outskirtspress.com

ISBN: 978-1-4327-9532-0

Library of Congress Control Number: 2012919990

PRINTED IN THE UNITED STATES OF AMERICA

CONTENTS

WINDAMER 1

TANTE LIEZE AND THE WILL OF GOD - Grandma's sister 4

HEINRICH - Grandma's brother 22

TAUNTE JOHT 40

THE DRUG STORE 61

SARAH 82

JAKE 102

SPRING STORM 130

THE APOLOGY 146

EVA 158

THE BAKER Grandma is the main character 181

GARDEN OF GRACE 195

A FAREWELL FOR AGANETHA 221

GUIDE TO LOW GERMAN TERMS AND PRONUNCIATION 231

WINDAMER

WHEN CATTAIL COUNTY, Minnesota, was established by the Territorial Legislature on May 23, 1857, prairie grass stretched over the rolling hills unbroken save by lakes, creeks, and a few Indian burial mounds. The whites, frightened off by occasional Indian massacres, did not move in until after the Civil War, when veterans began homesteading on land given them by the federal government in lieu of cash.

It was in fact a trapper who first settled in the area and who gave the town its name. In 1865 John Marsh, having taken a liking to the territory north of the Minnesota-Iowa state line because of its winding creeks and numerous small lakes ringed with cattails, well suited to trapping, and seeing that the gently sloping land was good for farming, should he later take a mind to it, built a strong log cabin on a rise covered with oak, elm, wild plum, and chokecherry bushes. The cabin overlooked a pleasant lake, which he named Big Minnow. A smaller lake five miles distant he named Little Minnow.

"Big Minnow!" his wife exclaimed when she moved into the cabin a few months later. She had attended school in the East and brought with her three treasures: a thick handmade quilt, a set of blue willow china, and a small box of ragged schoolbooks. Thumbing through the books, she came across the poems of Wordsworth and the name Windermere. "There you are," she told John. "That's a fittin' name.

Look how the wind blows little ripples across the water in the evenin'. Wind on the lake. Windermere." Marsh did not care one way or the other, and Windermere the name became, shortened almost at once to Windamere in the imprecise speech of the settlers. When in 1870 the town was platted, the county clerk shortened the name still further (unprotested, Mrs. Marsh having long since moved on) to Windamer.

Because it lay on a main railroad line between St. Paul and Sioux City, the little town survived. High-fronted stores and houses of gray lumber went up along muddy streets, lined up behind wooden sidewalks. In the fields, farmers mowed down the prairie grass and plowed up the yellow and blue clay. Horse-powered threshers harvested crops of hay, flax, and wheat.

In the years 1873 to 1878, Rocky Mountain locusts drove out the homesteaders. Their lands were bought up—acreage, buildings, and implements—for cash by incoming German Russian immigrants fleeing revolution and the draft, looking for good land. Others followed. They were religious people: Lutherans, Catholics, Mennonites.

A two-room schoolhouse was built in 1883. Teachers were stern. Laziness was not tolerated. Children learned to read, spell, write a beautiful slanting hand, and do sums; except the retarded Thelicke boy, who for his hopeless inability to learn was beaten daily and sent to sit by himself in the outhouse.

By 1900 the town was dotted with churches and tense with controversy. The conservative immigrants held stubbornly to old ways. They built house and barn together in the Russian style, farmed with immense energy, and on Sundays held long services in which sermons were read and musical instruments prohibited. Few ministers received salaries or were allowed to exchange pulpits. Footwashing was in; worldly amusements were out; and Sunday School, that new and foreign idea, was hotly debated. A formal and correct High German was the language used in Mennonite churches; but at home the families spoke Low German, a dialect which incorporated Dutch and English sounds.

Townsfolk of less stringent beliefs were more progressive. They met for worship in well-built churches, made business deals over coffee at the town's single eating place (later taken over by Bruno Steuke), and furnished their houses with pianos, flowered carpets and fine glassware. Their children went to the town elementary school and, after it was built, high school. Classes were taught in English. Small-town events, such as competitive ball games and band concerts in the park, were popular.

All business establishments except three—the hotel, the saloon, and one lumberyard—were owned by solid church-goers. The town had no theater. On Saturday nights the farmers came to town to shop, and on Sunday all businesses were closed tight as a drum, except the hotel and the saloon.

The first resident doctor arrived in 1921: a handsome man, single, urgently wooed by those single ladies who had no objections to his religious views, for he was Presbyterian. By that time a home for the elderly had been built, and a small hospital.

Four, five, sometimes six trains a day hooted through the town. Windamer was connected by rail to Chicago, Minneapolis-St. Paul, Omaha, and Sioux City. A crowd of townsfolk in black coats and hats standing near the yellow wooden depot, looking anxiously down the tracks for signs of an incoming train, denoted either the arrival of relatives from the Old Country or the departure of missionaries.

No Windamer farmer starved during the Depression.

TANTE LIEZE AND THE WILL OF GOD

HARD TIMES HAD come upon Tante Lieze Gunter. "As if your other troubles weren't enough," the women told her in Stoesz's General Store, standing between the counters in their square heavy coats and woolen head shawls. The pleasant odor of coffee, pinewood flooring, and new cloth hung in the air.

Tante Lieze closed her purse and picked up her shopping bag, ready to go home. "*Et jeyt*," she said in Low German. "It goes."

"But—in the basement! It's too damp. It isn't good. And what about Lentye?" The women shook their heads and clucked their tongues. "You can't leave her alone, surely?"

"*Na nae*, Frieda is with her."

Tante Lieze left the store and walked down the road, slowly because her knees pained her. Her hands, too, crooked and knobbed at the joints, reddened from much washing, hurt incessantly. Well, the women were right. It wasn't good, she knew that herself. It would have been better, much better, to continue living upstairs. It was much warmer and lighter up there. The basement was certainly damp, and not enough light got in—it was really almost dark when the snow piled up against the small high window. She frowned, remembering that the renters had let the water run over again—the linoleum under the sink in the upstairs bathroom was getting rotten, already breaking off in crumbling pieces and showing the black soaked wood underneath. If something wasn't done, even the flooring would soon rot through. She determined to speak to her brother Heinrich about it. He knew carpentry and would know what to do.

She walked with heavy steps along the uneven sidewalk, past the city park, deserted except for a dog sniffing about in the dirt, and along a row of white frame houses, each with a front porch reached by two or three wooden steps. The yards were a tangle of blackened bushes and dried brown stems. Under the hedges lay dirt-speckled patches of snow. Farther down, the sidewalk ceased and she had to walk on the road, avoiding the muddy ruts left by carriage wheels and the thin tires of cars. Now in the late afternoon a brilliant sunshine glanced off the white houses and the wet trunks of trees.

When she reached her own house, she paused to admire the blue cedar growing tall and shapely in the front yard. She twisted off a small sprig and put it in her bag. Then she went around to the back and descended the cement steps into the basement.

She stopped by the old iron stove in the outer room to make sure the fire had not gone out, stirred up the coals smoldering under a layer of ash, and moved the kettle forward to heat. She walked past the drain in the center of the floor to the washing machine, where she inspected bundles of clothes piled in a large basket, to be ironed yet tonight for Mrs. Abram Penner. Satisfied that all was in order, she moved toward the inner room and opened the door—carefully, so as not to bump into Lentye, who would have heard her coming and be waiting by the door.

But Lentye was not at the door. She had found a bright spot of sunlight in the middle of the floor and was sitting in it, laughing, her blind eyes lifted toward the little window above. She can tell there is light, at least, Tante Lieze thought. The cat was curled up in Lentye's lap, asleep.

Frieda was sitting at the table drinking coffee. Near her elbow a pile of dirty bowls, spoons and plates lay ignored. She wore a yellow cotton dress, cut low at the neck and adorned with a ruffle, badly sewed on. Bright pink rouge covered the hollows of her cheeks. She nodded in greeting when her mother entered.

Tante Lieze set her bag on the table, took out the sprig of cedar and put it into Lentye's hand. The girl immediately put it to her nose.

"*Joh*, cedar smells good," Frieda remarked, watching with interest.

"You fed her, then, Frieda?" Tante Lieze asked.

"*Joh*." Frieda began turning her cup around in the saucer. "Taunte Tina went home from the hospital. I heard it at the dime store from Mrs. Henshaw."

Tante Lieze took off her coat and shawl and hung them on a hook beside the curtain which hid the bed. Then she sat down on the sofa to take off her wet shoes, putting on instead a pair of knitted slippers worn through at the toes.

Frieda continued in her flat voice. "They opened her up but they couldn't do nothing. They just closed her up again and said she could go home. Doctor Schultz said to feed her good to keep up her strength. But she won't get no better. They didn't tell her about the cancer. She thinks she'll get better pretty soon."

Tante Lieze looked at her sharply. "You don't go and tell her. That's for the family to do, if they want to."

"*Na, nae*, I won't tell her." Frieda was arranging bread crumbs in little rows on the oilcloth. "Norah's having a terrible time. Taunte Tina won't eat. The room smells something awful . . . she don't always call them in time. Norah has to wash the sheets every day."

Tante Lieze was silent. She had found out from her sister Helena Jungas, who lived above the hardware store and had asked her up for coffee, that most of this was true. She got up and began clearing away the dirty dishes into a small tub to carry into the outer room for washing. "You should have cleaned up, you had time," she told Frieda crossly.

"*Joh*, I had time." Frieda watched her but did not move. "I thought it would be nice to bring Taunte Tina a new washcloth from the dime store. A nice new soft one with red stripes. They got new scarves too—silk ones, black silk scarves with nice fringes. You need a new scarf."

Tante Lieze retorted, annoyed, "I don't need a scarf."

"*Joh*, you need a new scarf," Frieda insisted. "The embroidery is all coming out of your old one." She pointed to the frayed green shawl hanging on the hook.

"It's good enough," Tante Lieze said shortly. She wished Frieda would go home. Frieda was a *plaupamuel*, a blabber-mouth. One daughter couldn't talk at all, the other rattled on all the time about nothing.

"I heard Helena got a new set of dishes," Frieda remarked. "Mrs. Teichrob saw them yesterday when she went up for coffee. A glass set—a nice new pink glass set. Johann brought it up from the store. You should tell Helena to give you her old set. All your cups have cracks." She showed her mother the crack in her cup.

"*Ach waut*!" Tante Lieze exclaimed. "I won't ask her for anything. You don't have to, either." She had found an old rag in the corner behind the cupboard and was wiping off her muddy shoes. Helena had once wanted to give her a coat some visitor had left behind, but she had refused it—she would much rather wear her own coat even if it was old and much too thick; she didn't need anybody's castoffs. She had not told Frieda about the coat, or every farmer's wife and even the geese and pigs would have heard about it, including the visitor who had left it behind.

She went into the other room to set the shoes near the stove to dry. Returning, she asked, "Was Lentye quiet?"

"*Na joh*, she was quiet. She likes the sun. It's warm. You should put the stove in here, to keep her warm."

Tante Lieze looked at her, exasperated. "If we put the stove in here she would burn herself. You better go now. You need to look after your children."

Frieda made no move to get up but sat running her finger up and down the crack in the cup. "I heard Mrs. Jauntz the preacher's wife from the Valley Church say God was punishing you. She said Dietrich was a sinner and now the child is suffering because of it."

"*Nae*! That she did not say!"

"*Joh.* She said it. I was standing near by her at the bakery. I heard her tell Mrs. Henry Braun that God is punishing you because of Dietrich. I heard her say it." Frieda nodded emphatically.

Tante Lieze was silent. Perhaps it was true. She herself had often wondered if God was punishing her, or Dietrich, or both of them, for their sins. She had not, in her youth, paid much attention to God. Her dreams had been of a large fine house, elegant gowns with lace and ruffles, fancy meals served on gold-rimmed china plates. But it had not worked out. It was Helena, her younger sister, who had the fine house above the hardware store. Dietrich's sins, however, had not been committed in his youth, but later. She never spoke of him to anyone. If the women attempted to commiserate with her for his desertion, she said merely, "*De es schwack* . . . that one is weak."

Nevertheless she answered Frieda firmly, "Lentye is not a punishment for your pa. She was born two years and more before he left." She looked again at Frieda. If God was punishing her, this empty-headed daughter with her shiftless husband and wild dirty children was more a punishment even than Lentye, who couldn't help being what she was.

The cat jumped suddenly out of Lentye's lap and sniffed at bits of bread fallen on the floor near the table. Lentye dropped her cedar twig and felt around for the cat, uttering hoarse cries.

"Here, take your spoon," Tante Lieze said. She put a spoon from the drawer into the girl's hand. Lentye quieted down and began rocking back and forth, waving the spoon.

Frieda, looking wise, piled up crumbs on the oilcloth. "She said God was punishing you."

"Frieda," Tante Lieze said wearily, "don't repeat everything people say. It's time for you to go home and do your work."

They heard the outside door slam, running feet. The door to the room burst open and a small black-haired boy rushed in. "Is Mamma here?" He ran to the kitchen cupboard, flung open the doors and began searching through the shelves.

"*Joh*, I'm here," Frieda said. She got up and took her coat from the couch.

Tante Lieze shut the cupboard doors with a bang. "Rudy, if you want something to eat, ask for it decently," she ordered.

The cat had run behind the couch. The boy, dashing after it, leaped on the couch, hung over the back and thrust his arm behind it, groping for the cat. Lentye banged her spoon on the floor and whimpered.

"Rudy, go outside—you're bothering Lentye," Tante Lieze commanded sharply.

"She's a baby!" he exclaimed. Abandoning the search for the cat, he jumped off the couch and grabbed at her spoon. Lentye spit and screamed. She would not let go of the spoon.

Tante Lieze caught the boy by the shoulders. "Shame on you! That's her spoon, she screams if she doesn't have it. Now go out! Right away! Your mother is going home too."

"Lentye's a silly baby!" he repeated; but turned and darted out the door.

Lentye was howling now in blind fury, throwing herself about on the floor. Someone thumped loudly on the ceiling above them. Tante Lieze hurried to the cupboard and took from a shelf a round white peppermint, which she thrust into the girl's hand. Lentye put the peppermint in her mouth and sucked on it; saliva began dripping down her chin.

"They don't like it when she screams," Tante Lieze told Frieda angrily. "I told you to keep your children away. They're much too rough—who can stand it?"

"*Joh,* I told them not to come here," Frieda said. She lingered a moment, then slowly walked out the door.

Tante Lieze picked up a washcloth to wipe the slobber from Lentye's face. Slowly, for her knees hurt badly now, she finished putting away the foodstuffs from her bag and wiped the crumbs from the oilcloth. Seeing that Lentye was quiet, she brought in the laundry from the other room. She spread the clothes one by one on the table, flicked water from a bowl evenly over them, using her fingers, then rolled them up tightly and returned them to the basket. Taking a pan of leftover *borscht* from the cupboard, she went into the outer room and put it on the stove to heat.

After supper she set her irons on the stove. When Lentye had at last fallen asleep on the couch—a sagging wine-colored wreck brought down from the back porch—she got out the ironing board and started ironing Mrs. Penner's washing, ignoring the pain in her hands.

She wondered if God was indeed punishing her, as Mrs. Jauntz had said. Mrs. Jauntz had probably heard it from her husband, a minister, who should know about such things. She had thought briefly about this after Lentye was born, but in the main had accepted her child as one accepts the difficulties of life. Was it true, after all? Was God mean in spirit, like some of the people in this town? After a while she remembered the man who had been born blind, not because of his own sins or those of his parents, but so that God's glory would be made known. She turned the thing over in her mind. At last, thinking of God's grace and glory, she became sure that something good would come of this deformed child. Lentye was born thus, she concluded, not as a punishment for anybody's sins, but because it was God's will. Why, she did not yet know, perhaps to teach other people compassion. As for Frieda, that was another matter entirely.

She ironed until very late: pillowcases embroidered with delicate blue roses, ruffled aprons, a man's starched white shirts; and then went to bed.

The next time Frieda stopped by, wanting a crochet pattern, Tante Lieze told her, "Lentye is not a punishment, I don't believe it. It is God's will she is this way. Something good will come from it. You can go tell Mrs. Jauntz that. Tell Mrs. Henry Braun too while you're at it."

But Frieda looked wise. "*Nae,* she said it was because of Dietrich, he was going out with that woman in Mankato."

Tante Lieze turned away. It was useless to argue with Frieda; once an idea got into her head it was set solidly in cement, there was no getting it out again.

The weather was unseasonably warm for several days. The roads dried. People put their fur hats back on closet shelves. Two women, the Heppner sisters, came to visit one morning, bringing with them a small accordion and a jar of canned crab apples for Lentye. "*Fael mal dank'schoen* . . . thank you very much," Tante Lieze said. She knew Lentye would spit the apples out all over her bib, but it was nice of them to bring something.

Lentye, knowing from the sounds that visitors were in the room, began to show off. She giggled, made loud noises, threw her arms about, and ducked her head in grotesque gestures. The women drew back. They looked at the girl, at the vacant eyes, drooping drooling mouth, dull yellow hair tangled on the misshaped head. "She won't let me comb her hair—the comb hurts her, she jerks away," Tante Lieze explained, ashamed.

The sisters shook their heads. "You have a heavy cross to bear, Mrs. Gunter."

"God made her this way," she replied after a moment. "Something good will come of it."

Marie Heppner asked doubtfully if she should play the accordion. Tante Lieze said it would be fine, Lentye liked any kind of music. At the first wheezing sound Lentye stiffened, turned her head and sat erect, listening. Her body sank into utter stillness, the thin useless legs folded under her. Watching her, Tante Lieze remembered that once when she was scarcely two years old, Lentye had listened thus to a small music box Helena had given her for Christmas.

When Marie stopped playing, Lentye began rocking restlessly. "Goh-gud!" she shouted, banging her spoon on the floor. "Goh-gud! Goh-gud!" The sisters, not comprehending, looked at Tante Lieze.

"She wants you to sing '*Grosser Gott, Wir Loben Dich*,' Tante Lieze explained.

"Oh, no, we can't sing," they exclaimed. But out of pity for the child, they sang in their thin elderly voices. Tante Lieze, thankful for their presence, joined in. The sisters left, promising to come again soon. They were greatly pleased that Lentye had liked the accordion.

In the afternoon Tante Lieze washed the Dunsmore clothes. With a long wooden spoon she lifted the heavy wet things in and out of the near-boiling soapy water and ran them through the wringer. The hot water scalded her hands and ran down her arms so that her sleeves, though folded back to the elbow, got soaked. She hung the clothes outside to dry in the wind. Afterwards she sat down at the table to sew up a rip in Lentye's nightgown; but her hands pained her and she put the nightgown aside.

Lentye was pulling herself around on the floor from table to cupboard, cupboard to sofa, tapping her spoon in queer little rhythms on the legs of the furniture. The cat lay on the back of the couch, watching through slitted eyes.

Someone knocked on the door. The footsteps had been so light that even Lentye had not heard them. It was little Carly, Taunte

Tina's granddaughter. She would not come in but peered through the half-open door at Lentye. "My mamma said, please come to see grandma as soon as you can," she said.

"Today?" Tante Lieze asked in surprise.

Carly didn't know. After a moment's thought Tante Lieze said, "Tell her I will come tomorrow about four o'clock, after I go to the store. Wait, I want to give you something." She took the coin purse from her handbag, found a nickel and held it out to the child. "Here, buy some candy at Uncle Klaas's store. But don't take long, your mamma wants you home."

The child advanced timidly into the room. She was wearing a red coat and a striped knitted cap with a white tassel. Eyes shining, she took the nickel and immediately ran out.

When Frieda arrived next day, Tante Lieze had already put on her coat and the frayed green shawl. A small jar tied into a cloth stood on the table. "Keep Lentye quiet," she told Frieda. She put the jar in her handbag and started for town. The air was pure and cold, fresh with the scent of evergreen trees growing in the front yards of houses along the street. The sky was overcast—it would snow again soon.

At the store Tante Lieze bought sugar, flour and coffee and asked the boy to deliver them to her house, at the back door. Then she set out for Taunte Tina's, seven blocks west beyond the creek. She wondered why Taunte Tina wanted to see her. They were not good friends, though everybody knew the old lady: she had been the midwife on call for years before Dr. Schultz finally came. Well, it was too bad, she wouldn't live long, they said.

When she reached the creek, she stopped on the bridge and leaned on the rail to rest. A few weeks ago the creek had been frozen over, a thick sheath of ice covered with twigs and dirt stretching from bank to bank. But now a clear rill was flowing down between the sheets of ice—she could see the pebbles under the water. Clear pure water running through the dark ice, like the something good that was going to happen in the midst of her troubles, she thought.

She found Taunte Tina's house, small, set well back in an untended yard. She climbed the wooden steps and knocked. Norah, the daughter, let her in.

She found herself in the kitchen. A fire was going in the old range at one end of the room, and baking pans were set out on the big table, along with an enormous brown crockery bowl in which dough was rising. Across one end of the table papers lay scattered—Carly's school papers, Tante Lieze saw, with drawings on them and large crooked words printed in crayon.

"Mamma wants to see you," Norah said, and showed Tante Lieze into the bedroom.

The sickroom smelled of medicine and old sheets. Tante Lieze sat down on a plain wooden chair and looked toward the bed where Taunte Tina lay, so shrivelled she scarcely made a hump under the heavy quilt. Her gray hair straggled over the pillow. She glanced at Tante Lieze, then turned her head away as if she did not want to see her, after all.

"It's not going so good, Taunte Tina?" inquired Tante Lieze.

"Not so good," Taunte Tina whispered, and began to cough. Norah came in to give her a spoonful of medicine from a bottle on the dresser, and went back out without speaking.

At length Taunte Tina turned toward her visitor and looked at her with dim, watery eyes. She began to speak in great haste. It was about Lentye, she said. Something had gone wrong when she was born. It had been her fault, she had not been experienced, and the labor had been so difficult, so very difficult. She stopped.

"*Joh,*" Tante Lieze said. She remembered well enough.

Taunte Tina went on, her weak voice urgent. It wasn't going right, she hadn't known what to do. There had been no doctor in town. Finally she had used an instrument to pull the baby out. There were hollow places, Lentye's head had a wrong shape? Yes. She should have waited and let the baby come of itself, that was always the best way. But Tante Lieze had been in such pain, the labor had already been so long, she was afraid Tante Lieze would die, or the baby, maybe both . . . it was her fault that Lentye was the way she was. Her voice died away.

Tante Lieze clutched her handbag with both hands, troubled. "It was a hard birth."

"*Joh,* a hard birth." Taunte Tina's dim eyes searched the other's face. At last she said, her hands moving restlessly on the quilt, "I was afraid to tell you . . . I thought it might be the child would grow out of it . . . I thought Dietrich would be angry . . . I should have told you."

"It wouldn't have changed her," Tante Lieze said.

"No, it wouldn't have changed her." The old woman shrank together; water welled in the corners of the faded eyes.

Tante Lieze heard a door close. A moment later, looking out the window, she saw Carly in her red coat run down the path toward town, the white tassel of her knitted cap bobbing above the bright brown hair. She watched until the child disappeared around the corner.

Then she turned back to Taunte Tina and said firmly, "I brought you raspberry jam from my garden. You can eat, *joh*?" She took the jar from her handbag and untied the cloth.

Taunte Tina's face twisted as though she would cry. "A little . . . I didn't expect . . . ."

"Norah can put some on bread for you for supper," Tante Lieze said. "Try to eat, you need the strength." She stood up and went to the bed. "You did the best you could, Taunte Tina. You helped many people. It is for God to forgive our mistakes, yours and mine, and everyone's." She held the thin hand briefly, nodded goodbye, and went out of the room.

In the kitchen, Norah was stuffing Carly's school papers into the stove. She looked very tired. "This is for your mother," Tante Lieze said, giving her the jar of jam.

Norah thanked her and went with her to the door. "Thank you for coming. She wanted to see you—she was worried about something."

"Tell her it's all right, what she told me," Tante Lieze said. "Tell her not to worry any more." Norah nodded and closed the door quietly.

Tante Lieze walked slowly with bowed head. She paid no attention to the road. It had not been God after all, but Taunte Tina—an accident, a thing that perhaps need not have happened. Lentye could have been like Carly. She could have been like her father, quick in speaking and thinking. God had not intended this misshapen child. It had been the hard instrument in the panicked hands of Taunte Tina.

At the bridge she rested and looked at the water. The clear running rill mocked her. It would snow again, the creek would freeze over and become ugly, covered with dirt and twigs. Nothing good would come of Lentye's misfortune, she thought; it had not been God's will at all. After a time she walked on. She did not notice that the way home was long or that her knees were aching.

She picked up the bag of groceries standing at the back door and started down the basement steps. Lentye in the other room began shouting, "Taybah! Taybah!"

"Sshh, I'm coming!" Tante Lieze went in and took off her coat, nodded to Frieda, who was sitting on the couch, crocheting.

Frieda immediately began to ask questions. How did Taunte Tina look? Did she have blotchy brown spots on her face like Mrs. Sukau had before she died? Did the room smell bad? What had she wanted Tante Lieze to come over for? Lentye wouldn't eat, she said, because there wasn't any sugar for the *tweeback*, she always had to have sugar.

Tante Lieze shut her off angrily and sent her home. She saw that

Lentye had pulled everything out of the lower cupboard again—the baking pans, blue enamel ladles, mixing bowls, everything lay scattered on the floor. Lentye was rocking back and forth, crouched on the carpet.

Tante Lieze gave her a piece of bread to pacify her until supper could be prepared, but Lentye threw the dry bread on the floor.

Tante Lieze hurried to make coffee; put two *tweeback* in a bowl, poured hot coffee over them and sprinkled them with sugar from the grocery bag. She tied on Lentye's bib and lifted her into a chair—the bib, made of flour sacking, covered the girl like a barber's cloth.

She fed Lentye spoonful by spoonful. Lentye slobbered happily and tried to grab the bowl, but Tante Lieze slapped her hands. By the time supper was finished, the bib was soaked. Tante Lieze shook the wet crumbs out of it and hung it up to dry. Lentye, satisfied, settled down on the couch with her spoon, crooning softly to herself.

Tante Lieze knelt beside her then and felt her head, the familiar lumps and hollows, the flat slant where the head should have been round. She felt carefully through the tangled hair until Lentye jerked away.

She put Lentye to sleep on the couch, straightened up the room, brought in the Dunsmore clothes, sprinkled the shirts and blouses, and began ironing.

As she ironed she saw, not the huddled figure asleep on the couch, breathing with a hoarse snoring sound, but a shiny-eyed child in a red coat and gay tasseled cap running through the trees. Oh, she would have ironed day and night to buy Lentye a coat, a fine blue coat trimmed with fur, with a hood . . . they would have run together to Uncle Klaas's store . . . the child would have been like Dietrich, bright and quick, able to make beautiful things with her hands, she would have learned singing, arithmetic.

Her heart smote her that Norah had burned little Carly's school papers. It was true that she herself had thrown away Frieda's papers, she had not thought much about them. But if she had even one from Lentye, with her name written in straggling childish letters . . . Norah should not have burned them, she was burning treasures.

Tears were running down her face. She had to wipe them away so that they would not drip on the ironing. Her hands pained, but she ironed steadily, the blue and white striped shirts, a child's dainty nightgown, a tablecloth with tatted insets. She noticed that one shirt had a dirty streak at the collar band—she would have to wash it again.

As she ironed she wept as she had in the early days when she first knew the child would never be right, and when Dietrich left her. Dietrich, who could never bear to be near anything ugly, a maker of fine furniture. When Lentye was born he had looked at her vacant eyes, her crooked head and slobbering mouth, and said, "That is no work of God," and refused to touch her. Two years later he had gone to Mankato to find work, leaving her to struggle at home half out of her mind with worry. She had heard rumors that he had taken up with a woman in Mankato; then he had disappeared, they said to the Cities. Well, Dietrich had been right, Lentye was no work of God.

She tried to recall the labor, so many hours, but she had been too dazed with pain to know what was happening. Later on everyone had remarked on the misshaped head but had assured her that the baby would surely grow out of it, lots of babies looked that way after a hard birth.

She finished the ironing, put away iron and board. Finding the leftover coffee still warm at the back of the stove, she poured it into a cup, got out her German Bible to read before going to bed, as was her custom. But instead of opening it she put her folded hands on it and forgot completely what she had intended to do. She leaned her head on her folded hands and sat a long while without moving. The coffee grew cold in the cup, the yellow light bulb burned steadily, casting shadows into the corners. Lentye breathed hoarsely on the couch. And still Tante Lieze sat at the table.

At last she raised her head and said aloud, "*Eck kaun den nich feyaewe.* I can't forgive them." She spoke softly so as not to wake Lentye, but her words traveled back through twenty years of trouble and forward through the gray days, who knew how many more? God of course forgave their mistakes, she knew, but it seemed to her too great a debt these two owed her, Dietrich and Taunte Tina. She had forgiven Taunte Tina in the afternoon, seeing her distress, but now that she had thought about it, understood the enormous loss she and her child must bear all their lives, the bitterness had become too great to bear. Yet forgive them she must.

And in the end, whose fault was it? Was it Dietrich's fault that he could not find work in this town, that he lived in a small house with two troublesome children, one foolish, the other deformed, with a wife whose hands were red and rough from scrubbing other people's clothes? He had come from a rich place in the Old Country, the handsome son of a furniture-maker, an artist, speaking High German—he was the one who had insisted that she, like her sister Helena who as a businessman's wife belonged to the upper circles, be addressed as *Tante*, not that miserable Low German *Taunte*. Could she blame him for leaving what he could not bear? And Taunte Tina, she had done the best she could, she had borne her own bitter thoughts all these years, poor thing. Where was the fault, then? Whom must she, in the end, forgive for this burden that had fallen on her like a mountain never to be moved? It seemed to her that God could have helped them all a little.

And if God had not willed Lentye to be misshaped, had created her perfect, but through a mistake she had been damaged, did God now have power to bring something good out of that mistake not willed by him? She did not know. As for Frieda, who knew what had gone wrong to make her the way she was. Perhaps God had not intended her to be that way, either.

At last she arose and with heavy steps prepared for bed. As she pulled aside the curtain to find her nightgown, she remembered suddenly that the last time Dietrich left home, one of his shirts had been dirty—she had found it rumpled on the floor of the bathroom and in anger had thrown it in his suitcase that way.

She put out the light and sat down on the edge of the bed and wept again in the dark, this time not because of Lentye or Taunte Tina, but because Dietrich had liked things nice, and she had let him go like that in anger, with a dirty unwashed shirt.

When Taunte Tina died a few weeks later, Tante Lieze went to the funeral, taking with her two loaves of rye bread for the lunch.

In the months that followed, when visitors came to encourage her and inquire after Lentye, she no longer said to them, "It is God's will, some good will come of it." When they tried to console her with such words, she turned away and was silent or began speaking of something else.

She found herself speaking less sharply to Frieda, and accepted from her one day a gift of a tea towel Frieda had decorated with lumpy red crocheted edging. Frieda was inordinately proud of her handiwork and made sure on subsequent visits that her tea towel was hanging where it could be seen.

While she was ironing one evening, Tante Lieze pondered over Frieda's unruly children, thinking that they too lived in an imperfect situation not of their own making and that possibly their little heads, like hers, were full of unsolved problems. She began inviting the children to the basement for supper. She washed their clothes from time to time, showed them how to turn the wringer—they thought it great fun. When spring softened the ground, she gave Rudy a little garden plot and showed him how to plant radishes and carrots. To her surprise, he showed interest and came by often to make sure no weeds were growing in his plot. One of Frieda's girls, Trina, found a soft brush and brushed Lentye's hair. Lentye did not object to the soft touch; and Trina would tie up the dull hair with a ribbon and say that

Lentye was pretty. Tante Lieze would look up from her ironing . . . yes, she was pretty, *gauns schoen* . . . and smile a little.

Of what Taunte Tina had told her she said not a word, either to Frieda, or her sister Helena, or anyone else in the town.

HEINRICH

IN THE STRONG sunlight of an early summer afternoon, the dark shadow of Tante Lieze's house lay across the yard, sharp-edged like a cutout of black paper. Heinrich, following the path toward the back of the house, stopped in the shade and set down his suitcase. Behind him, men's work shirts and pants hung on wires strung between two iron poles—the renters' things, or washing Tante Lieze was doing for somebody. In the neighbor's garden, bordered by straggling red and orange zinnias, a woman in a faded yellow sunbonnet knelt pulling weeds. She paused to watch him approach. Heinrich nodded a greeting, but she turned back to her weeding.

Heinrich picked up the suitcase—leather, old, with straps and buckles—and continued toward the back door. His face was flushed, his gait unsteady. He stumbled over the iron mud scraper but caught himself on the handrail.

He pushed open the basement door with his foot and started down the cement steps, shifting the suitcase ahead of him. At the bottom he abandoned the suitcase and started across the dim room, stumbled again at the floor drain and stopped with a furious exclamation. He could hear Lentye's scrabbling noises in the other room. Pulling a handkerchief from his pocket, he wiped his face and neck, and opened the door.

Lentye, sitting on the floor, listening with her head raised, uttered a harsh burbling sound. He stepped past without looking at her and sat down at the table.

Across the small room Frieda sat on the couch crocheting something out of violently pink string. She watched Heinrich with bright curious eyes. Her flat cheeks were highly rouged. "*Na*, Heinrich, w*aut deist*?"

Heinrich glanced at her, frowning. "Where's Lieze?"

"She went to Stoesz's. She was out of sugar again. She needs it for Lentye's *tweeback. Tweeback* soaked in coffee with sugar, that's what she eats. If there ain't no sugar, she won't eat."

Heinrich snorted. "Lieze shouldn't feed her that stuff."

"*Na nae*, she should give her something else. Nice vegetables from the garden. Lentye spits everything out . . . ."

He cut her off with an exclamation and leaned his head on his hands. Lentye, who had been listening intently, now crawled toward him. When her groping hands touched his trouser leg she stopped. "Ah—ah—ah!" she cried, pointing toward her mouth.

Frieda burst out laughing. "She wants you to give her candy. Yesterday Taunte Wiensche brought her corn candy in a little sack, from the dime store, a nickel worth."

Heinrich pulled the clinging hand away impatiently. "I don't have candy. When is Lieze coming back?"

"Oh, I guess pretty soon. She has to walk slow, her knees bother her." Frieda was surveying him with great interest. "You been drinking again? I can smell it."

Heinrich snorted but did not answer or look at her.

"Ah–ah," Lentye insisted, pointing at her mouth.

Frieda got up and rummaged in the cupboard. "You can give her this peppermint. Ma always gets nice white peppermints from Klaas. He gives her extra for Lentye."

"Give it to her yourself," Heinrich said, turning away.

Frieda put the peppermint into the groping hand. Lentye

began to suck on it noisily, drooling. "She slobbers something terrible," Frieda remarked.

She returned to the sofa. "Old Man Steuke was drunk again last week. I saw him when I was coming home from Dickman's. He couldn't walk by himself. Steve Olsen was holding him under the arms, from behind. Old Man Steuke goes to Quevli's all the time, he likes . . . ."

"You talk too much," Heinrich interrupted irritably. He got up, went over to the high window and peered out.

Frieda picked up her crocheting, looked at it, put it down. "I saw Mrs. Ortman at Ben Franklin's dime store. She said somebody could run over Old Man Steuke and he wouldn't even know it. She said Peters is in trouble too."

Heinrich jerked around. "Which Peters?"

"The one from Gessel. The preacher."

"You're crazy! He doesn't drink!"

"*Na nae*," Frieda said complacently. "He doesn't drink. He went bankrupt. He has to sell his farm at auction. Mrs. Ortman said . . . ."

"*Dommheit*! Peters isn't bankrupt!" Heinrich exclaimed. He sat down again at the table and put his head in his hands.

"*Joh, joh*, he is," Frieda affirmed. "Mrs. Ortman, she told me. She's second cousin to Peters' wife—they was both Radtkes. She said Peters don't know how to farm."

"Can't you make that girl stop slobbering?" Heinrich gestured impatiently at Lentye.

"Better leave her alone," Frieda advised without moving. "If she starts screaming you can't stop her. The people upstairs get mad. They pound on the floor with the broom. They told Tante Liesze they'd call the marshal."

"Yes, yes, I know all that," Heinrich interrupted, irritated. He got up and began walking up and down the narrow room, glancing out the high basement window.

Frieda settled back comfortably. "Mrs. Ortman said Peters' machinery is always breaking down, he don't know how to fix it, he just ties it together with wire. She said . . . ."

"There's nothing wrong with Peters! He's a good man!" Heinrich darted an angry glance at her, then sat down again, his back to her, frowning.

"*Joh, joh*, he's a good man," Frieda agreed. "Mrs. Ortman said Peters built his outhouse in the wrong place, the wind blows the smell right to the house. She said . . . ."

A furious exclamation from Heinrich stopped her. Lentye had crawled to Heinrich's chair and now sat pulling at his trouser leg. He jerked away. "Wash her!" he commanded.

Frieda rose, got a wet cloth from the outer room, and knelt to wipe the girl's face. Lentye squirmed away, whimpering. All at once she sat upright, listening.

"Ma's coming," Frieda announced.

Heinrich became aware of his sister's slow tread in the other room. A moment later Tante Lieze entered, carrying her shopping bag. The cat slipped through the door at her heels.

"*Goondach*, Heinrich," she greeted him. "Lentye, the cat's in."

Lentye groped for the cat. It sniffed delicately at her fingers, then jumped into her lap and settled down. Lentye leaned over it, crooning softly.

"I told Heinrich that preacher Peters from Gessel went bankrupt," Frieda remarked, "but he don't believe it."

"I didn't hear it," Tante Lieze said shortly. "Here's the flour sacks you wanted from the dime store. You can look at them at home."

Frieda fingered the small parcel with interest. "*Joh,* I want to make dishtowels. My old ones are wore out. I can put crochet around them to look nice, pink, maybe green."

"*Joh, joh*, that's good." Tante Lieze sat down and took off her shoes. "Just don't dry the kettles with them this time."

"*Na nae*, not the kettles." Frieda gathered her things into a crudely stitched black cloth bag. "Mrs. Ortman said . . . ."

"Frieda, you go now," Tante Lieze ordered sharply. She stopped abruptly, then said in a gentler voice, "Thank you for coming."

Frieda walked slowly to the door. "*Na joh*, I'll come again." She looked around the room for a moment and walked out.

"Once she gets talking there's no stopping her," Tante Lieze said. "I have to send her home. It's bad, but I can't help it."

"She's got no sense at all," Heinrich exclaimed. "George should keep her home."

"*Joh*—if he was ever home himself." Tante Lieze got two cups from the cupboard, fetched the coffee pot from the stove in the other room, and poured coffee.

Heinrich drank his at once. "I need a place to stay," he told her.

Tante Lieze opened the parcel of sugar and stirred some into her coffee. "What's the matter with Tohfeld's—she asking too much?"

"They told me to get out. They heard I was going to Quevli's again." Heinrich leaned his head on one hand and stared at the oilcloth, once yellow with a pattern of blue cherries but now faded and badly cracked.

His sister looked at him. "Don't blame them, Heinrich, they have children at home. Grandma Wiens might take you, she has a room. But listen, don't go to Quevli's. Drinking don't hurt some men, but you—"

Frowning, Heinrich rubbed his finger along the cracks in the oilcloth. "Where shall I go then?" he burst out suddenly. "At Quevli's at least I can joke a little."

Tante Lieze thought a long while, stirring her coffee. At length she leaned forward. "Why not go back to Montana? You can get a piece of land there. You could find work, you're a good carpenter. Teacher, too—a school might take you."

Heinrich shifted uneasily but said nothing.

"Helena takes good care of the girls. They're happy with her. She's got plenty room for them. When you're settled you can come back for them."

"Better I don't see them," he muttered.

"Go and see them. They need to see their dad." Tante Lieze shoved her cup aside and looked earnestly at her brother. "Heinrich, listen, go to Montana. You're a young man yet, you don't have to throw your life away. Build a good house, then come and get the girls . . . make a good home for them, so they can be proud of you. They would be ashamed to see you bum around like Old Man Steuke. You're a fine man, educated. You don't have to stay in this town." After a pause she added, "God will help you. I pray for this every day."

"*Daut meent aula nusht*!" he exclaimed vehemently. "It means nothing!" He got up and walked to the window. "Before Maria died I prayed, sometimes all night. I knelt on the floor in the wash house, it was freezing but I didn't care. I promised God everything if he would let Maria live." He turned abruptly and sat down. "Now I don't pray."

She sighed. "You should talk it over with a minister."

"Listen, I met Jauntz from the Valley Church in the park one day. I asked him, why did Maria have to die? How can I understand this? You know what he said? He wagged his big beard up and down and said, 'You didn't have faith, brother. The prayer of faith saves the sick.' I asked him, 'Then why is your father-in-law flat in bed with a stroke for seven years now? Don't you have faith—or maybe you don't want him to get well?' He said that was the Lord's will, we must accept it. What kind of answer is that, once this way, once that way?"

"Oh—Jauntz! What does he know!" Tante Lieze answered with some heat. "Have you talked with Peters, though?"

Heinrich seemed not to have heard her. He stared moodily at the table.

"Peters—did you talk to him?" she prodded.

He glanced at her in annoyance. "*Joh, joh,* I talked to him."

"What did he say, then?" She folded her hands and waited.

"He said, 'We must believe in the goodness of God because without it the universe makes no moral sense.'"

Tante Lieze glanced at him sideways to see if he was making fun of her. Deciding he was not, she asked, "What means that?"

He glanced at her impatiently. "God never does anything bad."

"*Ach waut*! Any *dommsta* in kindergarten knows that! That's all he said?"

He refused to answer, but sat picking small pieces off the cracks in the oilcloth. Lentye began to whimper. The cat had jumped from her lap and was walking daintily along the top of the bookshelf, behind a studio photograph of a young woman with dark hair and eyes, fashionable in a filmy high-necked blouse with a collar of pointed lace.

"*Na, du Kaut*!" Lieze exclaimed. "He'll knock your picture down. *Hei,* get down!" The cat leapt from the bookshelf and stood by the door, meowing. Tante Lieze rose to let the cat out, then took an old black handbag from the cupboard and gave it to Lentye. "Here, you can have your purse." Lentya jerked the purse open and emptied it on the floor—spools, clothespins, jar rings.

"What did Peters mean?" Tante Lieze asked with dignity. "I'm only a woman but I can understand something!"

"You don't understand anything!" Heinrich exclaimed. "Peters says we must believe God is good because if he isn't, this world makes no sense."

She thought it over. "*Joh, so es et.* That's how it is."

Heinrich shook his head. "Look at Peters. An educated man—he reads Russian, German, Bulgarian, writes for papers in Canada—how does he live? On a farm like a ditch digger. He doesn't know farming. He should have a church in the Cities—they pay their preachers."

"It's his wife," Tanta Lieze said. "She doesn't want to leave her parents."

Heinrich made a disgusted noise. "You go over, talk some sense into her."

Tante Lieze was silent. At last she said, "Listen, I want to ask you something. Why did God give me these children? A cripple and a blabbermouth. Why not bright ones like yours?"

"Go ask Jauntz."

She glanced at him, annoyed. "You read books, I thought maybe you found an answer somewhere." She paused. "I heard somebody said Lentye was born like that to punish me and Dietrich because of our sins. That's what somebody said, but I don't believe it."

He slammed his hand hard on the table. "They know nothing! Whatever some *dommkopf* says they repeat—the words don't go through their heads even, just slide in one ear and out their mouth, like a thresh machine. Who thinks around here?"

"*Na joh*," she said, "they're farm people, how shall they think like you? Don't take it hard if they're simple." She looked at his flushed face anxiously. "Most of them want to help."

He glared at her. "When Maria died, did they come to help? Her own sisters . . . they squabbled like bunch of chickens over the furniture. They wanted to send my girls, all four of them, little as they are, one here, one there, to work on the farms when they got old enough. That's the kind of help I got!"

"Ssshh," Tante Lieze said, jerking her head toward Lentye. "Anyway, it didn't happen."

He glanced angrily at Lentye, but lowered his voice. "Now they ask me, why don't you go to church any more? We never see you at church!" He snorted. "Nobody wants me at church but the old maids—they're the ones that want me. Widow Goossen invited me to dinner, she thinks I'll marry her because of her garden with the white picket fence. That crazy Sarah makes cow eyes at me on the church yard. I won't go. Anyway the preachers talk nonsense."

"You can't blame those women—too few men around, and you're educated," she told him.

"So when I go to Quevli's to talk with the men, they gossip all over town what a sinner I am and decide I can't teach school any more." He jerked around in the chair and stared at the wall. "Nobody can live in this town. They're even dragging out stuff from twenty years ago."

She sighed. "It's true. *Nusht fejaeta, nusht fejaeva.* Forget nothing, forgive nothing."

They sat without speaking. At last Tante Lieze said, "Go to Montana. The people are good. You can get a job, things will be easier. Helena will look after the girls, Johann has plenty of money, he doesn't mind. Just go. There's nothing in this town for you."

He stared at the floor. "I could try it," he muttered at last. "If it doesn't work out, Schroeder said he might have carpenter work for me over in Dumfrey." He turned to her suddenly. "My books—are they here?"

She stood up, rummaged under the bed in the back corner, pulled out a cardboard box. "Take them along, you might need them." She picked up a notebook with cardboard covers. "Look, your Sunday School teacher notes—a whole book full."

He glanced at the pages, covered with fine German script. "Give it to Jauntz, maybe he could learn something."

"Take your picture of Maria along too, this time." She gestured toward the portrait of the young woman on the bookshelf. Heinrich did not turn his head.

"You could take the 10:40 train Saturday night, or Sunday," Tante Lieze went on. "I can wash your clothes. But fix the floor under the sink upstairs before you go." She pushed the box of books aside and moved toward the cupboard. "Now I make you supper."

"Nay, I'll eat at Steuke's."

"Well, sleep here then. You can have the couch. Lentye can come with me in the bed."

Hearing her name, Lentye crawled whimpering toward her mother. "Ssshhh, you can eat in a minute," Tante Lieze told her.

Heinrich looked at the clutter on the floor in disgust. "You should take her to the Home."

Tante Lieze gave him an angry look. "I took care of her nineteen years, I can take care of her nineteen more."

Heinrich got up and went to the door. She hesitated, then walked after him. "Heinrich, listen, Peters is right. It will work out. God will help you."

"Any fool can say that," he muttered.

"And any fool can trample it under his feet!" she retorted. "But listen, don't go to Quevli's. Go see the girls instead."

"*Na joh*," he said, and hurried out.

The air was cool now, and fresh after the stuffiness of the basement. The sun shone clear in the west and a breeze had sprung up. The washing outside flapped on the wires.

Heinrich walked rapidly toward town past the neat white houses, each in its green yard planted with peony bushes, lilacs and evergreens. Here and there a woman worked bent over in her garden, wide in the hips, head tied up in a kerchief. Small children climbed shrieking on piles of dirt or chased each other across the yard. Heinrich walked by without speaking to anyone.

Near the park he heard hammering—Schroeder's men were building some kind of wooden platform in the middle of the park. He remembered that the German Band was going to play that night; everyone would be in town.

A woman was coming towards him, tall, smartly dressed. A girl in white stockings walked beside her, carrying music books. "It's Teacher Jentzen!" the girl cried, and stopped. Heinrich recognized her as one of his former pupils. He prepared to greet her, but the mother, eyebrows arched, took the child by the elbow and moved her firmly past. "But mamma, I want to talk to him!" he heard the child protest. The mother said something in a sharp tone and hurried her on.

Heinrich stared after them; then walked slowly to Steuke's Chow House. Abe Steuke was the son of the town drunk and had to keep bailing his father out of jail.

The small restaurant smelled of fried pork and coffee. Heinrich strode past the men sitting at the front counter and sat down at a small table in the back. A young girl in a white blouse and black skirt, blonde hair tied back in a flowered kerchief, took his order of *borscht,* bread and coffee.

A stout man in overalls and blue work shirt stopped, eased himself into the chair opposite, nodding genially at Heinrich. "You don't want to eat alone, company's free," he said. "I'm Congers from Gessel. Came for one of Johann's oil stoves for the wife. She's tired of burning wood." He put out a large hand.

"Heinrich Jentzen."

The farmer regarded him with interest. "The school teacher, eh? Wife died ten, eleven months ago? Guess you ain't married again?"

Heinrich glared at him.

"No offense. Life's better with a wife, all I meant. Somebody to cook, iron the shirts. Who's got the girls?"

"My sister Helena Jungas."

"Good, that's good. Johann's got the money, hardware store's doing good business. Helena's careful, got a mind of her own though, wouldn't want to tangle with her." Congers winked at Heinrich, who made no response.

The waitress came up with a bowl of cabbage soup and a plate of rye bread, which she set before Heinrich.

"Well, hel-lo," Congers said to the waitress. "What kind of *borscht* you got there? Not much meat, I see. Oh well, I got to eat.

Bring me the same. Tell Steuke to stir up the thick stuff from the bottom. Famine's in Russia, not here, tell him." He patted the girl on the arm. She smiled and walked away. "Wife cooks better soup," he told Heinrich, "but Steuke's girls is better-looking."

Heinrich poured water into his soup to cool it. "Listen, I heard Peters is selling his farm. You know him? Preacher in Gessel?"

"*Joh*, sure, I know him. My wife goes to his church. Me, I kinda give up on it. I go to sleep every time—work hard all week, Sunday, the minute I sit down I'm off. Anyway he preaches too high for me."

"Is he selling out?"

"Could call it that. He's bankrupt." Congers settled back in his chair, which began to tip. "Darn chairs. Why can't Steuke get something decent? Peters, you know, he ain't nothing of a farmer. Got his head in his books when he ought to be out fixing his machinery. Them things don't take care of theirselves. God ain't gonna work no miracles on machinery, not even for a preacher. Bad luck, too. We call him Hail Peters, always hails along that corner of land."

The waitress brought Congers' order. "Gimme some of that rhubarb pie," he told her, pointing with his knife. "And coffee." She nodded and left.

"What's he going to do?" Heinrich asked.

"Who, Peters? Work for Sloan, selling seed. Not much of a job but it's steady." Congers dipped a corner of bread into the soup and lifted it, dripping, to his mouth.

Heinrich watched him in disgust. He finally said, "Peters should get a job in the Cities. He's too smart to be selling seed for a living." He paused, studying Congers. "I hear they pay their preachers pretty good up there."

"Could be." Congers continued eating. "Got to admit, his wife looked a bit down in the mouth last time I seen her. Can't blame her. They're moving into the old Schmotzer place. It's a mess, I can tell you. Give their boys something to do, clean it up."

Heinrich ate in silence, then said suddenly, "How much do you pay him?"

"Pay who—Peters? What for? He don't work for me."

"No, no, your church. What does the church pay him for preaching?"

Congers wiped his mouth on his shirt sleeve and slowly leaned back. "Country churches don't pay preachers. Ain't got that kind of money. Preachers have their farms, gardens, like the rest of us. Of course we bring the family something—corn, sack of potatoes, clothes our kids grown out of. Try to see they're getting by."

Heinrich snorted. "Peters speaks four languages, has a seminary degree, and he's supposed to support his family on that lousy piece of a farm and live on handouts! You Gessel people are rich enough, you could pay him a good salary and never miss it."

Congers' eyes narrowed. "Other preachers getting along just fine."

"Peters is different. He's not cut out for farming."

Congers, taking his time, smeared butter thickly on his bread. Finally he said, "Don't believe in paying for preaching the Word. Man preaches for money, where's the Spirit of God? Old Vogle, preacher when I was a kid, used to say, don't mix money and the Word, it's like mixing soda and vinegar, nothing but fizz. Nope, he gets the Word free, he should give it out free. Don't want no money-crazy man behind the pulpit."

"I don't suppose you farmers might be a little money-crazy, considering the big accounts Al Shindle at the bank says you all got!"

Congers cast him a hard sidelong look. "Shindle's got no business talking about our bank accounts. Anyway we work plenty hard for it. Peters got some things to learn."

"Listen," Heinrich said, his voice rising, "I taught school, I know what it's like to study by oil lamp three or four hours every night. It's a different kind of work, but it isn't easy. Peters is no fool. He's an educated man. He could take over any church in the Cities."

Congers sat back, thumbs hooked into the bib of his overalls, and regarded Heinrich with cool amusement. "Why don't he, then? I'll tell you why. His wife won't leave Gessel because of her family, that's the whole of it. Man who can't manage his wife ain't worth a hill of beans. When I moved to Gessel I didn't ask my wife for no permission. If she'd of objected I'd of slapped her one. But—I didn't have to. She knows who wears the pants. I try to keep her happy, buy her a couch or stove now and then. That's what women need, a little present in one hand and the back of the other if they're sassy."

Heinrich looked at him with contempt.

The waitress brought pie on a small plate and a mug of coffee. Heinrich stared moodily at the floor while Congers ate. Finally he leaned toward Congers, gripping the table. "Listen, pay Peters enough so he won't go bankrupt. He's a good man."

"If it's the Lord's work, the Lord will reward him," Congers said easily, and beckoned to the waitress for cream for the coffee.

"Doesn't the Scripture say, don't muzzle the ox that treads the corn?" Heinrich exclaimed, his voice loud enough that several men at the counter turned their heads.

"Right handy with the scriptures, eh? I admire that. Look, nobody asked him to do all that studying. Preacher over to Muletown says he gets his sermons while he milks the cows Saturday night. Good farmer too. People respect him."

"That's what you call God's word—something the guy dreams up while he's milking?"

"Why not? He says the Spirit moves him while he's out there in the barn, sittin' quiet." Congers sat twirling his fork between his fingers, glancing toward the waitress.

Heinrich seized his head with both hands. "Bunch of mules!" he muttered.

Congers started up, then slowly relaxed, keeping his eyes on Heinrich. "Be careful who you call a mule. I got my job and you ain't.

Don't think we don't know about you." He paused to look Heinrich hard in the face. "Let me tell you, Jentzen, too much in the books, a man gets the big head. And that goes for you too."

"*Dommheit!*" Heinrich shouted, and banged his fist on the table—uneven on its legs, the table jumped, the spoons clattered in the bowls. The men at the counter stopped talking and turned around. The waitress, coming up with the cream, halted.

Congers half rose from his chair. Heinrich stood facing him, fists clenched as if to strike the man. Instead he said rapidly and with great intensity, "Listen, pay him something. Don't ruin him. He's a good man."

Congers said nothing, but took the cream pitcher from the waitress and sat down, still watching Heinrich. The men at the counter, seeing there would be no fight, turned back to their eating.

Finally Congers said, softly but with eyes like steel, "Nobody going to listen to you, Jentzen—getting fired for being drunk on the street ain't no recommendation for good works."

Heinrich turned on his heel, flung some money on the counter and went out.

It was growing dark. The street lamps had already been lit. Small children ran around shouting, trying to stamp on each others' shadows. Their mothers stood talking near by. Horse-drawn buggies and Ford cars drove down the main street. The stores, open to accommodate the farmers coming into town Saturday night, hummed with business. People hurried through lighted doors, congregated in the aisles between shoeboxes and stacks of overalls. Men standing in huddles laughed uproariously, slapping each other on the shoulder.

In the park, long planks had been set up on barrels in front of the brightly lit platform. A few people were already sitting. Young girls fluttered like white birds near the trees, arms intertwined. Young men in farm shirts strolled along the paths that crisscrossed the park. The band members were gathering on the platform, wearing natty straw hats with red and blue ribbons, white shirts with black armbands. A few were blowing into their instruments.

Heinrich stopped at the corner of the park. He was too angry to go back to Tante Lieze's. Instead he sat down on a bench outside the lighted area, behind a clump of bushes, and stared at the street, cursing Congers bitterly under his breath, as well as towns which bred such men. Behind him the instruments were tuning up, and people were settling onto benches waiting for the concert to begin.

His anger was giving way to black depression. It was not only the loss of Maria, but that other anguish that had started long ago in the university. He had read feverishly—commentaries, Menno Simons, the Pietists, in desperation even Lenin, books in German, Russian, English. "Of course God is there, why not?" Maria would tell him. He had scoffed at her for her simplicity, but his heart had nevertheless been warming slowly, moving nearer. Her death had been a betrayal without explanation or mercy.

It occurred to him that Peters might be there. He arose and walked slowly along the outer fringes of the crowd; in the shadows people would not stop to greet him, they were all busy talking to their friends and relatives.

The band suddenly, with a flourish of trumpets and the enthusiastic beating of drums, struck up a jaunty march. Around him people began clapping and stamping their feet to the rhythm. He walked toward the other side of the park, keeping to the darkness under the trees, but did not see Peters.

He did however glimpse Helena and the girls on a path leading toward the platform. Helena, wearing a smart summer coat, walked sedately with her head high, as always. Luetta and Marie walked on either side of her, clinging to her hands. Their older sister Erma skipped along arm in arm with her cousin Anna, Helena's girl; and behind them Johann walked slowly carrying little Edna. His four girls, happy, so like their mother.

He watched them find places on a bench. He should really buy the girls something at Ben Franklin's tomorrow and bring it over, he thought; see them for a bit, tell them he was going to Montana to homestead—though they might not understand that, maybe just say he was going away for a while and would come back.

He wanted urgently to find Peters and tell him not to take that low job but go to the Cities. If his wife didn't want to go, she could live with her parents until she changed her mind. He walked on, peering at the people standing under the trees. Most of them were talking with occasional glances toward the band, now playing a vigorous waltz.

A loud voice from the other side of a stand of tall bushes stopped him: "... should have seen him—thought he'd throw his soup right in my face, nearly started a fight right there." It was Congers. Heinrichs was unable to see him in the darkness but imagined the thick insolent face. Whom was he talking to?

"What was he mad about?" An unfamiliar voice, maybe another Gessel farmer.

"Wants us to pay Peters so he don't have to farm. Practically begged me on his knees." Loud male laughter. "Told him nobody was listening to a drunk who got kicked out of his job."

The anger Heinrich had felt in the restaurant seized him. With difficulty he stood where he was, breathing hard.

"Well, he's right, you should pay Peters," a woman's voice declared. "I feel sorry for his wife, the way they have to live." The voice, emphatic, critical, sounded like Grace Krahn.

"Yeah? Well, you just go on down and visit her and the two of you can have a nice little cry together." Congers' tone was patronizing.

One of the men spoke up. "Why was he so hot about Peters? His relative or something?"

"Don't believe so," Congers said. "Sticking up for Peters because they're both *ed-u-ca-ted.*" Cool, amused. Heinrich clenched his fists and took a step forward, but again stopped.

"Can't stand them high-and-mighty types myself," someone said. "No common sense, if you ask me. Well, I guess birds of a feather got to stick together."

Congers again: "Won't do 'em no good. Us farmers run this place and they might as well know it. Feel sorry for 'em, heads in the clouds, feet stuck in the mud. Peters, now, smart guy but a damfool of a farmer, you'd think . . . ." The group moved away in the semi-darkness under the trees.

The blood was pounding in Heinrich's head. When at last he could think more clearly, he walked hastily toward the sidewalk, pushing his way through the people crowding this end of the park, crossed the street and, almost running, made his way to Quevli's.

On Saturday night the west-bound 10:40 train hooted its way through town largely unnoticed.

TAUNTE JOHT

MRS. TINA ORTMAN and Mrs. Rosie Pankratz were in town on an errand of mercy. The afternoon was hot. Gardens and shrubs baked in the sun, hollyhocks hung wilting along fences, porches were empty, curtains hid the darkened cool interiors of houses. In the shade of a tree two small children were silently digging in the dirt with spoons. Near them a dog lay panting.

The two women walked along the shady side of the street. Their low-belted dresses, made of thin summer material, clung to their backs in damp blotches. Under their hats their faces were red and perspiring. Rosie carried a flowered cloth bag by its wooden handles. Mrs. Ortman held in her hand a sheet of paper covered with writing. Now and again they stopped, consulted the paper, and went into one of the houses along the road.

They were delivering pincushions to the elderly women of their church—the widows and shut-ins. The pincushions were made of knitted strips of brightly colored yarn, wound tightly into balls. They had not sold well at the July auction, and the sewing circle of the Parkview Mennonite Church had decided unanimously to distribute the surplus to deserving members. The bag was now nearly empty; only two remained, a pink-and-yellow and a lime green. However all the names had been crossed off the list. The women halted in the shade of a large cottonwood to consider what to do.

"Mrs. Abe Balzer's is left, and the one Taunte Richert gave us," Rosie said, peering into the bag. "I wish she hadn't given us one, we had it all figured out."

"It's a shame to take them back," Mrs. Ortman observed. "Mrs. Balzer'd be hurt." She paused and added, "Not that I care, her pincushion's that awful green, but she makes such a fuss."

Rosie took the list from her companion and studied it. "Maybe we could keep them ourselves," she suggested, frowning at the crossed-off names.

Mrs. Ortman grimaced. "I have my own. Anyhow, think what the ladies would say if they found out we kept some."

Rosie took a small handkerchief from the bag and wiped the perspiration that had collected under her hat. Her blonde hair clung to her forehead in damp curling wisps. "Mrs. Peske lives just over next to the hospital—she doesn't get around much any more."

Mrs. Ortman shook her head. "She's Alliance. They'd wonder why we came barging in."

"Well, I can't think of anybody. Maybe Taunte Willemsche?"

"She's nearly blind—what would she want with a pincushion?"

They looked out over the town: white frame houses drowsing in the shade of tall trees, sun-drenched gardens of peonies, potatoes and dill. The black earth looked gray in the baking heat.

"Taunte Joht," Rosie exclaimed suddenly.

Mrs. Ortman looked at her in surprise. "She don't go to our church."

"She used to, for a while, that's good enough. It's hot, I want to get home."

"You want to walk all that way to her place?"

"No—but can you think of anybody else?" Rosie put the list in the bag and looked at her friend.

"I'm not going inside though," Mrs. Ortman declared firmly.

They left the shade of the cottonwoods and went on down the

street, turning onto a narrow dirt road bordered by drooping sunflowers and weeds.

Taunte Joht lived near a swampy patch which the city fathers had not got around to draining. Her house, built on slightly higher ground, was approached by a walk made of planks laid endwise between her front door and the road. A growth of chokecherry bushes filled the yard and pushed up against the windows of the small house. Out back where a small area had been cleared, a few straggly rows of carrots and potatoes were visible in the tumbled black dirt. Still further back, hummocks of sharp-edged grass grew in the drying swamp. The smell of decay and muck hung in the air. Over the steaming vegetation hovered clouds of mosquitoes.

"We'll get bit to pieces," Mrs. Ortman said.

"They don't bother me." Rosie started down the planks. Mrs. Ortman followed, stepping carefully to avoid catching the heels of her shoes. They knocked on the door which, like the rest of the house, was made of rough boards weathered to a uniform gray.

After a few moments the door opened and Taunte Joht appeared—a small elderly woman in a long-sleeved cotton dress and dark apron. A piece of cloth was tied around her head. "*Na, goondach! Koamt nen!* Come in, come in!" she exclaimed, stepping back.

Rosie walked in. Mrs. Ortman hesitated; then, feeling mosquitoes settling on her back, hastily followed. Taunte Joht shut the door. "Lots mosquitoes," she said cheerfully. "Come, sit down, I find chairs." She swept a tangle of rags from one wooden chair and removed a pile of newspapers from another, the back of which was broken off. "Come, sit down."

But the women had stopped near the door. The tiny room was stifling. Clouds of steam rose from a huge boiler set on the stove, in which a red-hot fire burned as if it were the dead of winter. Perspiration began at once to trickle down their faces.

"I cook cabbage in," Taunte Joht explained, pointing toward

the stove. The table, they saw, was piled high with cabbages. Beside them lay a blackened cutting board on which was piled a heap of cabbage already shredded. Glass jars stood everywhere, some already filled and sealed. Taunte Joht pushed a tub of green dill out of the way with her foot and hurried to the sink. "Sit down, I make coffee."

Almost fainting from the heat, the women sat down. "Don't bother with coffee, we won't stay only a minute," Rosie said hurriedly.

"*Na,* why not? Already my stove is hot." Taunte Joht was dipping water into a tin kettle from a pail under the sink. "Outside hot, inside I make fire in the stove, don't make no difference." She set the kettle on the stove beside the boiler. The steam rising from under the lid of the boiler indicated cabbage cooking.

"It's much too hot to be canning," Rosie objected. "Wait a little till it cools off."

"Maybe, but the cabbage I got to cook today. Farmer Erickson brings cabbage from his garden, left over, maybe spoiled a little, I cut it off. Dill I grow myself, outside." She hunted in a cupboard for cups, found two and set them on the table.

The women eyed the cabbages, split, blackened, some visibly wilted. Bring her some good ones, you old Erickson, Rosie muttered under her breath.

"We just came to bring you something from the sewing circle," Mrs. Ortman said. "We're the Sunshine Committee. From the Parkview Mennonite Church."

Taunte Joht stood still. "For me something?"

Rosie took the pincushions out of the bag. "If you have use for one," she said politely.

Taunte Joht came over to look at the pincushions; wiped her hands on her apron, picked them up and examined them. "*Schoen, schoen*," she murmured, then looked up. "I don't go no more to church."

"It's all right, we have extra," Rosie explained hastily. Her face was flushed. "Pick the one you want."

Taunte Joht turned them over in her hands. "*Ganz schoen.*" At length she held up the pink-and-yellow. "A nice color, not? I use it."

Mrs. Ortman had folded a piece of newspaper and was fanning herself with it. She sat with her eyes closed.

"Mrs. Richert at the Old Folks Home made that one," Rosie explained.

"*Joh*? Taunte Richert?" She examined the pincushion again. "She knits good." She pointed toward the back corner of the room. "Me, I make a quilt for Jacob. My son."

The women looked where she pointed. On a small iron bedstead under the window were piles of old clothes—men's trousers, dark skirts, coats. Some had already been cut into squares. A crate on the floor overflowed with more clothes. A black dress hung over a string tacked up by the window, shriveled, bone dry. Something stirred in Rosie's memory, told to her by Helena Jungas. Taunte Joht had once gone to church wearing a black dress but had been shamed by the women for its being too short, and never returned. Was this the dress?

Mrs. Ortman looked about for a sewing machine. There was none. "Do you sew by hand?" she asked, surveying with evident disapproval the disorder everywhere—piles of old papers, dried dill in a rusty pail, cracked shoes, a pair of boots.

"*Yoh*, by hand," Taunte Joht said absently. She was looking at the green pincushion still in her hand. She held it up. "Maybe this one, you don't need? I give it to my son's wife? They have a new baby, one month old tomorrow." She looked at them, pride in her eyes.

Rosie glanced at Mrs. Ortman, who was again sitting with her eyes closed, fanning herself, and said quickly, "We're very glad for her to have it."

Taunte Joht placed the pincushions carefully on a shelf, two bright balls glowing in the dark corner. "*Schoen, schoen.*" She moved to the stove, removed the lid of the steaming kettle, and screwed the top off a jar. "Now I make coffee."

"No, please, we won't stay, but thank you very much," Rosie said hurriedly. "We just came by for a minute. You're busy canning."

"I got plenty time," Taunte Joht protested, halting with the jar of coffee grounds poised over the kettle.

But the women had risen and were moving toward the door. Taunte Joht set the jar down and hurried after them. "Wait, I show you my picture, then you go." She snatched from the windowsill a photograph of a young man with a dark beard, beside him a thin unsmiling woman holding a baby. Children of various heights stood around them, their arms straight down at their sides. The baby wore a long white dress edged with lace. "My Jacob's family. A nice picture, not?"

"Very nice," Rosie agreed, counting the children in spite of her haste: six.

Mrs. Ortman opened the door. "We have to walk home," she remarked.

"You walked?" Taunte Joht exclaimed. "It's too hot, you get heat stroke maybe. Wait, I ask my neighbor Mr. Sneer, maybe he can ride you home in his car."

"No, no, we'll rest in the shade," Rosie promised. "Well, goodbye. I hope your cabbage turns out good." The two women set off across the planks.

"I don't like you walk," Taunte Joht fretted, still holding the photograph. Rosie turned and waved.

The air outside, hot as it still was, now felt cool on their flushed faces. Partway down the road they stopped under a tree. Rosie took off her hat and fanned her face. "At least we got rid of the pincushions."

"Did you see the cabbage?" Mrs. Ortman asked. "All cracked."

"The jars looked good though," Rosie said. "She cuts off the bad parts."

They walked on. Mrs. Ortman stepped around a pile of drying flower stalks someone had thrown over the fence. "All that junk. She ought to throw it away."

"That's how poor people are," Rosie said. "They save everything in case they need it some time. Better be saving than wanting, my grandma Peters always said."

"All them kids! The baby was wearing a christening dress, did you see? Lutheran or maybe Catholic. The ladies won't like it."

"They don't have to know." Rosie plodded on, frowning slightly.

Mrs. Ortman grunted. "They'll find out. Well, here's my corner. I got pickles soaking."

They stopped at the corner. Rosie said, "I'm going home and get these hot clothes off and go sit in the cellar in my undies to cool off."

Mrs. Ortman raised her eyebrows. "What if somebody comes down?"

"I yell at 'em to stay out," Rosie said lightly. "Anyway, my kids are too little to pay much attention. Will you do the report this time? Maybe you can leave out that Mrs. Richert gave us an extra one, and just say we gave one to Taunte Joht as an encouragement to come back to church some time."

Mrs. Ortman agreed, and they parted ways.

At the next meeting of the Parkview Women's Sewing Society, Mrs. Ortman delivered the Sunshine Committee's report for the past month. She read from a hand-written page which would later be given to the secretary. The report included visits to several members in the hospital, to two Parkview widows, and to a mother with a new baby bringing a gift of diapers. The report concluded with mention of the pincushions. "We gave 'em all out," Mrs. Ortman stated, and read the names of all to whom pincushions had been given. There was a small stir around the circle of women.

"Who's Mrs. Joht?" a young woman inquired, looking up from embroidering a quilt block. She wore tiny glasses and combed her hair in puffs over her ears.

"You don't know?" An older woman was speaking. "The old lady from the swamp—she always wears a black hat with cherries on it. She goes around with bags of stuff from her garden to give to people."

"Oh, her?" The young woman laughed and cut a length of orange embroidery thread.

"Does she go to our church?" a stout lady in the front row, dressed in purple, inquired.

Mrs. Ortman cleared her throat. "She did for a while. Maybe she'll come back, some time."

"We should stay with our active members," the stout lady declared, looking around at the others. "She's got no claim. If she wants to receive from us, let her come regularly to church."

Mrs. Ortman, red in the face, explained rapidly. "We had extra. Mrs. Richert at the Old Folks Home didn't take hers. She had a whole table full, she makes 'em herself."

Rosie stood up. "We didn't know who else to give it to, all the names were crossed off. Mrs. Joht is poor, real poor, so why not—." She looked around at the ladies and added drily, "We didn't want to bring anybody's back," daring them to ask whose that last unwanted pincushion had been.

The women stirred and suddenly began talking to each other of other things. The chair-woman shuffled her papers. She said crisply, "Let us thank Mrs. Balzer for her comments and Mrs. Ortman for her report on a job well done. Now about . . . ."

Mrs. Balzer interrupted her. "If we start giving to every poor family in town there'll be no end to it, no thanks to us either—they'll just expect more the next time." She turned around so that all could hear. "Let them work, like the rest of us."

The ladies sat in silence. Some glanced at each other, raising their eyebrows. At last the chairwoman stood up and said loudly, not looking at Mrs. Balzer, "The committee will please consider Mrs. Balzer's remarks. We have one more item of business." She looked toward the back of the room. "We have with us tonight a representative from the Greater China Mission who will tell us about the need over there. The people suffer greatly in the cold winters. I believe Rev. Mott is starting a drive for usable clothing. Welcome, Rev. Mott."

A small man in a brown suit rose with a smile and came forward. He outlined his vision to help the peasants in northern China and Mongolia. The women voted unanimously to take part in a local clothing drive.

After the meeting the women crowded around Rosie and Mrs. Ortman. None of them, it seemed, had ever visited Taunte Joht.

"Did you go in? What was it like? I heard she collects rubbish from the dump and brings it to people."

"No, no, she brings stuff from her garden. She brought my aunt Kruger a jar of pickles once when she was laid up with a bad leg. Walked all the way."

"The mosquitoes must be simply awful down there by the swamp."

The young woman with ear puffs said, laughing, "My grandma rubs herself with kerosene to keep mosquitoes away. Keeps everybody away!"

The women laughed with her. Mrs. Dickman, neatly dressed in gray silk, spoke up. "The Johts used to come here to church once in a while. After he died she came in that black dress she wore to the funeral, only now it was too short—I guess she must have washed it and it shrunk so the petticoat showed. One of the deacon wives asked her if she didn't have a longer dress to look decent in the Lord's house, and she quit coming. We felt bad about it. The pastor's wife went over and offered to buy her a new one, but she got feisty and said she could worship God at home where it didn't matter what she had on." Mrs. Dickman sighed. "She never came back."

"Neither would I," Rosie said suddenly, with spirit. "My goodness, all that fuss because we gave her a silly old pincushion. Two, actually." She started walking away, head held high, suddenly paused and looked back. "One was the pincushion Taunte Richert gave us. The other one was Mrs. Balzer's. Lime green."

The women looked at her, startled, then began to giggle. "Serves her right," someone said. "Don't dare tell her," another put in, "or we'll never hear the end of it." The women dispersed to walk home in the long light of the warm summer evening.

Two days later Mrs. Ortman tendered her resignation from the Sunshine Committee, but was persuaded to stay on by the special request of the chairwoman, who invited her over for coffee and a particularly elegant silver cake served on real bone china from Canada.

During the autumn months the conversation at the Parkview sewing circle turned on relief clothes for northern China. Several women went from door to door collecting. The boxes in the church basement overflowed. Mrs. Balzer, by humble request of the circle, was put in charge of sorting. The pincushions were no longer mentioned.

The days became short and overcast. Freezing winds off the Canadian prairies swept the town. Snows fell, drifted up against the houses, and froze to the hardness of stone. Women put on their thick woolen coats and wrapped heavy shawls about their heads whenever they went out. The collecting of clothes for northern China ceased. Now and then Taunte Joht was seen in a man's gray overcoat and large boots, carrying her brown bag.

Then even the miseries of blizzards were forgotten in the excitement of the big event of that winter: the burning down of Johann and Helena's hardware store one freezing Saturday night in January.

Dozens of men worked furiously downstairs in the store, moving out stoves and washing machines, boxes of tools, kegs of nails. Others threw buckets of water on the roofs of adjacent buildings. The fire engine arrived but was not able to put out the fire because the pumps were frozen. The family, thank God, had been able to get out of their home above the store before the stairs caught on fire

The next day, Sunday, people on their way to church stopped to view the great smoking black pit in the middle of the business block. Sunday School rooms buzzed with talk: the fire had started in the barber shop in the next door basement, likely from an overheated stove . . . no, it was the oily rags on the floor of the garage next door that caught fire, which jumped the alley . . . everyone had got out . . . little Anscha had run into the flames to get her cat and would have perished had not Hoekema grabbed her . . . *na nae*, it was just the cat . . . the family had rushed out into the freezing night in nothing but their night clothes . . . no, no, they had been warned in time to put on their coats . . . Anscha's new piano, the one she got from her dad for Christmas, had got stuck on the front stairway trapping several men, heaven knew why Helena tried to save that heavy thing, the men could have died . . . that was entirely wrong, Helena wouldn't let them go for the piano, in fact the speaker had actually seen the piano, a dark shape, plunge through the flames from the second floor into the fiery basement.

Of special interest was the fact, attested to by Klaas since the items were in his drug store at that very moment, that the big family Bible had miraculously been saved, as well as six loaves of bread Helena had baked that very day.

By the end of the week it was reliably reported that Johann had bought the long-vacant Basinger Hotel as a place for his family to live. Meanwhile they were staying with Helena's sister, Tante Lieze—luckily the renters were away so they could sleep upstairs. The whole town knew by now, of course, that Johann had let his insurance lapse so that his store and home were a dead loss. How they would get by nobody knew. How the great had fallen, let it be a lesson to all.

At the next meeting of the Parkview sewing circle, it was suggested that some of the clothes in the basement be given to Helena Jungas for her children since (as had by now been verified) they had lost everything but the few things they had been wearing. Someone objected that much of the collected clothing was not very good. Mrs. Balzer sniffed at that. "If they're proud, let them go without," she stated firmly. The Sunshine Committee was asked to visit Mrs. Jungas to get the sizes of the children.

Thus it happened that on the next Wednesday afternoon Rosie Pankratz and Mrs. Ortman walked up the icy steps of the hotel in the middle of town, information having been given them that Helena would be there cleaning. "Must be filthy in there," Rosie remarked; "hotel's been sitting empty five, six years." Mrs. Ortman replied that beggars couldn't be choosers, anybody could clean out dirt.

They knocked. When nobody answered they tried the door, found it unlocked, and went in. The bare wood floor of the entry hall was black with dust trodden into a wet muck. They stomped the snow off their shoes and went through a half-open door into the main parlor.

The room was large with a low ceiling. In the light from two front windows they could see faded wall paper, badly water-stained and in some places hanging in brittle strips. The parlor carpet was covered with bits of rubbish. The wood floor around the carpet was badly worn and dirty, nearly black. The room was empty save for a hard bench of Russian make standing near the door and, at the far end, a steam radiator. Through an open door to their right they could see in the old dining room a clutter of tubs, washing machines, hardware and boxes—the stuff saved from Johann's store. The whole place smelled musty and wet.

"Gracious! What a mess!" Rosie exclaimed.

"She can be thankful she's got kids to help clean up," Mrs. Ortman observed tartly.

They spotted Helena at the far end of the room, halfway up the long flight of stairs leading to the upper floors, on her knees beside a pail of water. She had been scrubbing the steps but had stopped to see who had come in. Now she stood up, dried her hands on the apron tucked up around her waist, and came down, carrying the heavy pail. "*Guten Tag*," she said, using the formal High German.

Mrs. Ortman looked into the pail. The water was black.

"I'm Rosie Pankratz and this is Mrs. Ortman—we're from the sewing circle at the Parkview Church," Rosie explained. "It's too bad your place burned down."

"What's done is done," Helena said. She did not look as broken-hearted or sorrowful as they had expected. "I'm going to rent out these rooms. People from the train, salesmen, one night, two nights. If you hear of anybody—."

A sudden loud thud overhead drew their eyes upward. "Is that your girls cleaning up there?" Mrs. Ortman asked.

"No, they went to school," Helena said. "Mrs. Sukau came to help."

"They went to school?" Mrs. Ortman was clearly displeased.

Rosie was staring at Helena in astonishment. "You mean, run the hotel? That's an awful lot of work!"

"*Jah*—why not? My husband needs his money to rebuild the store. I can keep the family with rent from the rooms. We can live on the third floor." After a pause, Helena added softly, "I came here after the fire to start cleaning up, and a voice told me, 'Rent out these rooms and you will have bread.'"

The two women looked at each other.

"My girls can help me," Helena went on, speaking with determination. "In the day they go to school—I don't want they should get behind. It's enough if they help when they get home."

Rosie gazed with admiration at the firm full figure of Helena, standing straight in spite of weariness, old shoes, muddy skirt. "It's a good idea," she said, "if you can do it."

Mrs. Ortman spoke up. "You can tell us, maybe—did the piano get stuck on the stairs?"

Helena stared at her. "Who said that? The men wanted to move it out but I wouldn't allow it—the stairs are too narrow. You think I would let the men burn up because of a piano?"

"You hear a lot of stories," Mrs. Ortman mumbled. "It's a shame, brand new."

There was a pause. Helena waited expectantly. At last she said pleasantly, "Can I help you something?"

Rosie coughed slightly. "We thought . . . since you lost everything in the fire . . . our sewing circle has collected a lot of used clothes for China, we got boxes full, all sorted, in the church basement . . . we thought maybe something would fit your children, if we had the sizes."

"Oh." Helena gazed at the floor. Finally she shook her head. "*Danke*, we can get by. They saved the sewing machines. I can sew. Tante Lieze can help me. The girls wouldn't want to wear somebody's things to school—everybody would know."

"But . . . nine children to take care of!"

Mrs. Ortman spoke rapidly. "Maybe underwear or stockings—there's lots of stockings in them boxes, need only a little fixing. I saw some nightgowns, a little torn under the arms."

"*Nein, danke.*" Helena's blue eyes sparkled and she shut her lips tightly.

The women stood awkwardly, at a loss. "If you change your mind, let us know what size—shirts or anything, shoes too . . . we just wanted to help if we could," Rosie explained.

Helena smiled faintly. "I'll have rooms ready to rent out tomorrow. You can tell it around."

A knock sounded on the front door. "Excuse me." Helena hurried to open it, loosening her apron as she walked so that it hung straight. The two women waited to see who it was.

Taunte Joht stood there in her man's overcoat, carrying her brown bag. A frazzled dark shawl was tied under her chin; another shawl showed under it. On her feet were boots tied around with string.

"Taunte Joht!" Helena took her by the arm and pulled her forward. "Come inside, it's too cold out there."

"Cold in here too," Mrs. Ortman muttered, visibly upset by Helena's refusal of their clothing.

"I'll make your floor dirty, Mrs. Jungas," Taunte Joht objected.

"*Na nae*, plenty dirt already. Come, sit down, you shouldn't be out walking on such a cold day." She led the old woman across the room to the Russian bench.

Taunte Joht set her bag on the bench and looked around. "Lots room," she remarked with approval. Then she regarded the two women intently, and her face brightened. "You came too!" She turned to Helena. "They brought pincushions to my house. They walked . . . a hot day, very hot . . . I cooked cabbage."

Helena looked surprised. "You know them? It's Mrs. Ortman and Rosie Pankratz from the Parkview sewing circle."

"*Joh,* they told me." Taunte Joht was poking about in her bag. "*Ekj brocht die waut*—I brought you something." She lifted out a large package wrapped in newspapers. "For the children. Your house burned down, you got nothing." She set the package on the bench and resumed rummaging in the bag.

Helena carefully removed the newspapers. Inside was a large jar of canned cabbage, white, perfectly preserved. "For *borscht,*" Taunte Joht told her, and handed Helena a second wrapped parcel, in which was a loaf of brown bread.

Helena gazed at her with troubled eyes. "You have nothing

yourself, Taunte Joht, you shouldn't . . . at least eat supper with us, the girls can make the *borscht*."

"*Na nae*, I have *borscht* at home."

Helena touched the old woman's hand. "I didn't expect . . . you, a poor widow . . . *Fael mol dankeschoen*, many many thanks. But don't walk home! I can call Johann, Al can drive you. It's too cold, Taunte Joht!"

"*Ach waut*!" Taunte Joht started toward the door. "Walk I still can!"

"At least come in the basement and warm yourself up, we got the stove going down there to heat water. Rest a little."

"*Nae*, I can warm up at home, I got fire going." Taunte Joht nodded to the two women as she walked past them into the hall and opened the door.

"Be careful on the steps, don't fall!" Helena called after her.

Mrs. Ortman and Rosie stepped forward. "We'll be going now," Rosie said. "Tell Mrs. Sukau we said hello."

Helena turned, face flushed and eyes bright with tears. "She has nothing, but still . . . . Please, say to the ladies thank you but I can sew what we need."

The women picked their way down the slippery ice on the steps, clinging with gloved hands to the iron handrail. On the packed snow of the road it was easier going. They wrapped their woolen shawls around their faces. "Getting colder," Rosie said.

"Well!" Mrs. Ortman exclaimed after a short silence. "She don't want our clothes."

"I wouldn't either!" Rosie exclaimed. "It would be easier to make new than mend some of that stuff. My Alvina would never wear those dresses . . . everybody knows who had them before."

"I mend plenty stockings for my boys," Mrs. Ortman said bitterly. "Big holes, too."

"Fancy Taunte Joht walking all that way to bring Helena something," Rosie said. "I sure wouldn't have done it."

"From that dirty kitchen!"

"Oh, tush, the cabbage looked fine," Rosie retorted. "The bread too."

They reached the park. The walks had not been cleared; there was only a narrow path cut through the waist-high snow banks. The women walked single file until, further down the street, their ways parted.

"I can make the report if you want," Rosie said. "Wind's coming up—it's going to snow again tonight." She raised a hand in farewell, but Mrs. Ortman had already turned toward home.

At the meeting the following Tuesday, Rosie read the report of their visits, including the failed mission to Helena Jungas. As expected, Mrs. Abe Balzer expressed indignation at this indication of pride. The ladies in the back row smiled at each other and shook their heads. "No wonder she didn't want it, that old stuff," several women told Rosie afterwards. "Nobody gives away good stuff in this town—we use things up."

Several weeks later Rosie set out for the hospital on a dutiful round of visits. Mrs. Ortman had called saying she had a house full of company and could not go. Rosie herself had baking and laundry to attend to, but said she would go alone.

On arrival at the hospital, she was told at the reception desk that only one patient from Parkview Church was there, a John Ens with a broken hip in Room 7. Rosie felt she had nothing to say to this farmer whom she knew only by sight, but she had chosen a short scripture and written out a prayer—that would have to do. She hung her coat on one of the hooks provided for that purpose near the door, took off her galoshes, and walked down the hall toward 7. Passing other rooms with open doors, she glimpsed visitors: a mother knitting beside a bed, a young man in overalls talking to someone behind a curtain.

The door to 7 was closed. A nurse came by. "Want to see Ens?

He's on the bedpan, wait just a minute. Slipped on the ice and busted his hip. People shouldn't go out in this weather."

"Real slippery outside," Rosie agreed.

The nurse opened the door a crack and looked in, then closed it. "Might be a while. You can go see Taunte Joht if you want, she's next door in 8."

"Taunte Joht?" Rose exclaimed. "She's here?"

The nurse leaned against the wall, resting one foot comfortably against the wall behind her. "Came in Monday. Somebody stopped at her place, found her in bed half froze, fire was out . . . there was wood out back but probably she was too weak to get it. Pneumonia."

"I saw her a few weeks ago!" Rosie exclaimed. "She brought something to Helena at the hotel. Oh, dear. How bad is she?"

"Not too good." The nurse went to the door of 7, listened, and returned. "Hope he don't fall off the pan—broken hip ain't no picnic. You can go see Taunte Joht, she's awake. Not too clear though." She added, "Helena Jungas was here, looked pretty upset when she left."

Rosie entered 8, clutching her Bible. On the high white bed Taunte Joht looked very small. Her face was pale, cheeks drawn in around her gums. Her withered brown hands lay motionless on the white bedspread. A photograph was propped up against a glass of water on the nightstand—Jacob's family.

The nurse had followed her in. "*Na*, Taunte Joht, do you know who this is? Somebody to see you!"

The old woman's eyes wandered toward the visitor, unseeing. She said in a thin whisper, "Taunte Helena?"

"No, she went home. This is—what's your name? Rosie Pankratz. Come on, grandma, wake up, she wants to talk to you."

The dim eyes focused slowly. "*Joh*—from the church, they brought pincushions . . . ."

"A pincushion, hey? That's very nice." The nurse winked at Rosie. "Now lie still, grandma, or you'll start coughing again."

But Taunte Joht was struggling to raise herself, trying to see into the hall. "Where the other one is?"

"She couldn't come today," Rosie said. "I'm by myself." To the nurse she explained, "Mrs. Ortman came with me to her house."

"The other lady couldn't come," the nurse said loudly in Taunte Joht's ear. "Maybe next time." She helped her lie back on her pillows.

"Should I read to her?" Rosie asked, looking doubtfully at her Bible.

"Go ahead, why not? I'll go fix up Mr. Ens. Taunte Joht, the lady is going to read from the Bible. You stay awake now and lie still." The nurse walked out, leaving the door open.

Rosie read the passage chosen for the day, from Matthew 5: "Blessed are the poor in spirit for theirs is the kingdom of heaven. Blessed are . . . ."

Taunte Joht lay with her eyes closed. Rosie shut the Bible and looked helplessly at the shriveled face, wondering if she had heard. Her eyes fell on the photograph. "How is Jacob's baby?" she asked. She leaned closer and repeated the question.

Taunte Joht did not answer. Suddenly she turned her head and began to cough, her breath rasping in her throat. The nurse hurried in. Putting an arm behind the old woman's back, she raised her slightly. "All right, grandma, you'll be all right, it's almost time for your medicine."

The coughing fit passed, and the nurse eased Taunte Joht back onto the pillow.

"I'll go now," Rosie said hurriedly. "Maybe I can come again in a couple of days."

"She'll come again," the nurse said loudly, leaning over to pat the old hands.

But Taunte Joht caught hold of the nurse and began speaking rapidly. "*Joh*, those two, they came to my house . . . walking, it was terrible hot . . . I cooked cabbage . . . they brought me pincushions, two . . . *schoen, gauns schoen* . . .one for me, one for my Jacob's wife . . . they walked from town, so far . . . walking . . . ." Her voice murmured on.

On impulse Rosie picked up the photograph from the night stand and put it in Taunte Joht's hand. The old lady looked at it. Her words ceased, she closed her eyes and seemed to drift into sleep.

The nurse tapped Rosie on the arm. "You can see Ens now, he's all fixed up."

But Rosie walked past 7 down the hall, put on her coat, and went home.

Three days later the local paper carried, under an elaborate account of the wedding of the daughter of a prominent businessman in Dumfrey, a brief notice of the death of Mrs. Maria Joht. Rosie stared at the two lines of print for a long time. Then she clipped the notice to take along to the sewing circle as part of her next report.

At the meeting on Tuesday night, the chairwoman, supported by the unanimous vote of the sewing circle, commended the various committees for their work. She mentioned Rosie's visit to Taunte Joht in the hospital. "As it turned out, it was our last chance to do anything for her," the chairwoman said. "It was very good you went in. I understand you also went to the funeral."

Rosie listened dry-eyed. After the meeting she went home without speaking to anyone.

She put the newspaper clipping carefully into a drawer, then tore up the committee report and threw it into the stove.

Saying she would be back in a minute, she put her coat back on, went out the back door and sat on the porch steps. The night was dark but clear. She gazed at the trees, trunks and bare branches black against the dim sky, thinking of nothing in particular. A few lights were on in windows, here and there, shining across the snow. Above the town the bright cold stars hung in their appointed places. Rosie leaned her chin in her hands and looked at them. They were so far away, she thought—so calm, so beautiful. After a while she noticed among the white stars a yellow one, glowing like a jewel in the night sky. Tante Joht took her pincushion with her, she thought idly. There should be a lime-green one near by somewhere, though maybe she left that one behind for her son's wife.

She sat on the porch step, huddled in her coat, watching the stars, until one of the children came out looking for her.

THE DRUG STORE

WEDGED BETWEEN STOESZ'S general store and Mrs. Dehmler's hat shop was a narrow two-story white frame building with a high square front. Behind the words Dyck's Drug Store painted in a semicircle on the large front window, glass jars of peppermints and cinnamon sticks were arranged in rows, in front of them neat stacks of little boxes and tins—headache powders, camphor, salves and ointments. The wooden step in front of the door was worn. A few weeds grew in the narrow strip of dirt between the building and the sidewalk.

Klaas was standing outside in the early morning sunshine polishing his window with a small cloth when Helena Jungas came hurrying across the street.

"*Goondach*," he greeted her. "How is Johann? Is he sleeping better?" He put the cloth in the pocket of his apron and opened the door for her. Klaas was a short man, comfortably stout so that vests and aprons were a snug fit. His shirt sleeves were held up by black armbands just above the elbow. He wore round gold-rimmed glasses.

"Much better, *danke*." She had on a printed cotton house dress, somewhat rumpled as if she had moments before thrown off her apron to rush over. Her hotel was only a block away. "I just want some salve—I burned my arm on the stove pipe." She showed him a red welt on the inside of her arm.

Klaas walked around his showcase to the shelves behind it, filled with tins and boxes of all sizes. He selected a small flat tin and opened it. "Put some on, it'll heal you in no time."

Helena sniffed. "Smells terrible—what is it?" She rubbed a little on the burn, paused, opened her purse. "How much?" He told her. She snapped the purse shut. "I'll charge it."

"*Yoh,* sure," he said mildly, "you can pay me when you get back on your feet. Too bad about the fire. How is business? You getting enough roomers?" He wrote up her purchase on a paper beside the till.

"Four last night," she said, looking at her arm. "Salesmen—they left early. Good stuff you got here, Klaas." She moved toward the door, but instead sat down. For the customers' convenience Klaas had installed a few small chairs, old-fashioned with round wooden seats and ironwork backs.

"Listen, I heard you want to resign from the school board." She looked at him inquiringly.

Klaas took the cloth from his pocket and wiped the top of his showcase, slowly, moving aside the tall jars of peppermint sticks. At last he said, "I'm getting too old for their fights."

'What do you want to do—sit in here all day?"

His eyes wandered around the tiny shop, its well-stocked shelves, polished dark wooden floor. "Why not? It's a nice store."

"Who'll take your place, then? You have to be careful who's on that board."

He rubbed his neck thoughtfully. "Al Eytzen might do it . . . Bekker's nephew. Young guy, farms east of town."

"What, Al Eytzen? He's still wet behind the ears! He'll vote whatever way Bekker tells him, you can bet on it!"

"Well? Bekker isn't so bad. Does a pretty good job, Martin told me. Trying to help the town."

"Bekker has about as much sense as an iron post! If he wants to help the town, let him stand in the park to tie the horses to!"

Klaas chuckled. "The hotel isn't taming your tongue, I can see."

She laughed. "Well, it's true. But listen, the high school is going good. You got some new teachers, music and such. My girls like it. But let Bekker and his gang get hold of it, they'll set it back fifty years!"

"I went there fifty years ago, it wasn't so bad."

She leaned forward. "Klaas Dyck, now you're making fun. You know it and I know it, let them get hold of this town, we'll go back to horse and buggy days. Look at the Valley Church . . . they finally had a few Bible classes in English till Bekker's family made a fuss, they had to go back to German. Not that I talk English all that well myself, but let me learn if I want to! No, no, you stay on. Tell them you changed your mind."

She broke off when a small girl opened the door, followed by an older boy, both very blonde. "Hedy and Steven Erickson," Klaas said. "Children, this is Mrs. Jungas who runs the hotel now because her house burned down. You remember the big fire?"

The two gazed at her in wonder. "Did you jump out the upstairs windows?" the boy asked eagerly.

Helena laughed. "No, no, we had plenty time to get out."

The girl, beaming, held up a dime. "Uncle Sorensen gived us this. He's visiting and Mama is making pancakes."

The children began their inspection of the candy in the show case, walking back and forth, whispering and pointing at the candy corn, gold coins and chocolate mice, lemon and raspberry drops. "Take your time," Klaas told them. "It takes planning to spend a whole dime properly."

At last the boy straightened up and said in a business-like voice, "We want four pennies of peppermints, one penny of licorice, and a nickel of striped candy canes."

"Do you agree? I suppose it's your dime too?" Klaas asked the girl. She nodded and held out the dime, rocking on her toes. Klaas put the candy in a small paper bag and gravely handed it to the boy. "And how is Grandma Erickson? Is her head still hurting her?"

"It's a little better," the boy said.

"Only a little?" Klaas took a small packet from a shelf. "I want you should bring her this. Tell her to take some every day—the directions are written on the back, here." He pointed to the directions. "Just something to try, tell her it's free. And listen, be quiet in the house. Noise hurts her head. If you want to make noise, go outside. Let me see how quiet you can walk." The two tip-toed to the door. "Good, very good. Now then, be sure you show Uncle Sorensen our new beautiful high school. Tell him it cost thirty-two thousand dollars."

Helena laughed, watching the children run off. "Oh, you! You'll never get rich, giving away stuff."

Klaas sighed. "That's what Marina tells me. But what can I do? I can't help it. Anyway, why should I worry about getting rich? When I die someone else will get it. Better to help someone out a little, if I can." He took off his glasses, squinted at them, and began polishing them with a handkerchief. "I'm getting old, though. Not much an old guy can do."

Helena got up. "You're a good man, Klaas. We found out who our friends were when our store burned down." She stood regarding him affectionately for a moment. "You want to help the town, stay on the school board." She walked to the door.

"Wait!" Klaas held up a hand to detain her. "Marina wanted you to have dill next time you came in. Wait a minute, I'll get it." He hurried to the back part of the store and returned directly with a bundle of fresh dill tied together with store string.

Helena looked silently at the dill. "*Dankeschoen*, tell her thank you. The last time anybody gave me dill, it was Taunte Joht." Her eyes filled with tears. She took the dill and walked slowly out of the store.

Klaas watched her suddenly quicken her pace and veer off across the street. A moment later a tall, smartly dressed woman came into view, holding by the hand a small girl in a blue velvet dress. He laughed to himself. "Helena will be mad all day she didn't dress up," he said aloud. "At least she took her apron off."

The woman entered his store, pulling the child in with her. She nodded curtly at Klaas. "Got some Alpenkraeuter?"

Without hurrying, Klaas got down a tall square bottle filled with dark liquid. "Always plenty Alpenkraeuter. Whose girl you got there, Mrs. Penner?"

"Elsie's girl from California. They're visiting." She examined the bottle closely, reading the label. The girl stood sucking her finger, nose pressed to the glass of the display case.

"Looks like Elsie," Klaas commented.

Mrs. Penner opened the bottle and sniffed. "You got anything stronger than this? My husband crippled himself digging the garden. Hire somebody, I told him, but he's stubborn as a pair of mules. Serves him right, but still I got to take care of him. Julia, hurry up, choose something."

Klaas handed Mrs. Penner several tins of ointment. She opened and smelled them, smeared samples on her arm, frowned. "Let me see that other bottle—no, the one in the back. Oh goodness, that's hair tonic. Well, I don't know. You say this is good?" holding up one of the tins.

"Ben Hoekema said it fixed him . . . hurt his back carrying stoves at Johann's store the night of the fire." Klaas turned his attention to the child. "What can I get for you, young lady?"

The girl pointed to the ropes of red and black licorice. Mrs. Penner looked up. "Oh, my goodness no, you'll get that on your dress. Klaas, give her something that isn't messy." She turned back to the medicines, frowning. "I'll take this one and the Alpenkraeuter—if one doesn't work, maybe the other one will. Hurry up, Julia, we got to get home."

"Children get things done faster if you don't rush them," Klaas observed mildly. He put the medicines in a sack and set it on the counter.

"Don't touch the glass—you're leaving fingerprints! For goodness sake, Klaas, give her some lemon drops and be done with it," Mrs. Penner snapped, opening her purse.

"I hate lemon drops!" Julia said crossly.

"Raspberry all right, then?" Klaas asked her. "But next time wear an old dress." He put the candy in a small paper bag and handed it to the child. "Not messy," he assured Mrs. Penner.

She sniffed and was counting out money when the door was pushed open by a young man carrying a bundle of huge cardboard posters. "Mrs. Penner! Good morning to you!" He propped the posters up against the wall.

"Have a care, Deet!" she retorted. "You nearly poked me in the eye. What are you up to now, advertising yourself as the Most Wanted Man in the county?"

Deet grinned. His color was high, as if he had been walking fast in the wind. "Something like it. I'm running for town council. Can I put one of these in your window, Klaas?"

Klaas walked around from behind the show case and read the poster: "Dietrich Regehr will, if elected, serve in the best interests of Windamer. He will support the building of a gravel road to the lake, etc. etc."

"You'll vote for me?" Deet addressed both of them.

Klaas shook his head. "Why should I? I want somebody to build a nice new comfortable Old Folks Home for mamma and me to retire to. What do I care about your gravel road to the lake?"

"All you council men think of is spending other people's money," Mrs. Penner said tartly.

Deet grinned. "Better theirs than mine."

"The day you get on the town council, Deet Regehr, this town's in trouble," she retorted. "The trouble your pa had with you!"

"They say wild foals grow up into good horses," Klaas observed.

"Only if somebody breaks them!" She picked up her purchase and looked for Julia.

"Sharpest tongue in town," Deet said, nodding approval. "How about if I put you in charge of our road crew, you and Helena Jungas and Grace Krahn—then we'd get some work done."

Mrs. Penner glared at him and was about to answer when their attention was drawn to a commotion on the street. Two boys were dashing wildly toward the store, arms flailing. A moment later they flung themselves through the door. They both began screaming at once. "Uncle Klaas! The Watkins man hunged himself in the lumber yard!"

Klaas looked at one boy, then the other. "What?"

They danced about him in the excitement and importance of the news. "He hunged himself on one of the hook things on the wall," one said. The other added, brown eyes blazing, "His face looks all purple, his eyes are bugging out and his tongue . . . ."

"Did you see him? When was this?" Deet interrupted sharply.

"We just come from there. He's laying on the floor, the rope's still around his neck where they cut it off. We're going to the elevator to tell our dads." They started for the door.

"Wait, stop!" Klaas commanded. "You say the Watkins man? Mr. Lilla?"

"Yeah, him," one of the boys said. "We went to buy some nails for my dad and he was laying there. He's awful dead all right." They stood poised to run.

"I'd better go see," Deet said, and ran out.

By the counter Julia stood staring, clutching her sack of candy. Mrs. Penner began to say something but Klaas interrupted. "Boys, listen. This is a terrible thing. Don't go running around town telling everybody. Go tell your dads. Let them take care of it. You hear? Just tell your dads, nobody else. This might be a police matter, they'll want to investigate. Best thing you two can do is not say a word, not to anybody, only your dads. Understand?"

The boys looked disappointed. "How about the police? Can we tell the police?"

"Only if they ask you," Klaas said firmly.

The boys nodded. "Okay, we won't say nothin', just our dads and the police." They pushed through the door and raced away in the direction of the grain elevators.

The warning had come too late. People were already hurrying toward the lumberyard. Two of the clerks at the hardware store came out, hesitated, and ran down the street. At the corner Stoesz was talking to some farmers, gesturing and pointing, his grocery apron still on.

"Town won't miss him much," Mrs. Penner observed. "Never in church, fooling around on the road leaving his poor wife to shift for herself and all the kids. That Watkins stuff wasn't much good anyway."

Klaas turned around slowly. "Mr. Lilla was a good friend to Marina and me."

"Friend or not, he's damned for sure now. Come on, Julia, I want to get home." She herded the speechless, wide-eyed child out the door.

Klaas took a step toward them, then stopped and watched them go. I have to call Martin, he thought, and walked on unsteady legs to the back room where the telephone was. Martin did not answer. Klaas returned to the shop and sat down.

Before long Deet returned. "It was Lilla, all right. Abrams found him half an hour ago in a back corner behind a stack of boards. He used one of those iron hooks they hang rope on. Must have done it during the night or early this morning. They can't figure out how he got in."

"Poor man, poor man," Klaas mumbled. He passed a trembling hand over his eyes.

"I guess everything got too much for him," Deet said.

"Who's going to tell his wife?" Klaas paused, looked out the window. "Irma. She used to come in here when she was a little thing in pigtails. What's she going to do? They have five kids."

Deet shook his head. "It's bad, all right."

"Marina always bought from him," Klaas went on. "Real nice guy. He had some kind of trouble years ago before they moved down here from LeSeuer, and then that accident with the horses . . . but they said he was getting over it."

"I better see if I can help them with something. Martin's out there—he said he was coming over," Deet said, on his way out. At the door he paused. "Can I leave my stuff here? I'll get it later." He hurried away.

Klaas watched the people on the street standing in little knots, talking, gesticulating, looking toward the lumberyard. A tall man in gray shirt and pants ran across the street and opened the door. "Have you heard about Lilla? They're taking him to Corny's, want to get him out of sight as quick as they can. Half the town's out there gawking."

"Martin—I was going to call you," Klaas said. "What about Irma? Is anybody going down there? She needs to know."

"Stoesz is going with several ladies—they're probably on their way right now," Martin told him.

"Marina's working at the hospital today, she can go down later," Klaas said.

Martin nodded. "Corny's out in Gessel, old Tielman's funeral is today. I'm supposed to catch him before he comes back. You have a Gessel phone book? Deet said he'd see about a cemetery lot." Martin went into the back room, where he spent some time making calls.

He returned looking discouraged. "Corny said to bring him in, he won't embalm him though unless somebody's going to pay for it. Might be he'll have to be buried tomorrow. Which church do you suppose would take the funeral? Did he ever belong to one?"

Klaas shook his head. "Maybe. I don't think so. They'll have to ask Irma. But listen, Irma's going to need help. Somebody's got to notify his family, too—he has a couple brothers somewhere."

Martin frowned, gazing out the window at the street, where a group of people had gathered in front of the hardware store. "His brothers left LeSeuer long ago, they haven't had anything to do with the family for years. That's what he told me once. I can go over to the house and find out from Irma—maybe she knows where the brothers are."

After Martin left, Klaas walked over to his shelves and began poking about, taking medicine bottles down, putting them back. "Why did you do it?" he asked out loud. "You should have said something. Maybe we could have helped you." He took off his glasses and rubbed his eyes.

Someone banged open the door—it was the two boys, flushed and out of breath. "We wanna buy some likrish," they announced, digging in their pockets and producing coins. A third boy, thin and dark, wearing overalls, slid in behind them.

Klaas shook his head. "The store is closed for today."

"How come? It's too early!" they protested. "Anyway we just want some likrish."

"Not today," Klaas said. "I am closing the store out of respect for my friend Mr. Lilla. It will be closed tomorrow too."

The boys looked at each other. "He did a bad thing," one of them said. "My dad said they can't bury him in the cemetery with the regular people."

"They can't bury him from no church, neither," the other one said. "They don't bury no suicide guys from the church."

Klaas, who had been opening the door for them to leave, stopped. "Who told you that?"

"Oh, a bunch of guys talkin' at the elevator." The boys gestured vaguely. "You sure we can't buy nothin'? We gotta go—our dads said they was leaving in five minutes." The two dashed out and broke into a run, heading back to the elevator.

The thin boy remained standing by the counter. Klaas looked him over, then closed the door and locked it. "Well, Walter, what's on your mind?"

The boy glanced quickly at Klaas, then shifted his dark gaze to the floor.

"You want to sit?" Klaas asked. "I'm not going anywhere."

The boy rubbed his thin leg nervously with one hand. At last he said, "It's about him—Mr. Lilla—is he . . . ." He hesitated. "Was it real bad, what he did?"

Klaas did not answer immediately. He watched the corner road where a farm wagon was being driven toward the elevator. He heard the trot of horses, someone shouting in front of Stoesz's. "I don't know why Mr. Lilla did this," he said at last, "except he had a lot of troubles on his mind. His family came from Russia when he was a kid . . . he said his uncles and one of his brothers got killed by bandits—he was hiding behind a wagon and saw it happen. Then a couple years ago he had an accident, ran over a kid. After that he sort of went to pieces. Maybe all those things got going round in his head, he couldn't stop them. Maybe it got so bad in his head he couldn't stand it, and he had to stop it somehow."

The boy was watching his face intently. He nodded. "But . . . it's against God to kill yourself, ain't it? The men said suicide people can't go to heaven because they don't have no chance to repent. They said it was a rule in the Bible." His hand moved incessantly over his leg—a thin, tense hand, Klaas noted, overalls that were worn and patched and too short.

"There's no rule like that in the Bible," Klaas said, "you can go and look. There's plenty people in this town who like making up rules and then tell everybody else they're damned if they don't follow 'em. But maybe God sees things different. Maybe God has other rules he goes by. He looks at what's going on inside people."

The boy stopped rubbing his leg. "You think?"

Klaas said slowly. "God knows our frame, he remembers that we are dust. One thing I do know for sure, God has a lot more mercy in him than some of those men at the elevator."

The boy let out a long breath. Klaas looked at him more closely. "All the same, Walter, it's a terrible thing. It's terrible for his wife and kids. Lilla should have told somebody about his trouble, maybe they could have helped him. Another thing, you can never tell when something good is going to show up, next turn in the road." He studied the boy anxiously. "Like with your dad, now."

The boy started. A dark flush crept over his neck and face.

"Your dad, he's a bit too stingy with his money. He should have bought you new overalls a long time ago. Shoes too, and things for school. He shouldn't make you work all the time. He's a good man in a lot of ways, always pays his bills, takes good care of the farm. But he forgets about his family sometimes."

The boy gazed at the floor in silence.

Klaas began to fidget with his glasses—took them off, wiped them on his cuff, put them back on. "I've been thinking, Walter. I'm getting old. I was thinking about it just the other day. I need somebody to help me—you know, clean shelves, unpack boxes. Maybe you could work for me after school some days, maybe Saturdays. You're a smart boy, tall, you could reach the top shelves. I'd pay you, of course. When's your birthday?"

"August 19." The boy was listening though he kept his eyes on the floor.

"You'll be what—thirteen?"

"Fourteen."

"Fourteen. A good age to start earning a little money of your own. Well, what do you think?"

The boy looked up. "But Pa—I hafta work for him."

"I'll draw up a contract, hours and wages, how much he gets and how much you keep, and he'll let you come. I know that for a fact." The irresistible scent of money, Klaas was sure, would work this miracle. "If you agree, I'll talk to him tomorrow, next day for sure."

"I agree." The boy's face was serious, his hands thrust into his pockets in exactly the same way, Klaas noted, that his father's always were. Klaas put out his hand and the boy, looking up in surprise, pulled his own out of his pocket and they shook hands.

"And listen," Klaas said, "one of these days you'll be on your own and everything will be different. Remember that. Walter, it will be a real pleasure to have you working for me. I'm looking forward to it. In fact we could even start before your birthday. I'll talk it over with my wife and let you know."

Trying to rise to let the boy out, Klaas found he was too shaky to stand. "Here's the key," he said, throwing it to the boy, who caught it and unlocked the door, threw it back with a quick shy smile, and walked away toward the elevators.

Klaas leaned his head on his hands. "Look what you started, Lilla," he said aloud in dismay. He recalled that he needed to tell Marina about seeing Mrs. Lilla. He shut his eyes to concentrate on stopping the shaking. At length he found himself able to walk, went to telephone, and found that she had already gone on her own.

He relocked the door, pulled down the yellowing window shades, and went slowly upstairs to their apartment. Damnation, Klaas thought, should be reserved for a town that paid no attention to a desperate man. He himself had not sought Lilla out or talked to him for months, a year maybe. Most of what he knew about Lilla had been told him by Martin. But why hadn't Lilla said something? He should have told somebody.

There was a quick knock at the back door, and Martin ran up. "Irma's not talking," he said, out of breath. "She sits there like she doesn't understand what we're telling her. I couldn't find out anything from her about a church. I'll just have to find one that'll take him." Martin looked at him more closely. "What's wrong? You look like you got hit by a train."

"There's plenty wrong," Klaas said, "same things that've been wrong for the last fifty years. Those two boys told me the men are saying no church is going to have a service for him, being a suicide, and he can't be buried in the cemetery."

Martin sighed. "It won't be easy to find a church but I'll try." He got out a notebook and made a few notes, then started downstairs to use the telephone.

"What about a cemetery lot?" Klaas called after him.

"Deet's talking to Jungas." The office door closed.

Klaas sat down in the small upstairs parlor. From the window he watched the people going in and out of stores, talking, shaking their heads.

A few minutes later Marina came home. "Won't say a word, not a word," she told Klaas. "Just sits there like she's deaf and dumb. The poor kids. The older ones understand what happened, they sit there holding on to each other in the corner of that old front room. Littlest one is only four and keeps talking to her mother and pulling on her arm, but Irma won't move." She hung up her sweater and began bustling about the tiny kitchen. She called through the door, "What's Martin doing downstairs?"

"Trying to find a church that will do the funeral."

"He won't get nowheres. When poor Mr. Zielke shot himself, nobody'd touch the funeral. Had to be buried on the other side of the cemetery fence in a corn field." She got a sack of green beans from the pantry, laid them on the cutting board, and started chopping them up.

Klaas came into the kitchen and sat down. "That was twelve years ago. Maybe things have changed."

Marina did not reply, but scooped the chopped beans into a pot of water on the stove, threw in salt and a handful of dill. A fragrant smell filled the kitchen.

Some time later Martin ran back up without knocking. "Nobody'll take him. Listen to this!" He read from a piece of paper in his hand. "Presbyterian: pastor sympathetic but would have to get permission from elders, would take several days. Bargen Church: out of the question. Lutheran: pastor is away, his wife felt situation difficult to handle. Valley Church: Jauntz said definitely not; a man like that is under God's judgment and having the funeral in church would appear to condone his act. Alliance: nobody in the office. Parkview: Pastor Schulte would gladly do it but has some difficult members on the church council. First Mennonite: not sure, never faced this situation before. I even tried the Catholic church."

"What about the cemetery?" Klaas asked.

"Jungas and Stoesz are donating a small lot in the back corner next to the fence. People will talk but nobody will try to stop it—they're big men in town." Martin flung himself into a chair. "How can I go tell Irma no church will hold the funeral? She's so terribly ashamed already. God in heaven, what are they all thinking?"

"Maybe a small service in Corny's chapel," Marina suggested. The soup was bubbling on the stove. She got a loaf of bread out of a cupboard and began cutting thick slices.

"Might have to. I'll check with Corny. Be right back." Martin left. Some minutes later he returned. "No dice. Corny has the Mierau baby's funeral in the morning, and a lady from the Old Folks Home in the afternoon."

"Well, why not here, then?" Klaas said. "There's room downstairs if we push the show case against the wall. We could get in a few chairs."

The others stared at him. "Here!" Marina repeated, her soup ladle poised in mid-air.

"I don't know," Martin said doubtfully. "I suppose . . . there won't be many people, maybe it would work."

Marina ladled soup carefully into bowls and brought them to the table. "Sit down, let's eat." After a moment she said thoughtfully, "Well, why not? Used to have funerals in homes, didn't they, before there were funeral parlors? I could make a lunch . . . Mrs. Stoesz would help, maybe Helena if she has time."

"Town might make trouble. You have your business to think about," Martin said.

"What kind of trouble? We've had plenty trouble before . . . a little more won't hurt," she said, unperturbed, and blew on a spoonful of soup to cool it.

And so it was settled. Martin was to take some of the bean soup over to Irma today and ask if having a brief service at the store would be all right. It would be better than simply a graveside service. Everything would be taken care of, she wouldn't have to worry about a thing.

Marina served up coffee and pie, and Klaas began talking about Walter. "The Block kid was here—O.D.'s boy. He kept on and on about was suicide a bad thing. I began to wonder if he's been thinking of something like that himself."

"Oh, my goodness, that would be awful!" Marina exclaimed.

"Poor little guy has a tough time at home. Dad works him half to death, never gives him a penny. Clothes are old, patched, too small—the other kids probably make fun of him at school." Klaas picked up his coffee cup, looked into it, set it back down.

"Grace Krahn told me O.D's wife has to candle eggs to get money for shoes for the kids," Marina put in indignantly.

"What did you tell him?" Martin drank the last of his coffee. "No more, thanks."

"I offered him a job working for me," Klaas said. "Give him a way to get out from under his dad."

Marina set down the bowls she was carrying. "You what? You

can't afford to hire anybody! You're barely making it now, what with all those debts on the books."

"It was all I could think of right then," Klaas said. "Anyway I'm getting old. I've been thinking I could use help."

The three were silent. At last Martin said, "Some will object to us having a funeral in the store. It's like going against the church, I suppose."

"Maybe," Klaas said. "But we need to, for the family's sake."

"Poor Lilla." Marina sighed. "He never got over running over that kid—horses going wild . . . what spooked them, a shot, was it? Anyway he couldn't stop 'em. Still, he blamed himself. Couldn't sleep. Just stopped living."

Silence settled on them once more. Finally Marina, getting fidgety, got up to clear the table and began washing dishes. She put the rest of the soup in a large jar to give to Irma. "Be careful, it's hot," she told Martin.

"I'll let you know what she says," Martin said. He left, carrying the jar of soup tied up in a dishtowel.

Klaas helped dry the dishes. He hung up the wet dishtowel and said, "I'm going down to phone Peters, see if he'll do the funeral. I think I got his number somewhere." He went downstairs. Marina heard him talking.

Hearing a knock at the back door, she hurried down.

It was Helena Jungas. "The lunch can be at the hotel," she said at once. "More room there, you can't crowd them into your place. My sister Lieze is making the *zwieback*. Rosie from the Parkview church said she would bring sausage. You could maybe bring a couple pies?" They arranged the lunch, counting the number of people who might come, and Helena returned to the hotel.

Deet stopped by to get the latest news, said he would spread the word: short service at eleven o'clock at Dyck's store, burial at the cemetery, lunch at the hotel afterwards.

Early that evening a man and his wife came by. The man introduced himself as a deacon in the Valley Church but said his visit was unofficial. He and another deacon had spoken together after finding out the pastor had refused to hold Lilla's funeral. While unable to change the decision, they felt sympathetic to the plight of the widow and wished to help defray the cost . . . pay for the casket, for example, or whatever was needed. They had tried Corny's, but he had already gone home. Perhaps Klaas would let Corny know? The wife added that she would visit Mrs. Lilla when things settled down a bit, to see whether the family needed anything.

Klaas took off his glasses and rubbed his eyes. "It's very good of you," he said. "Irma will appreciate it very much. Right now she's not talking, you understand—she's grieving, and she's ashamed. Give her a few days. Kind words are what she needs most." He paused. "I'll call Corny tonight. The service will be here in my store tomorrow at eleven o'clock. If you want to come, you're welcome."

When Martin stopped in on his way home, Klaas told him that Peters had agreed to do the service, and that a couple had stopped by to offer help. "There are good people in this town, Martin," he said slowly. "I forget that sometimes. Maybe you should tell Deet to bring over a few more chairs."

"I don't suppose there's any law against having a funeral in a drug store," Martin said. "Don't know why there would be, but who knows. Do we announce this anywhere?"

"Deet's taking care of it," Klass told him.

The next morning Klaas and Marina tidied up the store—pushed the show case against the wall, covered it with a dark cloth, set a vase of garden flowers on it. Deet arrived with the chairs, which they arranged in rows. Mrs. Ortman from the Parkview Church walked in carrying a vase of roses, ferns and white daisies—from the Sunshine Committee, she announced. Marina, surprised, thanked her profusely and later placed the bouquet in a prominent position near the door.

Just before eleven o'clock Corny's men brought over the plain gray casket and set it up on trestles. Grace Krahn came in the back way with a spray of gladiolas from her garden, which she placed on the casket. A few people gathered in front of the store, looking self-consciously at one another and murmuring greetings; came in and sat down. Two had brought flowers in jars: roses, dahlias, red geraniums.

Mrs. Lilla and her children arrived at Klaas's back door—she had utterly refused to come the front way—and were escorted into the store, where chairs had been reserved for them. A thin-faced woman with heavy dark hair, Mrs. Lilla stared uncomprehendingly at the coffin. Beside her the three girls squirmed in too-tight dresses. The teen-aged sons sat unmoving, dark hair slicked back, staring straight ahead.

Rev. Peters arrived, wearing a worn black suit and carrying a Bible. After a brief silence, he rose to speak. He described Mr. Lilla's services to the community, his willingness to accommodate poor families who could not immediately pay for goods purchased. He spoke of God's care for the distressed, and read several scriptures of comfort. The group sang one hymn together. Before the final prayer Rev. Peters hesitated. "I would encourage anyone who owes Mr. Lilla to pay your bill, add perhaps a little more to help the family in this difficult time." He moved to stand directly in front of the Lilla family and with hands outstretched, spoke over them the benediction.

Afterwards the casket was maneuvered into Corny's hearse, and the mourners left for the cemetery. They wound their way to a grave hastily dug near the back corner just inside the fence. The sky was a serene blue. Sunlight glanced off the thin brass handles of the casket and warmed the weathering gravestones stretching down in rows toward the lake. The grass between them was dotted with dandelions.

Rev. Peters spoke a final prayer. The coffin was lowered and a spadeful of dirt thrown onto it.

Unexpectedly, Mrs. Lilla stood, twisted her hands together and looked up briefly at them all. "Thank you, thank you all very much," she whispered. "I didn't know what to do. He was troubled a long time. I hope he finds peace."

Helena Jungas put an arm around her. "*Jah,* we all hope. Now please, we will have a small lunch at my hotel before you go home."

Later Klaas and Marina went home to clean up. Deet had already removed chairs and trestles and moved the show case into place. Marina took a look around, and went up to the bedroom to lie down.

Martin came in. "Not many people, but more than I expected."

Klaas nodded. "I hope they stand by the family."

"I expect they will. Well, I'll take these flowers over to Irma's. You'd better rest a bit, Klaas." Martin picked up the flowers and left the store.

Klaas sat down at his desk in the small office downstairs. He meant to write, finally, his letter of resignation from the school board, but found his mind wandering. He thought about the folks bringing flowers, about old bills not paid; about the Lilla children, and their mother's whispered words of thanks, about Deet, about Lilla himself, and about Walter. He remembered that he must go over and talk to Walter's father.

He got up, walked into the store and stood by the window, watching the town carry on its business. Across the street, workers were putting up scaffolding, rebuilding a section of a roof. A group of boys watched them, jostling each other, until one of the workers shouted at them to move away. To the south the grain elevators gleamed in the afternoon sunshine. Beyond them he could see dark roofs of homes surrounded by cottonwoods, farther out the cornfields, barns, lines of trees along the creek.

Everywhere, he thought, the green countryside was beautiful, peaceful, things growing silently in the good dark earth under the brilliant sky. God's creation. But in the houses, wherever people were, there was trouble. In the Erickson farm house, the grandmother lay on her bed racked by head pains. East of the highway on his farm, O.D. Block drove his family to desperation. In the living rooms of this town, Mrs. Penner and others like her would this very evening be discussing, if not the damnation, at least the disgrace of Mr.Lilla, while in their small home Irma and the children grieved their hearts out.

He returned to his office and, sitting down at the desk, leaned his head on shaky hands. "I'm an old man," he said aloud. "I can't help the people in this town any more. Let Deet do it, or Martin. Forgive me, dear God, I forgot about Mr. Lilla. I didn't know it was so bad. Forgive us all. Somebody should have helped him." Covering his face with his hands, he wept.

When he heard Marina stirring upstairs, he rubbed his eyes with a handkerchief. Then he put on his glasses and wrote the letter of resignation from the school board.

SARAH

"**BEST TIME OF** my life, having babies," Mrs. Schultz said, slapping down a fresh batch of hand towels. She folded them energetically, one fold up, two over; then piled them on the trolley. "Nothing to do but sit in bed and knit for ten days. Only time I could rest."

"My sister in Iowa," said Mrs. Eidem, folding bath towels opposite her, "she has 'em easy—two pains and there they are, squalling. Never mind no hospital, just gimme the back bedroom for half a day, she says. Due for her ninth any day now. All them kids—jammed in an old farm house, running around like so many chicks."

The women were sitting at one end of a long folding table in the hospital's basement laundry room. A few windows high up let in sufficient light to work by. In adjacent rooms were boilers, washing machines and tubs, boxes of home-made soap, racks of long-handled wooden spoons, dippers and other utensils. Outside the windows were rows of long wires attached to iron posts, with clothespins stuck here and there.

At the other end of the table Mathilda Braun and Vena Karschnik were standing across from each other folding sheets. At a separate small table under the windows a round-faced woman sat slowly folding washcloths. Her yellow hair was puffed awkwardly around her ears in imitation of the style worn by younger women. She wore a print dress, and around her neck a string of large pink beads.

"Nine kids—that's nothing," Mathilda was saying. "My uncle Jonah in Canada had fourteen. Once when we went to visit there were so many kids, five of us slept on a Russian *sclopbenkj*, one on top of the other. Aunt Lina put a dresser up against us so we wouldn't fall off."

"You never!" Mrs. Schultz looked at her with suspicion.

"Uncle Jonah made us drink *schnapps* every night to make sure we'd sleep good, stacked up like firewood." Mathilda laughed merrily and the others saw that it was all a joke.

"Richert in 4, he's the one that needs the *schnapps*," Mrs. Eidem remarked. "Scratches himself nearly to pieces, he itches so bad. Skin comes off in big flakes, they have to sweep around his bed twice a day."

"Doc Olfert's using the wrong medicine," Vena said darkly. "The nurses say it takes the skin right off their hands—they have to wear gloves to put it on him. Think what it does to him. Here, Tillie, grab the other end of these sheets." The women lifted a heavy stack of folded sheets onto a second trolley.

The women worked in silence for a few minutes. In an adjoining room the huge mangle clanked and whirred.

"Have you seen Susie Engstrom's baby?" Mrs. Eidem asked. "It's got a purple patch on its shoulder big as a saucer. Susie keeps it dressed in high-necked things; she won't let anybody see the patch, she's so ashamed."

Mrs. Schultz clucked her tongue. "I heard about it. After all the miscarriages, she wanted this one so bad. She'll have to get used to it, though, it's not her fault."

"It's the baby I feel sorry for, when she grows up," Vena said. "A girl, too—makes it worse."

"When my sister's baby was born with a split lip, she cried for weeks," Mrs. Eidem said. "You can't imagine—even the top of his mouth was split open. When he tried to swallow his milk, it came pouring out of his nose. She washed her kitchen floor ten times a day. They were lucky though, got a doctor in the Cities who sewed it up so good you can't notice all that much any more, except his nose is a little crooked."

"Hard thing, bringing babies into the world," Mrs. Schultz observed. "You never know how they'll turn out. Got to love 'em and live with 'em."

She shoved an empty hamper across the floor with her foot and leaned on the table to rest. "Better not get married—eh, Sarah? You're not saying much today."

Sarah, the round-faced girl, was folding the washcloths slowly, laying each fold over her hand. In front of her were seven or eight piles of finished cloths. Mrs. Eidem came over to move the piles to the trolley. "Thinking about somebody, I can see!" she teased.

"She's got Friday off, girls—I bet a fellow's taking her out, that's what's on her mind," Vena announced.

"Who's after you now, Sarah? Come on, tell us, we'll keep it secret." Mathilda winked at the others.

Sarah's folding became even slower. "*Nae, nae*, nobody's after me," she protested. Her round face flushed pink. She smiled secretly at the washcloths.

"Wait—I heard Sarah say she was going away Saturday. I bet that good-looking guy at the creamery is taking her to the auction," Vena said.

Sarah giggled. "*Nae*, I'm not going to the auction."

"You can't fool us," Mrs. Eidem said, rapidly folding hospital gowns with the strings tucked inside. "He'll take you to the auction and buy you something, a vase maybe, or a necklace."

Sarah shook her head and touched the pink beads around her neck. "*Nae*, not to the auction. I'm going to Nick's farm to make buns for Lizzie's wedding."

Mathilda lifted her eyebrows. "Oh, a wedding! I suppose you'll have a new dress? Girls, wait till the men see Sarah in her new dress."

Sarah giggled louder. "*Nae*, I'm not getting a new dress."

"Well, then, a hat at least. You'll catch a man this time. Ollie Henshaw'll have to look out—somebody else'll get you if he's too slow."

The blushing Sarah kept her eyes on her washcloths. "Ollie Henshaw don't like me. He likes Gerty Buhr. He takes her on the lake in a boat."

"He's teasing you! What does he want with a young kid like Gerty? Didn't you see how he looked at you in church Sunday?" Mrs. Eidem loaded the hospital gowns on the trolley and reached for a tub of baby diapers.

"Who's taking you to the wedding?" Mrs. Schultz wanted to know.

"Nick. He's taking us," Sarah answered.

"Nick? Oh, Lizzie's dad . . . your father's nephew, isn't he? Well, you tell Nick you ain't going with him, you're going with Ollie."

Sarah giggled helplessly. The women's hands flew, folding and stacking.

"Any more out on the lines?"

"No, that's all. Six o'clock. We're done early."

The noise of the mangle stopped. A young girl came in with a load of pillow cases over her arm. "Got a clear place where I can fold these?"

"Give us each some, we'll help you," Mrs. Eidem said. The pillow cases were passed around. Mathilda examined one with a stain and flung it into the hamper under the laundry chute for boiling.

"It wouldn't be so bad if I didn't have to cook supper when I get home," Mrs. Schultz remarked.

"Fried potatoes and sour milk soup, that's what we're having," Mrs. Eidem said. "If Henry don't like it he can go eat at Steuke's."

"Well, girls, it's ironing uniforms and washing for the Old Folks Home tomorrow," Mathilda announced. "Gotta be here by six. Who's coming early to start the boiler?"

Nobody answered. "I'm wore out," Mrs. Eidem said at last. "My boy's been sick."

"I came early yesterday," Mrs. Schultz reminded them. The others were silent.

"Doft Penner, he likes me," Sarah announced suddenly.

The women looked at her in surprise. "Doft Penner! *Waut du sajst*! Not really! Not the handsome guy with the brown beard?"

"Well, why not?" Vena said. "His wife's been dead a year; he'll be looking around now, you bet."

Sarah giggled. "He wants to walk me home from choir practice."

The women exchanged smiles. "Be careful now, Sarah," Mathilda warned. "First it's a walk home from choir practice, then it's a walk by the lake, then it's a walk to the altar. Watch out! Don't let him kiss you, not the first time."

"*Nae*, he won't kiss me," Sarah protested, fingering her beads. Her cheeks were bright pink under the yellow puffed-out hair. "No, no, he won't do that."

"Wait and see, wait and see!" The women laughed and jostled each other, done with work now, putting on coats, scarves and galoshes. "Just don't you be in a hurry, we don't want you married off too soon. Who would keep us going down here?"

They walked up the basement steps and went outside, where they stopped, breath steaming in the cold air. "Who's coming to light up the fire?" Mathilda asked.

"Oh, I'll come," Vena said. Vena lived in the home for nurses next to the hospital. "If Sarah'll come too and tell me about Doft. No, Sarah, you don't have to come, I'm joking."

They laughed and went off in separate directions. Sarah walked home slowly, smiling to herself. Going around to the back door of the small house in which she lived with her parents, she went inside.

Her mother sat mending stockings in the living room by the

light of a table lamp. "*Na*, Sarah!" She put aside the mending and got up, holding her hip.

The father sat in his wheelchair in the corner facing into the room. His eyes were bright, his thin white beard combed smooth. "*De es nuscht*," he said, bobbing his head at her.

Sarah helped put supper on the table and wheeled her father into position while her mother put food on his plate. The old man's good hand trembled so that food often dropped from his wavering fork. Sarah sometimes assisted him, but tonight she paid no attention, and her mother had to help him eat.

Sarah said suddenly, "I don't want to wear my old brown dress for Lizzie's wedding."

Her mother looked up. "It's not so old, only from last year."

Sarah pouted. "I need a hat, with a veil."

Her mother glanced at her sharply and thought a moment. "You want to wear my new hat to the wedding? The blue one? It has a nice veil."

"*Joh*, it's a nice hat." Sarah smiled to herself.

"Did you get Friday off?" her mother asked. "Nick is coming at nine o'clock."

"*Joh*, I got Friday off." Sarah inspected her hands closely and began to pick at her fingernails. Her mother watched her, sighed, and rose to wash the dishes.

"Take Dad to the bedroom—I want to rub his feet," she directed Sarah. "You want your feet rubbed, Dad?"

The old man waved his good hand about and looked at them with his bright eyes. "*De es nuscht*," he said. Sarah wheeled him into the bedroom.

Before going to bed Sarah applied a thick streak of face cream to her cheeks and rubbed at them for a long time, smiling at her reflection in the mirror.

The next day she went to work early to help with the Old Folks

Home laundry. The women teased her mercilessly about Doft Penner. "Be careful at the wedding Saturday—he might want to walk you down the aisle too, after the bride!" Sarah blushed and smiled and shook her head.

On Friday just before nine Nick drove up in his mud-splashed Model A. "*Goondach*! Looks like a nice day, no wind for a change. How are you, Sarah? Here, take my arm, Taunte Bergsche, no use taking a fall, the steps are slippery. Uncle Berg going too?" He helped Sarah's mother into the car, then lifted the father out of his wheelchair and placed him in the back corner beside her, tucking blankets securely around his thin legs. "Sarah, you get in front with me—I like driving through town with pretty girls." Sarah, in a thick coat and shawl, got in slowly.

Nick joked with her the five miles to the farm, driving carefully along the ruts so as not to jostle Uncle Berg. "You're pretty lucky, working in the hospital, you know that? When a man is flat down, he can't get away, just got to lie there. He's glad for somebody to talk to. I know how it is, I was down for two weeks in the hospital once, got so lonesome I fell in love with all the nurses. You take your chance, now—pick a good-looking one, bring him a nice cold drink, pat him on the hand a little, next thing he'll be asking you for a date at the movies when he goes home."

Sarah protested, giggling. "I work in the basement. I don't go up there."

Nick steered expertly around a pile of blackened rope fallen off somebody's wagon. "Take my advice, but choose a farmer, not some city blockhead."

At the farm, while her parents rested in the parlor, Sarah went to help Hannah, Nick's wife, and their two teenage daughters in the kitchen—a large warm room with a row of windows overlooking the road to town running east along the windbreak. On the great round table in the center of the room, dough was already rising in two enormous yellow crockery bowls. "Come along, Sarah, we got plenty work for you," Hannah said, up to her elbows in a third batch of dough. "We've been at it since five this morning. There's an apron behind the door. Here's the recipe."

Sarah tied the apron around her waist, washed her hands under the kitchen pump, and began, very slowly, to measure flour into a bowl.

"Arpha, see if that one is risen enough," Hannah directed. "All right, put it on the pans. Pinch 'em off small, none of your elephants. Noreen, you fire up the oven a bit more. We're making six hundred *zwieback*," she told Sarah. "We figure three apiece. If they're hungry after that, they can go eat at home."

"*Joh*, three is enough," Sarah said. She lost count of the cups of flour and had to begin again.

Arpha and Noreen, working quickly, filled half a dozen long black flat pans with pinched-off balls of dough. They set the pans along the windowsills in the sun and covered them with clean dish towels. Hannah finished kneading, came over to assist Sarah. "Good, yours is ready, we'll set it near the stove to rise. Now if we can get the oven right—it acts up sometimes. Arpha, go get more wood, we'll need lots."

Arpha made a face. "Where's Arlie? Why can't he do something?" She dusted her floury hands on her apron and reached for a jacket hanging on a hook by the back door.

"Arlie's helping his dad fix the pig sty," Hannah said, setting a kettle on the stove. "My stars, a girl of fifteen and grumbles about bringing in wood. At your age I was out chopping it. Hurry up, now. Noreen, make the tops smaller, I don't want 'em sliding off."

Sarah's mother came in to help. "Not much left to do, we're well on the way," Hannah told her. "Sarah's doing your share. You just take it easy. Tell you what, there's a *Herald* on the piano, maybe you could read it to Uncle Berg—he'd like that."

By noon most of the baking was done. The oven was working well; the *zwieback* came out an even light brown. The cooled buns were piled into large dishpans and covered with clean cloths to be taken to the church next day. The rest of the buns were rising on the pans. Hannah set the girls to frying potatoes and sausage for lunch. They set the table with heavy china plates, put out bread, jam, and pickles, and called the family.

Nick came in with Arlie, a thin boy of twelve. They washed up at the sink. Nick carried Uncle Berg in and set him into a chair with armrests to prevent him from falling. Sarah's mother followed with the blanket for his legs. When she saw the food, she lifted her hands in protest. "*Nae, oba*, you went to too much work!"

"Just plain stuff today," Hannah said, laughing. "We'll do better next time."

Nick picked up a piece of sausage and squinted at it. "Awful bitty pieces you got here, Hannah. Guess we'll have to fill up on them *tweeback*."

"Nope," Hannah said firmly. "We got 'em counted for the wedding. What do you want to drink today, Taunte Bergsche—coffee?"

"Hot water," Sarah's mother said.

Nick snorted. "Hot water! Uncle Berg wants good strong coffee. Don't you, Uncle Berg?" He patted the old man's hand.

The old man smiled and waved his good hand to show he understood. "*De es nuscht.*"

The two girls looked at each other, trying not to laugh. "What does he mean?" Arpha asked.

"That's all he can say since his stroke," Mrs. Berg explained. "The words mean 'he is nothing,' but that's not what he wants to say. We can usually figure out what he's trying to tell us."

"He can't have coffee. It makes him sick," Sarah said.

"*Dommheit!*" Nick exclaimed. "My grandpa drank coffee, strong and thick with cream, till he was ninety. If they'd made it a little stronger, he would have made it to a hundred, sure."

They all laughed, except Sarah, who looked confused. "He's

making fun, Sarah," her mother said. She looked around the table. "Where's Lizzie, isn't she coming for lunch?"

"Oh, she's off somewhere with Irv," Hannah explained. "Getting flowers for the wedding, I think. No use talking to her these days, anyway—her head's flying around like a flock of birds, you'd think nobody ever got married before."

"When you get married," Nick told Sarah, "you be sensible. Don't go to all this fuss."

Sarah looked at her plate. "*Nae*, I'm not getting married."

"Good idea!" Nick applauded. "These girls of mine are both going to be old maids."

"Oh Dad!" The girls laughed and looked at each other.

"One thing sure, I ain't putting on no more expensive weddings," Nick declared. "You both gotta promise to elope."

"I'm having two bridesmaids and a bakery cake," Arpha cried. "And candles. I don't care what the church says."

"Well then, good thing you ain't getting married for another twenty years. Maybe by then I can afford it. Sarah here, that's another story. I'm ready any time, got her present all picked out. I'm going to give her that grandfather clock from Russia up in our bedroom. Eh, Sarah?"

"Nick, you stop teasing!" his wife commanded. She walked back and forth, bringing more potatoes, pie, hot water.

"Sarah won't get married," Mrs. Berg said quietly. "They don't ask her."

The joking stopped abruptly. After a pause the talk turned to other things—the unseasonable cold weather, the rising price of pork.

After dinner the old people were helped into bedrooms to rest. The girls cleared away, washed and dried the dishes. Sarah industriously wiped the big table. "You got a boy friend?" she inquired suddenly of Arpha, who was now lounging at the window examining her hands.

Arpha glanced at Sarah from under lowered eyelids. "Sure, lots," she said at length.

Sarah opened her mouth to say something, but the cellar door opened and Hannah appeared carrying a huge crock. "Arpha, put this butter in the molds," she instructed. "Noreen, get the rest of the buns done. I'm going to the henhouse for eggs." She left the kitchen, closing the door carefully behind her.

Arpha got two wooden spoons from a drawer, gave one to Sarah, and set about filling the molds. "I 'm going to have my reception in our garden, over near the fir trees."

"Huh, not me." Noreen slid a pan of buns into the oven. "I want pink and white bells over the bride's table. I got some pictures from a magazine."

Sarah was patting down butter, a spoonful at a time. She spoke up suddenly. "Doft Penner likes me." She looked shyly down at her red butter-smeared hands.

The girls glanced at each other but said nothing.

"He has a farm," Sarah added. Her cheeks grew pink.

"Last time you said it was Abe Mierau," Noreen said. She took off her scarf, smoothed her thick yellow hair, tied it back on.

"*Nae*, not Abe Mierau. No, no, he's going with Elsie Schmidt. He likes her."

"She makes it all up," Noreen told Arpha. "Don't listen."

"Did Doft Penner ask to take you somewhere?" Arpha asked Sarah.

Sarah blushed and shook her head. "He wants to take me home from choir practice."

"How do you know—did he ask you?" Arpha watched her with narrowed eyes, hands suspended over the butter.

Sarah smiled to herself but did not answer.

"Well, did he talk to you?" Arpha demanded sharply.

Sarah avoided their eyes. "*Nae, nae*, he doesn't talk to me. He stood close by, after choir practice, he looked at me . . . he . . . ." She stopped.

"They just look at you or something, and you think they want to ask you out!" Noreen said severely. "It's all in your imagination."

"Doft Penner likes me," Sarah insisted. She set her lips in a stubborn line.

Arpha burst out, "Stop imagining all that stuff! I heard say you make big eyes at the men, even the married ones—people laugh at you, do you know that? You shouldn't stand around where the men are; go stand with the women, it'd look more decent."

"I heard Doft's going to South Dakota pretty soon to visit some lady," Noreen stated. "He's not after you. He probably just happened to look at you while he was talking. You can forget about him."

Sarah looked at them, her pale blue eyes wandering over their young accusing faces. The color drained slowly from her cheeks; her shoulders drooped over the butter. "Doft Penner's going to South Dakota to see a lady?"

"That's what I heard."

Sarah's eyes grew watery. She wiped them on her sleeve. "Nobody told me," she murmured. "I didn't know."

"You've got to stop talking about all the men liking you," Arpha scolded. "You won't never get married, you're too old."

Sarah grew dumb. She worked on slowly, pushing butter into the mold with the spoon.

The back door opened, letting in a draft of cold air, and Hannah hurried in. "Arpha, get the leftover pie from the pantry to send with Taunte Berg. Dad's ready to go. Sarah, thanks a lot—just leave it, we'll finish."

"Is Doft Penner going to South Dakota to visit a lady?" Arpha asked.

Hannah paused, on her way to the parlor. "I wouldn't be surprised. He's been writing to a Mrs. Reimer, a widow. Why do you want to know?"

Arpha did not answer, but looked at Sarah and lifted her eyebrows in triumph. Sarah's face drooped. She walked slowly to the door.

The old people were helped into the car. On the way home Nick tried to tease Sarah. "It's your turn now, we'll do the same for you. I'll make the sausage myself."

Sarah did not respond.

The next day was clear and warmer with a gentle wind, so that the roads began to dry off. The wedding was in the little country church Nick's family attended. Nick came early for Sarah and her parents.

Sarah, wearing her brown dress and her mother's blue hat with the veil, was ushered with her mother to a front row on the women's side. She sat wedged in tightly between her mother and a stout woman in black silk. The tiny church was full; even the extra chairs placed behind the back benches and in the outer hall were occupied. A girl in a high-necked lavender dress was playing the piano. On the small stage were baskets of greenery and yellow daisies. The audience rustled and whispered.

The minister came in. The music changed, and from the back of the church Lizzie, smiling, walked in. Her white gown reached just below the knee, above white stockings and shoes. She wore a short veil with strings of white beads looped across her forehead, carried red roses tied with a long ribbon. Beside her walked Irvin Epp, a muscular young man in a dark suit.

Sarah's face flushed; her eyes brightened and then grew watery. She looked earnestly at the young couple standing before the altar. The minister, an elderly man with a white beard, was talking to them, a Bible open in one hand. Sunshine from the windows gleamed along the polished altar rail and lit the bride's fair hair. Sarah gazed at the filmy veil, at the graceful curve of Lizzie's arm in the satin sleeve, the groom's straight proud back. She fidgeted with her hat. The stout woman, turning her head in annoyance, nudged for more room. Sarah squeezed herself together and sat holding her purse in her lap with both hands.

Afterwards at the wedding supper, her parents were assisted to a special table. Sarah stood in line on the narrow steps into the basement until at the third sitting an usher pointed her to a place across from an old gentleman. He was eating noisily using his fingers. *Zwieback* in blue bowls, plates of ham and saucers of dill pickles stood at intervals on the long tables. Middle-aged men in white aprons pushed between the crowded benches with kettles of coffee, joking with the guests. There was a general noise of many conversations. "They're opening gifts!" someone shouted over the din. Guests rose to make their way upstairs to watch.

Sarah put on her thick coat and went with them. Unable to push through the crowd to watch the gift-opening, she went outside. In the yard people stood in little groups, talking. Shrieking children chased each other. The young people, including the piano player in the lavender dress, had gathered near the parked cars and carriages and were talking animatedly among themselves.

Not far from Sarah, the young farmers stood in the short stiff grass, conversing, their thumbs hooked into their heavy jacket pockets. Unconsciously Sarah edged closer. After a few minutes she heard other men talking behind her. She turned her head and saw that one of them, a tall fellow with untidy brown hair, was looking at her. At once she dropped her gaze, searching the ground, smiling a little to herself. After a few minutes she lifted her eyes to seek out the man, but he had turned away and was speaking to an elderly gentleman in a felt hat.

Arpha had come up and was standing three feet away with a tall bare-headed boy. She was staring hard at Sarah. Catching Sarah's eye, she frowned and shook her head reprovingly; then walked on, hanging on the boy's arm and laughing.

Sarah's shoulders drooped. She went slowly back to a group of older women standing by the wall of the church, where there was shelter from the wind.

Nick found her and escorted her to the car, saying her parents were tired and needed to leave. He was in high spirits. "What did you think of my Lizzie, eh? Finally got her married off. Of course we're going to have to sell her dress to pay for the wedding. I'd offer it to you, Sarah, cheap, but I don't think it would fit."

Sarah did not respond.

At home her mother said, "The ladies said the blue hat isn't right with the brown dress. They don't match."

"*Nae,* they don't match," Sarah agreed, and gave her mother back the hat.

Early Monday morning in the laundry room the women sighed, wished it were Sunday again, stood with hands on hips surveying the heaps of dirty laundry. "Three new babies over the weekend," Vena explained. They started reluctantly to work at the steaming tubs and began teasing Sarah about Doft Penner.

"Well, and did he hold your hand at the wedding? What did he say?"

"I'm jealous," Mathilda declared. "I had an eye on him myself."

Sarah shook her head slowly. "He wasn't at the wedding. He's going to South Dakota to see Mrs. Reimer."

"What? Mavis Reimer, the widow? She's got three kids, maybe four. No, no, don't give up yet. Besides, he's not the only fish in the lake. There's Jake Fehderau and that other Jake, the little one—kinda dried up but a good wife would do wonders for him. He could build you a nice house out by the creek."

But Sarah refused to be aroused. She sat at the table without looking around, face heavy and eyes dull, grating bars of home-made soap into a bucket.

The women glanced at each other, studied Sarah with worried

eyes. Their talk drifted to the ill folk upstairs, the work waiting for them in their gardens, troubles with their children. Perspiration ran down their faces in the heat of the laundry room.

In the afternoon Vena dragged a hamper of towels over to the table beside Sarah. "I'll help you fold these," she offered. After some hesitation she asked kindly, "Are you feeling all right? You're too quiet today."

Sarah did not answer. Vena tried again. "Something happen at home? To your dad, maybe—another stroke?"

Sarah shook her head. "*Nae*, nothing happened to him." She gazed at the towels, began more slowly than ever to fold them.

On their way home after work, the women talked among themselves. "Something must have happened, at the wedding, maybe. She sits there like a stone. Like our calf when it got hit on the head." They considered asking Sarah's mother, but decided they would wait a few days.

Two days later Vena astounded them by announcing that she was engaged. "Yep, he proposed last night on the telephone," she cried. "We've been writing each other for a year now, and here all of a sudden he pops the question. Over the phone! Can you beat that? I laughed so hard I could hardly answer him. All those nurses listening, too!"

The women stopped work and clustered around her. "Who is he? You're a sly one, keeping it all dark! Come on, we want to know."

It was a certain Harvey Duerksen, spelled 'ue,' she said, in Wolfpoint, Montana. She had not said anything to anyone because marrying was the farthest thing from her mind, until he started sending chocolates in the mail a few weeks ago, and a fine time she'd been having, hiding them from the those snoopy nurses.

Talk was brisk that day. The women offered Vena advice on every conceivable aspect of housekeeping, child-bearing, husband-pleasing, and even, in lowered and sometimes scornful voices, on certain intimate matters. "Whatever you do," Mrs. Schultz concluded, "don't shame him in front of other people, and don't do spring cleaning when he's home—men hate the house turned upside down."

"Well, Mathilda," Mrs. Eidem said, turning to her, "you got any secret flirtations going on we ought to know about?"

Mathilda, unblushing, continued ironing uniforms. "Not me. Not gonna spend my life looking after a man, wait on him hand and foot, sit by his bed for hours when he's old and sick. Nope, not me. Not that I haven't had my chances, but I turned 'em all down."

"*Nae*, she don't want to get married," Sarah murmured. The women glanced toward her. She had stopped work, was leaning forward listening to them with a longing, hungry look. The women were ashamed at having forgotten about her.

"Just as well, too," Mrs. Eidem said loudly. "Being married ain't all it's cooked up to be, let me tell you. Sarah, here, she won't have to worry herself silly over some guy, trying to figure out what he wants for supper every night. You just stay the way you are, Sarah, it's fine."

Sarah turned slowly away.

Shortly after this Sarah's mother took ill and could no longer care for her husband. Sarah told the women she couldn't come to work anymore, she had to help at home. "That's too bad!" Mrs. Eidem exclaimed. "We'll miss you, that's for sure." The other women agreed. They suggested that Tante Berg see the doctor, or if he was too busy, Klaas Dyck at his store—he had helped lots of people, they affirmed, and never charged except for the medicine.

Over the noon hour the next day Vena hurried to town to buy a parting gift: a photograph album with a bright fancy cover. The women presented it to Sarah after work. "You can put pictures of your family in it," they told her. Sarah thanked them with dull eyes and walked home with the album under her arm.

Vena suggested one day at work, several weeks later, that someone should really go to see the Bergs, see how the old dad and mother were doing, and Sarah, whom several of them had seen at church but had not spoken to since she stopped working. Mrs. Schultz offered to go with Vena later in the week.

They walked to the small house, bringing roses cut from Mrs. Schultz's garden. Sarah answered the door. "Can we come in? We brought some flowers for your mother," Vena said.

Sarah opened the door. Her mother was taking a nap, she told them. Her father couldn't get up any more, he had to stay in bed. She went to the kitchen to look for something to put the roses in.

The women looked around. A humble home: calendar prints on the walls, worn gray couch with a few patchwork cushions, old rocking chair, in the corner the wheelchair no longer in use. On a small table beside the couch lay the photograph album they had given Sarah. Vena picked it up, cocked an eyebrow at Mrs. Schultz, who was frowning "no," and opened it.

Pasted carefully on the pages were small objects: a bit of lace, a corner torn off a blue napkin, an invitation folded in half, pressed flowers. The women puzzled over the odd collection until they saw that the invitation was to a wedding and guessed that the other items, too, represented weddings. Photographs from the *Herald* had been carefully cut out and glued down: pictures of brides, families grouped outside the church, wedding cars decorated with white streamers, bride and groom in formal poses, announcements. "Lizzie's flowers," whispered Mrs. Schultz, pointing to a pressed dry red rose tied with a white ribbon. On further inspection the invitation proved to be Lizzie's as well.

"I saw Sarah at the wedding," Mrs. Schultz murmured. "She was wearing a brown dress and her mother's blue hat, veil and all. I wondered why Tante Berg let her go that way." She sighed.

The women looked at each other. At last Vena said quietly, "Poor girl. The one thing she wants and never will have."

Sarah returned, holding a canning jar. Her eyes traveled over the women and the open album. "My wedding book," she explained. She set the jar down and stuck the roses into it.

"Be sure to put in some water," Mrs. Schultz murmured with a worried glance at the jar.

"You like to look at these pictures and things?" Vena asked, watching Sarah closely.

"*Yoh,* I like to look at them. Before I go to bed."

Mrs. Schultz said, "It's very nice, the way you arranged the pages." She added lightly, "Save a few pages for yourself. You know, some day . . . ."

Sarah slowly raised her eyes and looked at them, first one, then the other. "*Nae,*" she said. "I won't get married. They don't ask me." She took the album from Vena, closed it, and put it firmly back on the little table.

After a moment Mrs. Schultz said gently, "You have a nice home here. Your mother and your dad need you. It's enough, isn't it, Sarah?"

Sarah did not answer.

Her mother called from the bedroom, wanting to know who was there.

"We'll come back another time," Vena said hastily. "We miss you at the hospital, Sarah. It was more fun when you were there. But you're doing a very important thing, taking care of your parents. A lot of girls wouldn't do it."

"Come and see us at the hospital some time . . ." Mrs. Schultz began.

But Sarah was already on her way to the bedroom.

The women went out and closed the door behind them. They walked in silence for a time. Vena said, "Sarah knows. She won't joke any more. It's like she grew up, or maybe gave up." After a moment she added, "I liked her better the other way. She liked being teased, as if she had hope, at least a little, even if it wasn't sensible—and now that's gone."

"All the same, I wish there'd been somebody for her," Mrs. Schultz said. They ceased talking and walked back to the hospital.

Mr. Berg died at the end of the summer. After that Sarah and her mother were often seen walking along the streets together, very slowly, the old mother having remained in poor health. They became a familiar sight, inseparable, wearing similar coats and hats, so that at a distance it was hard to tell them apart.

JAKE

HE PEERED AT himself in the small dresser mirror: sharp pinched face, thin neck in a stiff white collar, black hair that for forty years had kept falling over his forehead into his eyes. He jerked at the knot of his new tie; it seemed to him the knot was too bulky, it stuck out oddly under his scrawny Adam's apple. He pulled it off. The old one was even worse, out of style with its broad red stripes. He considered going without a tie, then hastily put on his black bow tie—if no one else was wearing one, he could easily unsnap it and put it in his pocket.

He opened his top drawer to look for a clean handkerchief. Should he tell where he was going, this time? She always wanted to know. It was a choice of evils: the hurt looks if he didn't, the questions and disapproval if he did. His mother would certainly not approve of a party at Cloudy Lake, even in a church. She said it was a worldly town; the churches were Lutheran and everybody smoked. Only one step away from Catholics, she said, which was heathenism with all that incense and painted images. He explained that Lutherans had no images, only a cross. She retorted that they went to dances, and that was that. He decided not to tell her, at least not until afterwards.

He rubbed Vaseline into the falling hank of hair and combed it tightly back. Feeling he had done his best, he went out to the kitchen, but stopped at the back door, frowning in his worry that he had forgotten something . . . handkerchief, comb, a little money. He could think of nothing else, except the nagging uncertainty about the tie. The door to the basement was open; he could hear his mother and Mathilda fussing around with jars. He went out, backed the car out of the tiny garage, and took the right-hand turn to Ben's.

The air was cool for summer. Across the fields the sun was setting in a blaze of purple and tender pink. He felt a sudden rise of satisfaction. This was how it should be: he, wearing a suit, driving his car out of town to be in the company of men. Men of the wider world (Cloudy Lake being twice the size of Windamer), men with new ideas and broader horizons, men of business and affairs. He hungered to be with them. There would undoubtedly also be women at the party, but at this moment they did not concern him.

A mile down the highway he turned off onto a small dirt road, drove up to a weathered farm house surrounded by crab apple trees, and honked.

Ben came out at once and got into the car. He wore a plaid farm shirt open at the throat and smelled of shaving lotion. Jake realized with a pang of anxiety that he had forgotten shaving lotion. "Hiya!" Ben greeted him. "Thanks for the lift, my jalopy's acting up again. By gum, a black bow tie!"

Jake did not answer but drove carefully out of the yard and back down the dirt road to the gravel highway. On the way to Cloudy Lake he asked Ben nervously, "Don't they wear bow ties?"

Ben laughed. "Anything. Collars, ties, no ties, work shirts. Nobody cares." Jake envied him. Ben was broad-chested, strong, confident, he spoke easily, always had a girl he was going out with though he was putting off getting married, came and went as he pleased, living by himself on the old farm.

He drove slowly on the gravel road to spare the car, which he had spent two hours the day before polishing until the small black fenders gleamed. After a while Ben said, "Can you hike it up a bit? It's a ways."

During the forty minutes it took to get to Cloudy Lake, Ben rambled on about the distressed state of the economy. There was sure to be a crash, he said, followed by a depression; all it would take would be a run on the bank. Farmers had been too greedy for profit. He didn't think Windamer would be too hard hit because the German Mennonites were conservative with their money. Jake, steering the car into deepening twilight, had no time to answer.

The yard of the Lutheran church was full of shiny blue and gray cars. It occurred to Jake that his Ford, though he had polished it with such care, was hopelessly old-fashioned. It was black, small, and old. "Where should I park?" he asked Ben anxiously. Ben pointed down the road, and they pulled up under a tree just past the church, a large building with a steeple.

Ben strode to a side door, pulled it open without knocking, and went in. Jake was careful to stay behind him. He dreaded those first glances . . . people looked at him as if thinking, 'He's too pale, white in the face, a dried-up shrimp, is he a man or a boy or what?' The room was noisy; people stood everywhere talking, holding glasses and small plates. Nobody paid the slightest attention to the newcomers except a large man in a white apron, who waved them toward the refreshment table.

Jake hastily observed the clothing of the young men. It was true, they wore all sorts of things—suits with tight-fitting trousers, open shirts, even overalls. One or two had on bow ties. It was all right, then.

A group of them were standing toward one side of the room engaged in a heated discussion. They were all tall, Jake saw, very tall and handsome with fair hair and mustaches—Norwegians, probably, or Swedes. Jake began to feel small and insignificant, out of place, an undersized Mennonite in a forest of good-looking Scandinavian Lutherans. His heart sank at the thought of standing among them.

He tried to stay behind Ben, but Ben pulled him forward and introduced him: "My friend, Jake Braun. His dad is a big wheel in MCC."

The young men paused, greeted him politely and went on with their discussion. One of them, standing with his hands in his pockets, was surveying the others with amusement. "Well, they're organizing a strike in Willmar, why don't you join up? You read Turner's speech (he struck a pose), 'The Travail of Democracy in Distress, the Fires of Revolt Burn!'"

A stocky man in striped overalls laughed. "You go ahead and strike, Severson. I'm trading my corn for cattle. Not that they have much of a price either way, but I figure to come out ahead."

"Buck looks out for himself, never mind causes," another said.

"Don't hold with strikes, is all," Buck returned.

Jake grew interested. At home politics was a subject of conversation only when his father was home; then friends would come over to discuss national and European affairs until late at night, conversations he listened to with interest. He edged closer, contemplated making a remark; he read the Mankato papers, he knew a few things. At a pause in the conversation he said suddenly, "The Minnesota farmers . . . we're doing better than most, we should hang on and not sell out." He was hot, perspiring.

The others glanced at him. "Exactly," Severson said. "We're all eating pretty well. Small farmers are lucky this time. It's the big businesses running on loans that aren't going to make it."

"I dunno," a fourth man said. "Heard some farmers down southway gonna be burning their own corn for fuel, come winter."

Jake's heart was beating violently. The success of his first remark made him wish to say something else if opportunity offered. He leaned forward, listening intently.

However Ben came over and pulled him toward the food table. Jake followed reluctantly. They filled their plates with sandwiches, potato salad, pickles and pie.

On the other side of the room the girls had seated themselves in a circle of chairs, plates of food on their laps. Fluffy light skirts hung gracefully over the edges of the chairs, not quite to the slender ankles and white shoes. The girls were laughing among themselves.

"Hey, Ben," one of them called, "take some of that fried chicken—I made it special for you!" She was a tall girl wearing a flimsy blouse with a drooping collar.

'Not me!" Ben retorted. "I'm looking for sauerkraut. Anybody bring sauerkraut?" He went to sit beside the tall girl.

Jake found a chair near the wall. He balanced his plate awkwardly on his knees and looked for a place to put his coffee cup.

A few minutes later a girl dropped into the vacant chair beside him. "I'm Evelyn. Here, let me hold your cup for you, I'm all through." She took his cup from him and held it in both hands.

Jake panicked. What were the right things to say? "You shouldn't have to . . . I can put it on the floor."

She laughed and began asking questions about his family. He answered between bites, stammering out nervous little runs of words. He was from Windamer . . . lived with his mother and sister . . . a small place by a creek, almost in the country . . . no, his father was alive, he worked for MCC, he was gone most of the time.

"What's MCC?" Evelyn wanted to know. He saw that her eyes were blue, her eyebrows arched, blonde hair curled down her forehead or swept smoothly back over her ears. Her cheeks were pale, slightly pockmarked. He could not guess her age—twenty-five? Thirty? Her dress, green with puffed sleeves, suggested fashion—not like the plain housedresses his mother and Mathilda always wore at home.

Disconcerted by her presence so close to him, he struggled to put thoughts into words. "Mennonite Central Committee—it's a relief agency, they're trying to get the Mennonites out of Russia . . . things are pretty bad there, revolution and famine and . . . thousands of them, yes, to Canada and Minnesota . . . his dad was raising money to help them pay their travel debts."

"Oh!" she exclaimed, "that's wonderful, what your dad's doing. Are you Mennonite?"

Jake felt vaguely ashamed. He did not know what Lutheran opinion of Mennonites was. "Well, yes, my family . . . ."

She interrupted. "Do you have chickens?"

Jake hesitated, relieved that she was not appalled at his being Mennonite, but chickens? He hated the squawking things. "A few," he admitted. "My sister takes care of them." He wondered why she was asking about chickens.

Evelyn took a small sip of coffee. "Oops—this is yours. Sorry!"

"It's all right," Jake assured her, nodding several times to let her know it was certainly all right.

"You say you live with your folks?" Her voice was light. She continued to sip his coffee, watching him over the rim of the cup.

"Yes, I . . . I do most of the outside work." A garden, a couple fields of corn, what did that amount to? Those tall Norwegians probably had hundreds of acres, tall white houses, assuredly did not live with their mothers. Distressed, he said the first thing that came to his mind. "Across the creek there's a flat place, a pasture. Maybe . . . I thought I could build a house there."

"Oh—do you build?" Her voice was admiring, warm.

"I can build a little. Ben, over there, he's a contractor, he could help."

"Well, goodness, why don't you go ahead? It sounds wonderful. A house by the creek!"

"Yes, I . . . maybe I should." It amazed him how a dim thought, one that seemed extravagant and impossible, far too expensive and far too daring, should suddenly become, when she uttered it, a clear and sensible plan. What was so difficult about it? First, of course, he would have to build some kind of bridge over the creek.

"Goodness, I've drunk all your coffee. I'll get you some more." She jumped up.

"No," Jake protested, but she ran gaily to the table and came back with the cup full of coffee, a few grounds swirling at the top.

Her eyes were alight. "Know what I'd do on a farm? I'd put up lace curtains, like in town. I'd have flowers all around the house, and a white picket fence, and a patch of grass. I'd have lunch out on the grass every day, or under the trees by the creek. What do you think?"

Uncertain how to answer, trying to balance his plate on his thin knees while handling the heavy coffee mug, Jake asked, "You live in Cloudy Lake?"

"Oh!" She made a face. "Aunt Mattie's Boarding House for Young Women. Awful place. Drains keep plugging up, water runs all over the floor. I can't get my window open, it's painted shut. I nearly die up there, it's so hot. Cheap, though. You know the Red Rooster grocery? Town square, south side. That's where I work."

Jake felt immensely relieved. She was an ordinary working girl after all. The smooth hair style and fashionable dress had deceived him. He felt now that he could talk to her.

"My folks live in Philadelphia," she went on. "Dad's a railroad worker. They live in a poor section, houses jammed up against each other, garbage in the streets. I hate the city. Ever been in New York? It's worse than Philadelphia. I want to live here in Minnesota, on a farm." She jumped up again, went off to the table and brought back some tiny cookies filled with red jam. "Here, I made these, try them. That's lingonberry jam."

Jake thanked her, nervous at being the object of so much attention. Ben, he noticed, was still talking to the tall girl. The young men were wandering around, mugs in hand, helping themselves from the food table or teasing the girls. One or two were standing just outside the door, smoking.

"A poem, Tina!" someone shouted. The others began to clap,

until a girl in a shirred shirtwaist stood up, making a face, and began to recite a poem in another language. She was interrupted at every line by bursts of laughter.

Evelyn nudged Jake. "What is that—Norwegian? Can you understand it? Tell me what's so funny."

Jake shook his head. "I just know German." He felt left out. But then she didn't understand the poem either.

One of the young men who had been arguing politics now sauntered over to an old piano in the back corner and began playing. The music was sprightly, rhythmic. Several of the group stood, paired up, and—to Jake's dismay, his mother's words ringing in his ears—began to dance. He stared at the floor, cold with dread that Evelyn might ask him to join them. To his great relief, she did not, but instead wandered off to talk to the girl who had recited the poem.

He glanced suddenly at his watch. Almost nine! It was time, certainly time, to go. It would take nearly an hour to get home driving in the dark. He caught Ben's eye and motioned toward the door. Ben screwed up his face in protest, talked a while longer while Jake fidgeted, and finally got up.

Evelyn had returned. She touched Jake's arm lightly. "You're coming to the next party, aren't you? There's one every month."

"I don't know," Jake said, anxious about the time.

"Well, come. I like talking to you," she said. "I'm going to bring a shoo-fly pie—that's an Amish thing."

Now Ben was arguing with the man in the white apron, giving him money. Was he expected to pay? Ben had not said. He hurried over, pulling his wallet out of his pocket.

"No, no, all taken care of," Ben said. "They don't charge anyway. I was just making a donation for wine next time." He winked at the man in the white apron. Jake put his wallet back.

On the way out, remembering in time, he turned to say goodbye to Evelyn. She waved from across the room, where she was standing by herself near the circle of chattering girls.

As they walked to the car Jake asked uncertainly, "Will that man—the cook . . . will he bring wine next time?" Drinking, worse than smoking or even dancing . . . his mother was sure to find out.

Ben laughed. "Who knows? Maybe he will. On the other hand, maybe he won't."

The night air was chilly, and Jake shivered. He had a hard time starting the car. Finally Ben had to push it down the road a little way, then jump in while the car was moving. The lights fell in a feeble circle on the gravel.

"Looks like Evie took to you," Ben said. "Friendly kid. Clerks at the Red Rooster. She keeps saying she'd rather quit and go live on a farm—not by herself, of course."

"That's what she said," Jake murmured, pleased that he was included among those to whom she told these things.

"Comes on a bit strong, sort of puts the fellows off, but she'd make somebody a nice little wife," Ben said.

Jake steered cautiously over the bridge outside Cloudy Lake and thought of the bridge he must build across his creek. "How old is she?" he mumbled, trying not to sound too interested.

"What? Oh, how old. I don't know. Maybe thirty-two, -three." Ben yawned, leaned his head back, and after a few minutes was asleep.

Jake kept his eyes on the road, putting aside his worries about the party, wondering about Evelyn. "I like talking to you," she had said. It hadn't seemed to bother her that he was small, couldn't balance his plate on his knees, couldn't think of things to say. He recalled with pleasure her bright hair, the lighthearted way she had drunk his cup of coffee. She had touched his arm. He recalled that he had come to this party to be with other men. That too had been a pleasure, to have his remark accepted by these tall men of the world. Yet now it was Evelyn who dominated his thoughts.

But what did Ben mean, she put the fellows off? Did she act like this with every strange man? Was she the kind to flatter a man, lead him on, then cut him off? Mercilessly, cruelly, against his will, he began to relive that other scene, though he had made up his mind never to think of it any more.

He was standing at the corner of his father's apple orchard dressed in his best suit. He had washed, combed his hair, shined his shoes, brushed the second-hand suit as best he could. His cousin Abe had promised to come by in his car with Marian Esau and Amanda Bartel and pick him up for a youth meeting at Heron Lake. That meant he would sit next to Amanda in the back seat on the drive over. She wouldn't sit with him in church, of course, but he would walk in with her and the other young people would see it. His heart pounded at the thought of Amanda. He admired hopelessly her curled brown hair, her jaunty walk, her dainty clinging white dresses. She never noticed him, but if he was next to her in the car she might, out of politeness, talk to him a little.

He had stood in the tall grass at the unplowed corner, waiting. When Abe's car appeared down the road, trailing a small cloud of dust—he would be slowing down in a minute—Jake smoothed his hair back for the twentieth time and stepped forward. He realized suddenly with dismay that Abe wasn't slowing down . . . he was waving, both girls were waving, but the car wasn't stopping. Abe drove right by, on down the road, stirring up the dust. Shocked, outraged, deeply humiliated, Jake had stumbled toward home. The girls must have told him not to stop—they didn't want him in the back seat, someone would have to sit with him. Waves of heat passed over his face and neck. He began to cry, stumbling through the furrows of the orchard until he reached the washhouse and sat inside it until he could calm himself.

Now, peering ahead at the road in the dim light of the headlamps, Jake felt his face growing hot. He told himself that Evelyn was not like that, not at all. Anyway it had happened long ago. He tried, by recalling the pleasures of the evening, to return to his former pleasant mood.

The car bumped through a pit in the gravel. Ben jerked awake. He looked at Jake gripping the steering wheel, and laughed. "What's on your mind?"

"I . . . was just thinking about something." Jake looked about, not sure where they were until he saw Thiezen's windmill glimmering some distance down the road. Two miles further he turned off onto Ben's road, waited till he got off, yawning, and drove home. He put the car in the garage and let himself in the back door.

His mother was still up, as expected, sewing a shirt, waiting for him. She allowed him to lock the door and hang up the car keys before she spoke. "You didn't say you were going anywhere. It's late. I was worried you were in an accident. I almost called the hospital."

'It's not so late," Jake muttered, and went toward his bedroom.

"You should at least say where you're going!" She would ask and ask until she found out.

There was no light under Mathilda's door. She must have gone to bed, having to rise early for her job at the hospital laundry—time enough tomorrow for her teasing. The evening which had gone so well trailed off into unhappiness.

But why? he thought, preparing for bed. It was his own fault. He had allowed the recollection of his humiliation to disturb the drive home. A man of forty, yet he let his mother pry into his affairs and his sister to poke fun at him. Such things would never happen to Ben. Ben simply wouldn't allow it. Evelyn was right. The first thing to do was build his own house across the creek and find some privacy. His father had given him the land. He had money in the bank, enough to get started. His mother couldn't legally stop him.

He lay in bed making plans about the bridge over the creek. "I like talking to you, come again." He turned over on his stomach to avoid nightmares and slept without dreaming.

At breakfast his mother, stirring oatmeal at the stove, said nothing. Her mouth was set in a tight line of disapproval. Mathilda was drinking coffee at the table, wearing her coat, ready to leave. She rounded on him. "Whenever did you get home last night? Out with some girl, I bet! What's Gertrude going to say?" She cocked her head and regarded him with sparkling black eyes.

"*Ach waut*!" his mother exclaimed. She plopped his bowl of oatmeal on the table and went back to the stove.

"Come on, who was it?" Mathilda jumped up, put her cup in the sink and headed for the back door.

"I don't have a girl," Jake said angrily. "I went somewhere with Ben." Why did they have to ask about everything? He was a man, not a child. He pretended to study last week's *Herald*, although he had read it twice, while he ate the oatmeal.

"Gotta go, I'm late." Mathilda ran out, slamming the door.

His mother walked back and forth doing kitchen work in dignified silence. She would be like that, he knew, until he told her where he had been. He got up and went out the door.

"Potatoes need hoeing," his mother called after him.

It was still early. He walked down to the creek to take a look. The water trickled sluggishly between roots of trees, very low at this time of year; but clear, so that he could see the sand and pebbles at the bottom. Across the creek, slightly further down, was his piece of land, at present rented to a neighbor as pasture.

It would take careful planning to build the bridge. He could, of course, lay planks across for the time being, but eventually he wanted a proper bridge with an arch, like those he had seen pictured in books. It would have to connect somehow with the road. He would build the bridge at the far end of his land for more privacy.

He returned to the garden, picked up a hoe and began loosening the black dirt around the potato plants. His mother's lemon lilies and white dahlias were still in bloom, and there was a pleasant scent of green undergrowth in the still air. In their enclosure the chickens were pecking at the dirt, making their contented little clucking sounds. Evelyn would like it here.

He certainly should get a new suit, though. He was dissatisfied with the one he had worn to the party. It looked baggy, too big, as if he had shrunk. He tried to think if a wedding was coming up—that would be an excuse to get new clothes

His mother called from the back door. She needed four yards of unbleached muslin for quilt backing and three spools of thread; she had already telephoned Franz's. He could take the car and go pick them up, charge them as usual. Snipping her words off as if she were biting thread.

Jake cleaned up quickly, thinking he would look in at Peterson's Men's Wear before coming back.

But the clerk at Franz's Dry Goods, Gertrude, the thin, fortyish woman Mathilda had picked to tease him about and whom he disliked, detained him with questions. She had relatives in the German refugee camps, it seemed, and was worried about them. Fidgeting lest people come in and see him talking with her, Jake answered that his father would be home in a few days and she could ask him personally. By the time he escaped with his mother's parcel it was nearly eleven o'clock.

He stepped quickly into Peterson's and looked around. He was surrounded by men's suits hanging on racks, shirts and ties on display on various counters. Nervousness over the lateness of the hour, however, prevented him from looking at the suits calmly, and he left, saying he would return another day. Peterson asked about his father. "A great man, doing an important work."

They all admired his father, Jake thought, driving home. It was his misfortune to have such a miserable excuse of a son. Jake suddenly remembered the day he had stood before the principal of the Bible School in Canada, where they had once lived, and spoken of his resolve to be a missionary. The principal had looked at him, at his thin neck inside the bulky home-knitted sweater, and said gently, "I think your family needs you at home." Jake had walked out, defeated. Even for the mission field they needed tall men with strong voices, men who could attract capable wives. Remembering that event, Jake drove home at a reckless speed.

At supper that night Mathilda baited him once more. "What were you doing in Peterson's? Don't deny it. Gertrude saw you go in there."

Jake looked at her almost with hatred. "I need a new suit pretty soon," he said loudly.

"*Ach waut*!" his mother exclaimed. "You have a good enough suit. If anybody needs a suit, it's your dad, always in public like he is."

"He's stepping out, no doubt about it," Mathilda stated. "I bet you anything he was at a party last night, that's why he wants new clothes. Where was it?"

They would have to know some time or there would be no peace. "Cloudy Lake. A church social."

His mother, scraping pans in the sink, looked at him reproachfully. "*Nae oba*! You know what kind of place that is. They drink. You should know better."

"They didn't drink!" he said, intensely irritated and afraid of the next question, which he might not be able to answer truthfully.

Mathilda began washing dishes. "Oh, Cloudy Lake, is it? Lots of pretty Swedish girls over there. Blondes by the dozen. Who did you . . . ."

His mother interrupted. "That Ben, he put you up to this, I suppose. How many girls has he gone with, and not married yet! Smokes too, I heard."

"Gertrude will be real disappointed if you go off with some girl at Cloudy Lake," Mathilda said brightly. "I don't know why you don't like her—quiet, works hard, has a nice little house."

"She's an old maid," Jake muttered.

"You're no frisky calf yourself," she retorted. "She's only forty-one—just the right age."

"Mathilda, you leave him alone about that Gertrude," their mother scolded. Gertrude was from Parkview Church. According to his mother, Parkview was suspect because, though a branch of Mennonites, they had retained the catechism.

"Well, there's plenty other girls in Windamer," Mathilda went on, a mischievous gleam in her eye. "How about Sarah Berg? She'd have you in a minute, now Doft Penner is getting married again. Or what's wrong with Angie Swanson?" She flipped a dish towel from its rod near the stove and started drying the dishes.

Jake got up without answering and went to his room. Girls in Windamer—of course there were girls. Angie was fat; besides that she always had a cold and no handkerchief. Marie at the bank, whom he admired, was his double cousin. As for Sarah, mooning around the men, he would be the laughing-stock of the town if he were ever seen with her. The younger girls, the clear-faced pretty ones, they were still in high school or gone off to Bible School—they walked by him as if he were invisible. He felt like an old fisherman circling and circling the same small pool.

No, let them complain. He would go to Cloudy Lake and try to see Evelyn, who had come to sit by him of her own wish. I should finish night school and get a government job, Jake thought, and wondered why he hadn't thought of this before. He still had his engineering texts.

He took out a pencil and, sitting down at his desk, began making lists of figures, writing quickly in the pool of light from his desk lamp. He took down his books to look for designs for bridges. He stopped at the photograph of Ammanati's stone bridge over the

Arne, in Italy. The tranquil beauty of it excited him: the low rounded arches, the piers jutting out in strong triangles, the carvings. That was how bridges should be built. The foolish wooden things they kept putting up around Windamer got washed out with every flood. If he got an engineering job, it would be with bridges. He leafed through the book, looking for formulas calculating pitch and stress. He fell asleep thinking he might go to Cloudy Lake next week to say hello to Evelyn at the Red Rooster.

"The chicken house . . . I thought you were going to fix it," his mother said first thing next morning. It was Saturday. "Dad's coming home on Wednesday. He'll wonder what you did all this time. The lawn mower is still jammed, too. I'm surprised you don't look after it."

"We should buy new boards for the chicken house," Jake said, looking with distaste at his oatmeal. "All we do is patch up. One of these days the whole shed will fall down."

"Tell your dad—not me!" his mother snapped. She slammed the kettle on the stove. She'll be like this till I apologize for going to Cloudy Lake, Jake thought.

He went out to the chicken shed. It was a hazy, humid day, the kind that oppressed him with the sense that the whole world had bogged down and nothing would ever happen. He wished a thunder storm would blow in and clear the air.

He found a couple of old boards in the long grass behind the garage and hammered them over the broken places in the chicken shed, not bothering to line them up straight, putting nails any old place while the chickens fluttered about, squawking. He hated seeing the patched-up shed, but his father paid small attention to such things, and his mother opposed cash layouts. On his own place he would build carefully with strong new boards, he thought. He checked the wire netting around the chicken yard. If there was one thing he detested it was chickens on the loose, leaving droppings all over.

Before tackling the lawn mower he went down to the creek. He walked along it looking for possible sites for a bridge, and found several. A few trees would have to be cut down, and both banks would have to be shored up with cement to prevent collapse. It was quiet here under the trees with the water gurgling over the stones, a few minnows darting about.

Feeling more cheerful, he returned to the garage to work on the lawnmower, a rusty old piece of machinery his father had brought home from a farm auction. Not that they had much of a lawn, just a patch in front of the house.

The wished-for thunder storm rolled around on Monday night, leaving behind a refreshing coolness. The rain, though slight, would help the garden and fields.

Immediately after breakfast the next day, Jake went out and raked the wet dead leaves from under the bushes. At nine his mother left for her Tuesday sewing circle; she would not be home until after three. Jake went to his room and changed into a clean shirt. It had a patch under one arm where he had torn it on a fence, but there was none other. He combed his hair, took the car out and left for Cloudy Lake.

The sun lay warm on the corn fields. The stalks would grow to seven feet and more this year, Jake thought, though with prices still slipping, a good crop was like being given with one hand that which was immediately taken away by the other. Still, the long sloping tasseled fields were a pleasant sight.

Two worries nagged at him, however. The first was the possible impropriety of visiting Evelyn without an invitation, only four days after the party; she might think he was hurrying things too much. He tried to think of an excuse for coming to the town—ask her to recommend a dress shop for his mother, perhaps. The second was the possibility that someone from Windamer would see him and report to his family.

He found the Red Rooster without difficulty and parked across the street. He felt suddenly that it had been foolish of him to come. Evelyn would greet him politely, wondering why he was there, and that would be all. He would have to turn around and drive all the way back home, for nothing.

He crossed the street and, walking by, glanced into the open door of the small grocery. Evelyn was not in sight. Relieved, he turned back and entered, and stood just inside the door to look around. The store smelled of newly ground coffee, sawdust, apples and sausage. A tall, very thin man in a white butcher's apron stood behind the meat counter talking to a stout woman, who stood with her back to Jake. The woman looked vaguely familiar. Jake wondered, in sudden panic, if she was from Windamer. He moved behind a stack of wooden barrels—dried fish, by the smell. He saw Evelyn then, arranging tinned goods on a shelf near by.

She turned, spied him, and immediately put down the tins. "Jake! How nice! Wait a minute, I'll tell Mr. Robbins I'm going for my break. We can go to Tiny's for coffee." Without waiting for an answer she ran across to the thin man, said a few words, and ran back. "Come on, then!"

Jake followed her, hoping the stout woman hadn't noticed. Evelyn pulled him into a small corner restaurant with a few tables and stiff wooden chairs. "Do you drink coffee? Oh, of course you do. How about a doughnut? Alice, coffee and two doughnuts!" She leaned her elbows on the table. "How's your family? Has your father come home yet? You don't know how lucky you are, living in the country. Our rooming house drains ran over—whole place smells awful. We were up scrubbing floors half the night."

"I . . . I'm very sorry," Jake stammered. In the daytime now she looked older, pale and tired. He wanted to help her somehow.

She made a comic face. "Mattie doesn't like spending money on repairs. She won't do anything unless we threaten to move out. You know anything about drains?"

"I fixed ours once . . . maybe I could . . . ."

"You did? Really? No, let Mattie hire somebody. Here comes our coffee."

The waitress brought two mugs and a plate with two doughnuts. Recalling the patch under his arm, Jake picked up his cup with the arm held close to his side; then, feeling silly, transferred the cup to his left hand.

Evelyn paid no attention but chattered brightly on. "Listen, if you ever want to build your own place, I'll help you plan it. Men never know where to put the cupboards. I know a man who built his own house and put one little cupboard, just one dinky thing, in the kitchen over the sink. His wife had to go out and buy a tin thing so she had someplace to put stuff."

Jake let her talk, watching her now lively face, marveling that she was sitting there speaking to him in this way. She had snatched a paper napkin and was drawing on it. "See, this is how it should be—entry here, door to the kitchen, stairs . . . wide ones. Downstairs bedroom, two upstairs and . . . ." She stopped suddenly and jumped up. "Goodness, I got to get back or Robbins will dock me. Are you done?" She drank her coffee hastily. Jake saw that she had not touched her doughnut. "Here, take this home, I don't want it. Alice, put it on my charge account. No, really, I always do that—put your old money back in your pocket. But listen, come buy some of Robbins' sausage. He makes wonderful sausage—people from all over come to buy it. Are you going to come again? Let me know and I'll arrange my day off."

Jake followed her back to the grocery, stammering his thanks. She disappeared into a back room. He decided to buy two pounds of the sausage for tomorrow's supper, since his father was coming home. This would be a good excuse for having left home. It was smoked German sausage, firm and fresh. Mr. Robbins wrapped it in pink paper.

He drove home with the package beside him. He hadn't felt so happy in years. Evelyn hadn't turned him off, she seemed to like him, he had no idea why. Jumping up instantly like that, taking him out for coffee . . . though he really should have insisted on paying. Next time he certainly would insist.

It occurred to him that he had said none of the things he could have said; in fact, almost nothing at all. She had done all the talking. It was just as well. If she was talkative, it would do for two. He began to make plans to call her until he realized he did not have the number of her rooming place. He could hardly call the grocery store. Why had he not thought to ask for the number? He would certainly do so at the next party. With these thoughts circling in his mind, he drove up to the house and put the car in the garage.

To his dismay his mother was already home. His father had tried to telephone the house and, finding nobody home, called the church with the message that he was coming a day early—today. The train was due at 5:10, only three hours away. Where for heaven's sake had Jake been? He had said nothing about going out! The front yard needed mowing. Was the mower fixed? No, they didn't have to meet the train; Dad wanted to walk, he said, after sitting so much.

Jake put his package on the table. "I bought it for supper for Dad. They said it's very good sausage."

His mother looked at him sharply. "Where did you get it?"

He did not answer, but went to his room to change into old clothes to mow the lawn. Thank goodness the mower was repaired. Let her find out later where he'd gone—with Dad home, she would have other things to think about.

Mathilda came home early. The two women rushed around cleaning and cooking, while Jake swept the porch and fed the chickens. The pungent smell of frying sausage filled the kitchen.

Just before six Rev. Henry Braun came walking home from the depot carrying a small battered suitcase and a bulging briefcase. He greeted them all. While his wife, in a flutter, put supper on the table, he went to change since his clothes, he said, smelled like smoke—the man in front of him had been smoking until told to stop.

They sat down formally, Rev. Braun at the head of the table. Hurrying, smiling, his wife served the sausage, nicely browned, with noodles and onions. Rev. Braun dripped vinegar over the noodles. "It's all very good, mother," he said. "Good Mennonite food. Is that rhubarb pie?" He looked up and smiled. She met his eyes, almost shyly, her face softly lit. After a moment Rev. Braun said, "Have you all been well?"

While he ate, he told them that he had collected a good sum of money in North Dakota and Montana, considering the scarcity of cash. The people's hearts were stirred by the plight of the refugees crowded into barracks in Germany, and families trying to escape from Russia into Canada and the United States. Other families were separated, waiting desperately for news of husbands and sons seized by the Communists. "How fortunate we are," he concluded, smiling around at them all.

Jake spoke up. "Gertrude Reimer wants to know about her relatives in the camps. Have you heard anything?"

His father thought a moment. "I'll have to check my notebook. I may have some news."

When supper was almost over, Mathilda leaned back and announced, "Well, now I know who Jake is seeing in Cloudy Lake." Jake started and stared at her in dismay. How in the world did she find out these things? "Shall I tell?" she asked merrily, looking at Jake. When he said nothing, she went on. "I met Mrs. Teichrob coming to the hospital to see her husband this afternoon. She said she went to Cloudy Lake today to buy sausage from Robbins, and she saw Jake—our Jake—walk out with the pretty little clerk. Ain't so, Jake?"

"*Nae oba*!" his mother exclaimed. "That's where you bought the sausage?"

Mathilda tilted her head and watched Jake. "Come on, you might as well tell us her name."

It was no use. Jake steeled himself and said, "Evelyn. I don't know her last name. I just know her a little, I'm not . . . ."

"Stevens," Mathilda said. "From Pennsylvania. Mrs. Teichrob asked Robbins."

His mother looked at him in disbelief. "Stevens! What sort of name is that? What church is she from?"

"I didn't ask her," Jake said. "I just barely talked to her." His face began to wear the stony stubborn look that infuriated his mother.

His mother got up and began to clear the table. "Father, what do you say? While you're gone, our Jake sneaks out and takes up with an English girl in Cloudy Lake."

His father said nothing, but sat picking his teeth with a toothpick. At length he replied, "It's not always good, mixing with the English. They have different ways."

The mother burst out impatiently. "Look at that Herman Voth's wife—Sadie Green she was—can't talk German, can't cook German either, wears low-cut dresses. Old Grandma Voth is so ashamed, she won't invite them when she has other company."

"But Alec Bergen's son married a Pennsylvania Dutch girl," Mathilda put in, raising her eyebrows conspiratorially at Jake, switching sides. "If he can get away with it . . . ."

"Your father in MCC, on the mission board!" the mother cried. "It would shame him before the whole conference! What is this girl—Lutheran?"

"The important thing is if she's a good Christian," the father said, reproving his wife. "They ought to take Sadie Voth in. She's a fine woman."

"Hmph!" Jake's mother fell silent, her mouth shut in a tight line.

Jake looked at his father with respect. A wise, open-hearted man. No wonder he was highly regarded. Jake felt a glimmer of hope.

The mother burst out once more. "These English girls don't know how to work. What do they know about farming? Paint their faces and spend their money, that's what they do! You'll end up in the poorhouse!"

"*Na*, Mother, Jake hasn't said anything about getting married," the father said mildly. He turned to Jake. "Just be sure what you're doing, son. It's hard for English girls to fit in here. We're too clannish." He sighed.

His mother said nothing more but moved about with quick, hard steps. Mathilda, glancing at her father, was silent. She helped her mother put the food away and wash the dishes.

Jake wanted to get back in the car and drive away. The tension in the house, already in the first hour his father was home, was his fault, he thought. Yet it was Mathilda who had brought it up, for no good purpose. A lot of this was her doing, he thought angrily.

He went into the living room and sat down. Perhaps his father would strike up a more pleasant conversation about something—his trip, people he had met. But his father had taken a pile of papers out of his briefcase and was studying them. Jake picked up the old *Herald* and turned the pages. After a while he got up and went to his room.

How could he bring Evelyn here? His mother would observe the girl narrowly to see if she painted her face, cooked *borscht* properly. She would never accept a Lutheran girl, if that's what Evelyn was. Perhaps she wasn't Lutheran, but Episcopal, perhaps nothing at all. A heathen, his mother would exclaim. Mathilda would make fun of everything.

It occurred to him, poking around without interest in his engineering books, that Evelyn had talked a great deal about the house he might build, but asked nothing about him. She had hardly looked at him while she talked. Maybe she just wanted a place so she could get out of the rooming house. She might make similar advances to any man who had a house.

He sat doodling with a pencil on an old envelope. It wasn't likely, after all, that a pretty woman like her would fall in love with a dried-up bachelor like him. He could imagine her bustling about a house, putting doilies under vases of flowers, making a garden, serving lunch under the trees . . . but lavishing kisses on him, he couldn't for a moment imagine that. But then, perhaps it didn't matter so much. If she was content with a house, it might work out.

Maybe, though, something was wrong with her. Why hadn't one of those tall Norwegians married her by this time? There might be an explanation: she was an outsider. Those Scandinavians were just as clannish as the Mennonites. She didn't speak Norwegian or Swedish, her father was a railroad worker in a foreign city. Her name, Stevens. What was that—British? He knew how she felt—who was more an outsider than he, Jake? It wasn't only nationality that made people outsiders. If you were too skinny or too ugly or too poor, or couldn't understand Low German jokes, the town went on its way, leaving you in the dust by the side of the road. He felt a moment's pity for Sarah Berg, laughed at by the men.

He threw down his pencil and went to the living room to say goodnight to his parents, who were talking together softly in the lamplight, his father having laid aside his papers. On his mother's face was the same unaccustomed softness he had glimpsed in the kitchen. He lingered a moment, thinking that even now in their later years his parents felt tenderness for each other—the love he himself yearned for. But their business seemed to be private, and he returned to his room. Mathilda had already gone to bed.

He undressed, forgetting to turn the light off. The sight of his skinny legs disturbed him. He grew hot at the thought of letting Evelyn see him . . . thin legs, shriveled neck. It occurred to him that pleasing a woman would not be easy . . . she might laugh when she saw him puny in his pajamas, scorn his advances . . . as for anything more, he wouldn't know what to do. His parents never talked to them about such things. He turned off the light, got into bed and stared desperately at the ceiling, ashamed that he knew nothing about a woman. He would have to ask Ben. For Ben it would all be easy. And for those Norwegians. They were handsome, tall, strong, they knew how to joke with girls and probably a lot more besides.

He pulled up the quilt and curled up for sleep, but instead he began thinking about Hiram Hawkins. Hiram, who had tormented him in grade school. Jake had not been ashamed of his body before Hiram began to bully him. In fact, people commented what a quick, energetic child he had been. "Hey, you runt, come here!" Hiram, huge as a bear, calling him. Jakey, in first grade, shrinking against the wall of the one-room school, the other boys tittering, waiting for the fun. Hiram advancing, smirking; picking Jakey up by his overall straps, carrying him to the janitor's room, swinging him up and setting him down hard in the sink among the stinking wet mops. The boys mocking with shrill laughter until they heard a teacher coming, and ran. Jakey climbing out, crying with rage and humiliation, his pants soaked from the mops. Tomorrow it would happen again. It happened every day, until Big Al came to school. He said to Hiram, "Touch Jakey Braun once more and I'll kill you." Big Al was bigger even than Hiram, and Hiram obeyed. Big Al later became a bootlegger, but Jake had worshiped him for years. Still, the shame had remained. He always undressed in the dark. Tonight, worrying about Evelyn, he had forgotten to turn out the light.

He turned over on his stomach to avoid the nightmares and eventually fell asleep. He began to dream . . . he was standing in a pit up to his waist in dark water, in the middle of the town, people rushing by not noticing him, his father looking at him in a blank, bewildered way; he was reaching out his arms, a teenaged boy in a drenched shirt, crying out in a strange voice, "Nobody wants me! *Nobody wants me*!" Panic overwhelmed him in the dream,woke him. Sitting up, sweating with pain and misery, he argued with the dream.

His father wanted him, at least spoke respectfully to him. Ben was his friend. And Evelyn . . . but at the thought of her, shame again rolled over him, hot, black, wave upon wave. After a time he realized he was cold and lay back down under the quilt.

At breakfast he spoke little but sat picking at the fried eggs and cracklings left for him on the table. Mathilda had left very early—it was her turn to start up the boilers in the laundry room. His mother and father were outdoors looking at the garden.

Afterwards his mother went to the basement to do laundry. His father sat in the living room, cheerfully reading reports written in small crabbed handwriting. When Jake went in to ask what work needed to be done, his father looked up pleasantly. "It all looks very good, you have taken fine care of our little farm. Take some time off. Maybe this afternoon we can walk to the fields to see how the corn is doing." He returned to his reports.

Jake, slightly cheered, went into the front yard just as Ben drove up. "Hiya Jake—I'm driving in to Cloudy Lake this afternoon, want to come along?"

Jake shook his head. "My father's home," he said in explanation.

"Somebody'll be disappointed!" Ben said, and drove away whistling.

"What did Ben want?" It was his mother, standing in the front doorway.

"He's going to Cloudy Lake, asked if I wanted to go along. I said no."

"You're not going?" She looked pleased. She came outside and stood by him. "We have a nice place," she remarked pleasantly, after a silence. "Dad said you were taking good care of things. It's a mercy you're here to do it. Dad's never home. I see you fixed the chicken shed."

Jake said nothing in response, knowing that the reason for her present approval was his refusal of Ben's offer. After some minutes he mentioned seeing the cornfields with his father later that day. "*Na joh.* That's good," his mother said, and went inside.

Relieved to be alone, Jake walked away through the orchard toward the creek. He was ashamed of the ramshackle way he had fixed the shed, but she didn't seem to care or even notice. It was his disobedience in defying her fixed opinions that she wouldn't tolerate. He walked over the rough ground to the creek.

Picking up a stick, he poked at the clear water, stirring up small gobs of mud that floated away and left the water running clear once more. He watched idly as the neighbor's cows came to drink, easing themselves down the bank and then taking the last steep bit in a heavy rush so that water splashed around their legs. He walked further to look across the creek at the place he had thought to build . . . a small house, plain, carefully built, the boards measured and fitted.

He sat down on the bank. Maybe he was wrong about Evelyn. She might not, after all, secretly laugh, despise him as a husband . . . it was possible she too was ashamed of something, a fault or disfigurement . . . how eagerly he would tell her it didn't matter, not at all.

But even then, how could he bring her here? His mother and Mathilda would wear her down to shreds. His father, being away, could not protect her.

A heaviness settled on him. He could see no way to get out from under the weight of his family. He did not know what to do. He thought about the bridge he wanted to build, a shapely arch built on cement piers sunk into each bank, here where the creek narrowed. But unless he built the house, and why build it if not for Evelyn, there would be no reason to build a bridge. His thoughts, unable to come to a resolution, wandered off.

He stared at the water sliding smoothly by, rippling over sand and pebbles, as it had in all the years since he had played there as a small boy. Suddenly, as in a vision, he saw with absolute clarity that if he did not do this, did not at least build something of his dream, house or bridge, with or without Evelyn, he would slide forever into the dark pit of his nightmare. It must be done, he must do it, whatever anyone said, or he was lost.

He jumped up, ran down the bank, and with a stick began to make marks in the sand at the place where the nearer pier should go . . . deep crooked gashes, into which the water flowed as fast as he made them.

SPRING STORM

A FRESHENING WIND stirred the new leaves drifting like light green lace across the heavy trunks of the trees on Mrs. Dickman's front lawn. Over to the north the horizon was growing dark, gray and violet, threatening rain.

In the front room of her tidy white house, Mrs. Dickman stood with the coffee pot poised over the table. She looked inquiringly at her guests. Both politely declined more coffee. She set the pot down and passed the lemon cake. "Ladies, please help yourselves. Don't hold back." The cake made its round and Mrs. Dickman replaced it in the center of the table. She was about to pass the *pirozhky* when Mrs. Penner spoke up.

"I don't mind moving back here—I have lots of relatives. I'm just worried about my asthma," she informed Mrs. Dickman and, across the table, Tante Lieze. "I told my man, if it's as bad here as Montana, I'm going to California to live with Elsie." Her quick black eyes darted about inspecting, for the third time, the small living room. All was decently in order. Lace doilies were pinned in place on the arms of the blue velvet couch and chairs, the fern on its wooden stand was set neatly in a corner, the china figurines in the glass-fronted cupboard stood in formal rows. The windowsills, she had noted earlier, were free of dust.

Mrs. Dickman forgot to pass the *pirozhky*. "There's something about asthma in my mother's cookbook," she said, and rose to get it from a drawer in the china cupboard.

"Cookbook? It has recipes for asthma?" Mrs. Penner looked amused.

"Well, it's not just a cookbook, "Mrs. Dickman explained. "It tells about medicines, and how to clean house—all sorts of things. Ma said it was better than old Pankratz's doctor books."

She laid it on the table: an old book, heavy, with the top cover missing. She turned the yellowing pages carefully. Putting her finger on a paragraph she read: "Sufferers from asthma should get a musk-rat skin and wear it over their lungs with the fur next to the body. It will bring certain relief. This remedy was sent to us by a lady in Minnesota, who used it with great success."

Mrs. Penner burst out laughing. "A muskrat skin? Pooh! What would that do!"

Mrs. Dickman looked offended. "Sometimes old things work best," she said with dignity. She closed the book and laid it aside. "My mother doctored all ten of us from this book—croup, measles, everything. We all made it through."

Mrs. Penner shook her head. "I'm not going out to catch no muskrat, that's for sure. I'll go get something from Klaas Dyck. What do you think, Tante Lieze?"

Looking at her own knobbed fingers, Tante Lieze replied slowly, "Old folks have to live with their troubles."

"Liezje has arthritis bad in her hands," Mrs. Dickman explained to Mrs. Penner.

"Well, I told Hank, no use suffering from asthma in a little dump of a Minnesota town when we can go live with Elsie in California. She picks oranges straight off a tree in her back yard every morning for breakfast. But Hank wants to farm. Corn and cattle, that's all he knows. Stubborn as an old donkey. It'd take a tornado to move him off that farm, let alone to California." Mrs. Penner made a face and helped herself to the *pirozhky*.

Instantly Mrs. Dickman passed the plate around, apologizing for having forgotten, and for the sticky brown spots on the plate. "The juice kept leaking out," she explained in some distress. "I made better ones last week."

"Put a spoonful extra flour in the apples," Mrs. Penner advised. She rearranged the ruffle down the front of her green voile dress and turned to Tante Lieze. "I hear you have a girl that isn't right in the head."

"Two of them," Tante Lieze said shortly.

"*Na*, Liezje, don't say that," Mrs. Dickman reproved her. "Frieda means good, even if her tongue runs on a little." She turned to Mrs. Penner. "Lentye's the one. She was born that way."

Tante Lieze turned to Mrs. Dickman as if to say something, but instead began to stir the coffee in her cup, set the spoon down, and drank the coffee. Mrs. Dickman immediately offered her more, but she shook her head.

"You take care of her yourself?" Mrs. Penner asked. "Couldn't you put her in a home?"

Tante Lieze pondered the question. "She couldn't go to a strange place—she'd get all mixed up. I'm used to her, she's company for me."

Mrs. Penner turned her attention to the tea set. The dishes were of fine china, white with gold rims and delicate pink roses in the center. "*Na*, Dicksche, why use your best set? We might break something. We could have eaten in the kitchen, that would be good enough." She lifted her cup and inspected the marks underneath. "From Canada, looks like."

"I'm tired of eating in the kitchen with Jasch," Mrs. Dickman answered, laughing. "Let me get out my good set once in a while, for company at least."

"It's her wedding set," Tante Lieze said. "How many years now?"

"Forty-three. Nothing broken yet." Mrs. Dickman smiled and pushed back the white hair that had escaped from her combs and curled gaily across her temples.

Mrs. Penner set her cup back in its saucer and glanced out the big front window. "It's going to rain," she informed them. "Look at the wind." The others looked. The curtains were blowing inward now in lacy swirls. Outside, the smaller branches were whipping back and forth in a flurry of leaves. Mrs. Dickman rose and lowered the windows.

"We need the rain," Tante Lieze said. "The ground is too dry."

"Rain . . . but I hope it don't storm," Mrs. Dickman said, sitting back down. "Last time half the trees in the park had branches broke off, not just little ones—big ones. A big branch from one of Harder's trees tore off, just missed our garage." She pointed to a side window which looked out over the neighbor's spacious grounds. "Jasch told young Harry to get his trees cut back, but he never did, said he liked trees to grow natural or something silly. Harry's a good businessman, but in some ways he don't have much sense."

The others followed her gaze. Across an expanse of green lawn and surrounded by immense cottonwoods, the Harder residence stood: a handsome two-story house with front and side porches, pillars painted white, hedges trimmed. A gravel drive led to a garage and sheds.

"Harry Harder? He lives there?" Mrs. Penner looked out with bright, curious eyes. "Getting rich, is he? Or did his dad buy him that place? I heard he married the Voth girl. I remember he was crazy for her already in grade school. Mrs. Harder told me once, 'He's made up his mind.' He was only fourteen or fifteen."

Mrs. Dickman and Tante Lieze looked at each other. Tante Lieze said in a voice with an edge to it, "He had his mind made up all right."

Hurriedly Mrs. Dickman put in, "They got married six years ago. Katrina, her name is. She isn't very well. Can I get you more coffee? I have some hot in the kitchen."

Mrs. Penner looked interested. "What's wrong with her? Last

time I saw her, that was before we moved to Montana, she was a pretty little thing, hair tied up in ribbons, bounced all over town like a young colt with her skirts flying around her ankles. She ain't got consumption, has she? No, I don't want any more coffee."

"No," Mrs. Dickman said, after a pause. "She's been to plenty doctors, they can't find anything wrong."

Tante Lieze was watching the lilac bush outside the front window, in full purple bloom, now tossing wildly in the wind. "The wind is tearing up your lilac," she told Mrs. Dickman.

"Female trouble?" Mrs. Penner persisted. "Does she have any kids?"

"Two boys—Robbie and little Harry. Robbie's four, Harry is going to be two." Mrs. Dickman sighed, looked uneasily at the leftover *pirozhky,* then at her guest. "She had an easy time with them, no trouble."

Mrs. Penner eyed them with sudden suspicion. "Don't tell me Harry's taken up with another woman."

"*Na nae,*" Mrs. Dickman hastened to say. "He likes her well enough. You should have seen the wedding. Flowers all over the place. He took her to the Cities to buy a dress, silk, rows and rows of tucks and lace. They served a big dinner afterwards under the trees at the old Harder place, three hundred people at least. And lunch in the evening for those who stayed over. Must have cost old Harder plenty. Voths did what they could, but you could see it was a Harder wedding."

"Well, old man Harder has plenty!" Mrs. Penner observed. "Always gave that boy of his anything he wanted. Still, it's foolishness spending all that money on a wedding, don't hold a couple together no better than the old way." She laughed and reached for the lemon cake, sending Mrs. Dickman off into another flurry of plate-passing. "You know how my aunt Justina got married? The preacher asked Sunday morning after the sermon if anybody wanted to get married, and Justina got up on the women's side and Uncle Aaron on the men's side, and they went to the front, and the preacher married them, and then they went back and sat down, she on the women's side like before, and he on the men's side. She was wearing her black Sunday dress with maybe a necklace or something extra. Been together nearly fifty years, golden wedding coming up. Sixty-three descendants, last count."

Mrs. Dickman laughed. "My ma told me a preacher got up one Sunday and asked for those who wanted to get married to stand up, and one man got up, and six ladies."

Mrs. Penner cocked an eyebrow at her. "Now Dicksche, that's just a joke. Don't make fun of the old ways. Old Harder didn't have no fancy wedding himself; they were all poor as mice in them days. Look at him now, thinks he owns the whole town. So—Katrina's sick, you said?"

Tante Lieze was gazing out the front window, watching the lilac toss and shiver in the wind. A shower of petals covered the ground beneath it. Somewhere upstairs a branch scraped against the roof. "I better get home," she said firmly. "It's going to rain."

"Take the rest of the *pirozhky* to Lentye," Mrs. Dickman told her. She stood up, indicating that the meal was over.

But Mrs. Penner didn't budge. "I want to know about Katrina," she demanded. "Something's going on. You better tell me. I'll find out one way or another."

Mrs. Dickman cast an anxious glance at Tante Lieze, who had closed her mouth firmly and refused to speak. At last she turned to Mrs. Penner. "It's Harry."

Mrs. Penner regarded her with curiosity. "*Na*, Dicksche, how can she be having a hard time with Harry? He's a nice boy. He still likes her, you said. Good to the kids, I suppose, buys her anything she wants?"

"Emma, there are things you don't know," Mrs. Dickman said

with some asperity. She paused. "Katrina used to be engaged to John Falk. From the Alliance Church. The Falks live in the old Klein house on the dirt road north of town, next to Egg Tchetter—you know, the hatchery man."

"Yes, yes, I know," Mrs. Penner said impatiently. "This Falk fellow. Tall and stringy, brown hair always falling in his eyes? Katrina was engaged to *him*?"

'Yes. He was going to Africa as a missionary with the Alliance. Katrina was only nineteen, but she was all set to go to Africa with him. She'd have gone to Timbuctoo with him, if he'd asked her!" Mrs. Dickman picked up a piece of cake and began absently to break off crumbs.

"Africa!" exclaimed Mrs. Penner. "Ain't that the place where they eat caterpillars, drink water out of them crocodile rivers? I'd never in this life let any girl of mine go there!"

"The Voths was against it, of course, their only girl," Mrs. Dickman said. "So they all decided that because she was so young, John would go first to build a house, start things up, then come back after a year or so and they would get married. That way it would be easier for her."

Mrs. Penner waited. "Well?"

Mrs. Dickman looked down at the pile of crumbs on her plate. "Did I do this? My goodness. Yes, well, John said he would write to her as often as he could, not knowing what the mail situation was, you know. Katrina cried an awful lot, but they agreed on it, and John left and she started going to Bible School. She sewed some dresses because John said they couldn't buy much over there. Made a nice quilt, embroidered tea towels, said she wanted some pretty things even if she was in Africa." She stopped and sighed.

"So?" Mrs. Penner prompted.

Mrs. Dickman hesitated, then said slowly, "She stopped getting his letters."

"Found himself a woman out there, did he?" Mrs. Penner said, winking at Tante Lieze.

"*Na nae*, Emma, how you talk!" Mrs. Dickman looked at her with indignation.

"Well, it happens!" Mrs. Penner retorted. "Cousin of Hank's, one of the Schroeder girls, she went to China, married a Chinese, never came back."

"No," Mrs. Dickman said emphatically. "John wasn't that kind! He wrote and said he was living with some other missionaries, learning the language, planning on building a small house and starting a garden. He said it wasn't easy over there, but he was learning their ways. Then she didn't get any more letters. They just stopped. Katrina didn't know what to think. I'd see her walking into the post office with her head up, hopeful and talking to people, cute as a button in her blue coat and little white fur hat. And she'd come out going real slow, staring at the ground, crying. My, that girl was unhappy. She got pale and thin as a stick. I could have cried for her, but I figured she'd just have to be patient, maybe the mails couldn't get through."

"Don't tell me. He got sick—attacked by one of them wild animals?"

"It would have been easier," Tante Lieze muttered.

"No. That was the year," Mrs. Dickman said in a peculiar hushed tone, "that was the year Harry Harder worked in the post office."

"Well?" Mrs. Penner looked from one to the other. Tante Lieze sat gazing at her knobbed hands.

"Harry stopped the letters," Mrs. Dickman said finally.

"He did what? What do you mean, stopped the letters? Whose letters?"

"Harry stopped John's letters. When a letter came for Katrina, Harry took it out of the mail and put it aside so she never got them. He could do that, working at the post office." Mrs. Dickman brushed crumbs off the tablecloth and looked Mrs. Penner straight in the face.

There was a long silence. Finally Mrs. Penner shook her head. "He wouldn't do that. Harry's a good boy. We're related to the Harders, you know—my mother's an Enns, and the Ennses were all cousins to old Harder's first wife. Church people, all of them. I don't believe it."

"Katrina asked Harry straight out," Mrs. Dickman said firmly. "He burned the letters."

"Why did she marry him, then?"

"She didn't find out till after the wedding, or she never would have," Mrs. Dickman said. "She never wanted to marry Harry. But the letters didn't come, and Harry was over there day and night, he bought her all sorts of expensive stuff—he was really crazy for her. Her family liked him, they thought maybe John wasn't coming back. They never wanted her to go off to Africa in the first place. So finally she gave in."

"Sounds okay to me," Mrs. Penner said. "Harry's a good-looking guy, strong, steady job. I bet half the girls in town were after him."

"She seemed happy enough at first," Mrs. Dickman went on. "Invited folks to dinner, always went to church. She made a big garden, and pretty soon she was expecting. So we all thought it turned out for the best after all. And then all of a sudden John showed up."

Mrs. Penner laughed. "Hoo-eee! I bet he was surprised to find his girl safe and snug in Harry's house!"

At this Tante Lieze turned her back on Mrs. Penner and gazed steadfastly out of the window. The dark clouds were directly overhead. The wind was blowing bits of debris in the air, whining shrilly through the trees, but as yet there was no rain.

"It nearly killed him," Mrs. Dickman said. "Katrina had stopped writing because she didn't get any letters, so he didn't know anything. I'll never forget it. Our sewing circle invited him to speak the very next day after he arrived from New York. We had four quilting frames up, and Katie was at the same frame I was. The ladies were joking about her expecting the baby, and she was blushing away. She was showing a little, wearing a green silk dress, real loose, with a lace collar, hair done up on top of her head. Then John walked in. He saw her right away, and she saw him—she got so pale, I thought she'd faint. The chairman asked the ladies to give their names. When it was her turn, she spoke up loud, like she was angry, and gave her married name, looking straight at John. He just stared at her a minute, and then he turned to the next lady real quick, and began wiping his face with his handkerchief, and he gave his talk jerky-like. The ladies thought he was just tired, but I had other ideas. Katrina was watching him the whole time. She put in about ten stitches, and we had to take them out afterwards, they were so crooked."

"Well! And how did she find out about the letters?"

"She must have talked to John. I suppose they put two and two together, and later she went to Harry and asked him straight to his face if that's what happened. My, Katrina was upset. She cried so hard, we thought she'd lose the baby, the way she carried on. John didn't stick around long. His folks told me he traveled around the churches for a couple months and then went back to Africa. As far as I know, he never married."

Mrs. Penner folded her napkin and shook the crumbs out of her lap. "Well, I can't see that it's so bad. She'd have had it a lot worse with Falk out in that heathen place. If she has any sense, she'll live with Harry and be happy. Look at that house. Full of good furniture too, I bet."

Tante Lieze turned from the window and glanced angrily at Mrs. Penner. "He's a hard man, that Harry."

"*Leewe Tiet!*" exclaimed Mrs. Penner. "When I think how I used to work in the fields like a hired man, pitched bundles, everything! Don't you think I could cry right now if I wanted to? You think I'll ever get to California? Hank'll sit on his stupid farm like a clod till we die! Katrina'll have to make up her mind to it . . . if she's going to sit and mope because she'd rather go live in a mud hut in Africa, if I was Harry I'd say, go ahead, go on out there! Why should he slave away if she's going to make herself unhappy over some brown-haired nobody of a missionary!"

Tante Lieze turned on her. "He's doing the Lord's work, and you know it."

"He was silly to choose Africa over her and leave her behind, a pretty girl like her, to sit and wait for who knows how long! What did he expect?" Mrs. Penner looked Tante Liesze coolly in the face.

"I tell her Harry wanted her so bad, that's why he did it—she should leave off being so bitter," Mrs. Dickman said, looking deeply troubled. "But she won't hear a word of it. She says he was wicked to have tricked her like that. Anybody with eyes could see it was John she wanted."

"Well, it's a sin to let your family go to ruin just because you don't like the way things turned out," Mrs. Penner declared emphatically. "Probably God wanted it this way. Who knows what would have happened to her in Africa? Died of malaria, most likely."

"What if it was your girl, your Elsie?" Tante Lieze asked, with an angry look.

"I'd tell her the same: smarten up and make the best of it. The bed's been made, I'd tell her, and you find a way to lie in it! I got to go, the rain'll be starting any minute. Better shut your upstairs windows, Dicksche." She stood up and put on her coat and scarf.

"Come again, don't wait for an invitation," Mrs. Dickman said, but without conviction.

She handed Mrs. Penner her purse and opened the front door. A gust of wind tore at Mrs. Penner's scarf; she grabbed at it with one hand and set out.

"That's another one like Frieda, can't see past the end of her nose," Tante Liesze muttered. When Mrs. Penner was out of sight, she turned to Mrs. Dickman. "Katrina's outside with the boys. Over there."

She pulled back the drapery of a side window, and they saw, across the back lawn under the trees, a small figure standing motionless on the grass. Her face was lifted—she seemed to be searching for something on the horizon. Her long brown skirt and thin blouse whipped about in the wind. Behind her a stocky child in a blue cap stumbled along, picking up objects and throwing them a short distance. A taller child, a boy, was dragging a red wagon through the grass. "She's been out there a long time already," Tante Lieze said. "I didn't want Mrs. Penner to know it."

"She sits under that tree, maybe two hours sometimes," Mrs. Dickman said. "Once she told me Africa is that direction. I don't know, maybe it is. I don't know what's going to happen to her. Some days she just sits in the kitchen and stares, doesn't look out for the kids, nothing. I go help her when I have time. I bring the boys here—they like to dig in my garden." She looked at Tante Liesze in distress. "The thing she can't stand is that his family don't care. She says old man Harder thinks it was pretty smart, the way Harry got her. Mrs. Harder gets mad because the house is dirty—you know how she is, flies in a temper if there's a spot on the carpet. They don't hardly come over any more. When they do, Katrina goes all quiet, hardly says a word."

"What about young Harry?" Tante Liesze asked.

"Oh, he pretends everything's okay, she'll get over it. Takes her to doctors in the Cities. Sides with his folks, tells her to buck up. Stays away from home, works in his dad's business. What can he do? He knows it's his fault."

Under the enormous cottonwoods the figures looked small, moving about on a stage of dark blowing grass against the backdrop of the tall house. The wind blew at the boys' coats; they seemed not to mind but kept pulling the wagon and throwing sticks. Spats of rain spattered on Mrs. Dickman's window. "They should go in," she murmured.

The two women returned to the table and sat down.

"I worry about the boys," Mrs. Dickman said. "They're too quiet. Robbie, that's the older one, he hardly ever laughs, sits in the garden by himself and digs in the dirt. Little Harry doesn't talk a word yet. Katrina told me she can't bear to look at him because his hair is light and thin, like his dad's. I told her, Katrina, you have to take care of them! It's not their fault. They have nobody else, only you. She said she would try, but she shivered, like it was a terrible thing."

"Can't her mother help out? She shouldn't be by herself so much."

"Katrina doesn't want her. Lydia keeps saying what's done is done, it can't be changed now, she'll have to do her duty to the family. Her folks were plenty mad at first. Katrina wanted her dad to sue, or help her get a divorce, but of course he wouldn't. He said it was forbidden by the church to go to court, it would be a great shame on the family and a sin. So Katrina thinks they're against her too. Lydia has cried her eyes out many a time, I can tell you. But she still thinks it was for the best. She was dead set against Katrina going to Africa with John. She figures Katrina ought to count her blessings instead of feeling sorry for herself."

Mrs. Dickman paused. "Katrina said once she could maybe forgive Harry if he would even once admit he did wrong, apologize even a little, but he won't. He's stubborn like his dad. And the whole family sticks with him. They blame her for not making things good for Harry, he being a young businessman in town—they're embarrassed how the house looks, and the boys, hair not combed and such."

"Harder is their name, hard they are," Tante Lieze said. "Who can stand it?"

"What can she do?" Mrs. Dickman cried. "She's set against

Harry, she won't hardly talk to him—but she has to live with him, she can't go be with John."

Tante Lieze gazed out the window at the wildly tossing lilacs. At length she said quietly, "She can't give up. She has to go through what's in front of her."

Mrs. Dickman took another look out the side window. "I wish they'd go in. Look how it's raining. Maybe I should go tell her, she forgets everything sometimes."

"*Na nae,* Dickscha, it's not so cold, they'll just get a little wet. When does Harry get home?"

"Oh, he's gone off with his dad to look at some farms south of Mankato. It'll be late."

She sighed and turned to face her friend. "I don't know what to say to her, Tante Lieze. I tell her the Bible says we must forgive even our enemies."

Tante Lieze thought it over, shook her head slowly. "Forgive—it's not so easy. It's a hard thing."

Mrs. Dickman, remembering what Tante Lieze had gone through, was silent. Finally she said, "Katrina thinks God doesn't care about her. She said at first she used to pray every day for God to help her love Harry and his folks, but she stopped. She asked me, how can John tell the Africans God loves them if He let this happen to us? Or maybe God is too busy saving Africans and doesn't pay attention to the awful things going on in this town."

Tante Lieze studied her hands, folded in front of her on the table, and did not answer.

"A while back she used to scream at me," Mrs. Dickman went on. "Over and over, 'Why didn't God stop him? Why didn't he stop him? We promised our lives to God for Africa, we were willing to give up everything! God can do anything, He could have stopped him!' I didn't know what to tell her."

"Yes, why?" Tante Lieze repeated slowly. "God didn't stop the terrible famine in Russia . . . my aunt starved to death, and a lot of others in my village. He didn't stop that bandit Makhno—how many of our people did he murder in Molotschna, even the old couple that brought him up, he walked in and killed the old man. Sometimes at night I think about them."

Mrs. Dickman shuddered. "I don't let Jasch read me those reports, I can't sleep. I don't know, Liezje. I don't know the right things to say. Would you maybe talk to her?"

"*Joh*, I can try." Tante Lieze paused, and added, "The next day Mrs. Harder will come along and sweep out what I say, like with a broom."

"I just wish Jasch would go tell that young Harry a thing or two!" Mrs. Dickman cried suddenly, with surprising energy. "Maybe even beat him up! Some days I even want to do it myself!" She jumped up and began carrying plates into the kitchen.

Returning, she picked up more plates, set them back on the table and sat down. "I get scared, Tante Lieze. Last time I went over she looked at me so wild, so strange. I told her, Harry did you wrong, it was a sin what he did, the whole town knows it. But be patient. God will find a way for you. She got angry. She said, 'There's no way, no other way. I have to live here in this house till I die.' I'm scared maybe she will die. I don't know what to do."

The shrill whine of the wind had given way to a hard splatter of rain driving against the walls of the house. Mrs. Dickman rose, stooped and peered through the window. Then she said with relief, "They're going in, thank the Lord. They'll be wet as jaybirds by now." She watched a few moments longer, and sighed deeply as if, now that Katrina and the boys were safely hidden in the house, which was itself half-obscured by rain and the falling darkness, she need not worry about them for a while.

Tante Liesze was silent for a long time. At last she said, "I used to worry day and night when Dietrich went off and left me with

Lentye. Now I tell God, you let it happen, you are stronger than the evil, you find a way."

Mrs. Dickman looked out at the rain and gathering darkness. "Go talk to her, Tante Lieze, you're the right one." She picked up the plate of leftover *pirozhky.* "These are for Lentye. I'll wrap them up in something. You'll get soaked walking home, though. You better wait a bit."

"*Joh,* I can wait. Frieda's at my place," Tante Lieze answered. "Summer storms don't take so long. I can wait it out."

Tante Lieze sat by the table and watched, from the front window, the wind ripping the purple blooms from the outer branches of the lilac. The ground around it was covered with petals. The inner part of the bush, sheltered by the house, was spared: there the long lavender flowers lay more quietly, a deep rich purple, shining in the rain. Her own troubles she could bear, she thought, but this young girl, what had she done?

Having cleared the table, Mrs. Dickman came to sit beside her. Together they waited for the storm to pass.

THE APOLOGY

AMANDA—DEAR AMANDA, THE darling of the town, at their twenty-fifth wedding anniversary, beautiful as the day she was married, wearing in fact her wedding dress today, her figure still slender though bewitchingly rounded now—sat at the head table with her husband Marlin Junke in chairs decorated with white satin bows. The high school auditorium was full to the doors. People sat elbow to elbow at long tables covered with white paper and loaded with platters of sausage, buns and rye bread, bowls of potato salad, glass dishes of pickles, fancy plates bearing frosted cakes cut into thick slices. Vases of yellow and white chrysanthemums were placed along the tables. All faces were turned toward the head table, where Amanda and Marlin's son Thomas was making the opening remarks.

"We are honoring," he was saying, "the silver wedding of a golden couple." There was a ripple of laughter—all knew what he meant. Marlin Junke was the prosperous owner of the town's new and thriving automobile business, honored member of the bank and hospital boards, deacon in his church, of unimpeachable character and judgment. Amanda, dear Amanda, who supported him, helped the poor and pitied the unfortunate, winsome in all her ways, walked the town streets with bright words of greeting for everyone. Marlin had chosen well; and so, at seventeen, had she.

From behind a crystal bowl of deep pink roses, Amanda surveyed the room, noting this face and that. Some she had not seen for months perhaps, and a few from North Dakota (Junke country) were here on their first visit in years. She was happy to see them all. They were all so kind, she thought, to come on a Saturday in the middle of harvest in warm weather, yet here they were in their best clothes, leaving combines and corn pickers waiting in the ripe fields. At various front tables were the numerous relatives who had come from near and far—musicians, teachers, nurses, farmers. This had been the union of two respected, vastly talented families. The other guests looked them over with friendly, often envious eyes.

Marlin, she became aware, was glancing at her out of the corner of his eye; strong silent Marlin who adored her, so handsome today in his dark suit with a white flower in his buttonhole, dark brown hair graying only slightly at the temples. The audience was laughing. What had Thomas said? Something about Marlin holding his wife by the hand so that she would not slide down from her chair and climb out the window . . . an allusion to a story he promised would be told later, though everyone already knew it. She smiled to herself. It was a story worth telling.

At the back of the auditorium a row of men with white dish towels tied around their middles leaned against the wall waiting to serve the coffee. In the kitchen, she knew, were great bowls of food which would replenish the platters on the tables as fast as they were emptied. It was all so well arranged, all planned by their three efficient children, the work all done by volunteers from the church and bank and hospital. Mrs. Grace Krahn had supplied the flowers from her garden, and the ladies of the Parkside Church had baked the cakes.

Thomas sat down. A quartet of cousins from nearby towns, led by cousin Abe, sang a hymn of thanksgiving. Rev. Schulte of the Parkside Church rose to say grace, and the meal began. Heads turned toward the food, forks clinked, platters were handed around. The men in white aprons carried around coffee in blue enamel kettles. Voices rose in conversation, neighbors and friends greeted one another, discussed the harvest and the weather, told jokes in Low German.

Amanda herself was not hungry. She leaned forward a little and glanced down the table at their daughters: Ellie in a fashionable navy dress, sitting beside her husband Frank, and beyond her Trudy, charming in rose pink, talking to Carl. Both girls happily married, she thought with joy. Frank was a skilled mechanic who worked in his father-in-law's business, and Carl a young farmer with an exceptionally productive spread of land on the other side of the lake. At the far end of the table was Thomas, the MC, seated now with his slender black-haired Annette from Quebec. He was already in a prominent position at the bank, for all his joking ways. All three of them had sturdy young children, all were involved in a church. Somehow she had always known it would be this way. She would marry Marlin, and they would have a wonderful family, and all would be very well. The words came to her mind: to those who have, more shall be given. So much, so very much, had been given.

She glanced affectionately at Marlin, sitting stiffly with his broad shoulders squared back, not because he was so dignified (as people thought), but because he was so shy. She was comfortably aware that she was quite as beautiful as her daughters: her hair was still a soft brown, the high old-fashioned lace collar of her wedding dress hid the few age-lines at her throat, the corsage of pink roses at her shoulder heightened the delicate color of her cheeks. And added to all this was her own serene, hopeful frame of mind. Happiness was her nature. For all this she was fervently thankful to God.

The others at the head table were talking, laughing, passing buns and pickles, drinking coffee. Marlin, beside her, lifted an eyebrow at the scant food on her plate (he was well into a second round) and offered to serve her more sausage. She shook her head, smiling at him. "Later, perhaps," she said.

Her gaze wandered to the back of the auditorium. She noticed, at the end of one of the long tables, a stout elderly woman of proud bearing, wearing a dark gray hat with feathers, apparently explaining something to one of the serving men. A young woman sitting beside her was talking vivaciously to a farmer across the table; and further down the bench, crowded up against the back wall, was a small man wearing a bow tie. Amanda noticed him especially because of his pale, thin face and the black hair falling across his forehead, which he kept pushing back with a nervous gesture. He seemed not to be talking to anyone, but rather gazing about at the busy noisy crowd in a timid manner. Amanda could not recall their names, though they looked familiar. It wasn't possible, of course, to know everybody, but still it disturbed her not to know their names, people of her own town.

Marlin's younger brother Jonas was now telling the story of the Great Escape, when Amanda was fifteen. Most people had stopped eating and were watching with amusement the tall, jolly-faced farmer, the family story-teller.

"Marlin was stuck on her from about fourth grade—he never said so, but we knew it because he always walked by her house on the way to ball games. She'd be skipping rope out front, maybe, or swinging on that creaky porch swing. It wasn't the shortest way to the ball field, but that's the way he always went. So here he is, sixteen years old by now, close on seventeen, and he thinks it's high time to ask this girl out, but there's nowhere to go in this town, at least nowhere that's allowed by his parents and most especially by HER parents (laughter), except the *Jugendverein*—the Young People's Meeting—on Sunday night. A wonderful place to learn to know a girl. You could walk her there, and maybe, if it was a liberal congregation, even sit by her (laughter). Well, so he gets up nerve and asks her can he walk with her to the next *Jugendverein* at the Alliance Church. And she sees no reason why not, lots of girls are wild to go out with this handsome though very quiet guy, might as well find out if he's any good, does he have a tongue to go along with his good looks, which are considerable (laughter).

"So a couple weeks later she walks with him through town along with several other young couples. She's wearing this frilly light-colored summer dress all over ribbons and tucks, and white stockings, you know how young girls used to dress, long sweet curls and so forth. Marlin's higher'n a cloud, minding his best manners, attempting a conversation about cows and the price of corn and such, which is what the men of this town always talk about when they're doing serious courting (laughter). And about the time they get to the Alliance church, Amanda gets cold feet. After all it's her first real date, and what's she to do sitting for an hour or two (programs were long in those days) next to this tremendously serious-minded boy. Besides, she realizes she's had it up to her eyebrows with church for the day, the morning service having been two-and-a-half hours long (laughter).

"So what does she do. At the front door she excuses herself to go comb her curls which she says are mussed up from the wind, which there wasn't any of, but the mirror is in the ladies' coat room behind a door, and fortunately this room has another door to the babies' crying room, which is fortunately open, so she quietly walks into the baby room, climbs out the window, and walks home (much laughter).

"All this time Marlin is waiting outside the door of the ladies' coat room. He's getting nervous as everyone else is going in and the benches are filling up, and he doesn't want to sit clear in back, and he's wondering what on earth is taking this girl so long. He walks a little way along the benches to see if maybe she got confused and sat down somewhere, but she's not there. Finally, very red in the face, he asks his cousin Arlene to go see where Amanda is. And Arlene reports, after full investigation, that Amanda is nowhere, but a woman in the baby room saw a girl climb out the window and walk away, and very shocked she was too, the girl being almost grown up and in her Sunday clothes. Marlin is miffed out of his mind, for sure. But I gotta hand it to him, he stuck with this feather-brained chit (laughter), and about two months later he tried again, and this time she sat with him the whole evening, and you can see how it turned out."

Marlin had turned a deep red from forehead to neck. Amanda turned to him and smiled, and squeezed his hand. It had all been so long ago, and such fun.

What Jonas did not know, nor anyone else, was that it was she—not Marlin—who had set things in motion again. When Marlin, out of wounded pride, or fear, did not approach her for several weeks, she simply walked up to him one day and asked him to take her to a movie she wanted to see. Not in Windamer, of course—most churches forbade movie-going as of the devil— but over in Cloudy Lake. The astonished boy had agreed. Then she had quietly, without his being in the least aware of it, put the reins back in his hands and allowed him to do the asking from then on.

"It is my understanding that he proposed to her in the apple orchard, which had been recently plowed so they were standing ankle deep in dust," Jonas was saying. Under the same tree, Amanda thought, smiling to herself, where the shy boy had kissed her for the first time. There were, after all, many things her children didn't know, nor had her parents back then.

Jonas's speech ended to a burst of clapping. A women's trio came up and sang several light-hearted songs. Thomas told jokes about old married couples. Then he asked several people to come up front to pay tribute to the honored couple. At about this time one of the strong young grandchildren, being cared for at a distant table by friends, emitted a piercing howl and had to be carried out, to the delight of the audience. "Future board member," commented Thomas.

While Martin Dyck of the town council was making a few laudatory remarks about this still-youthful couple and their positive influence on the community, Amanda let her gaze wander back to the man by the wall. He was sitting sunk into himself, staring ahead. He seemed to be immobilized, as if, she thought, he would move or speak only when told to do so. She compared him with strong silent Marlin beside her. No woman, she thought, would be likely to choose that small, dejected man—no light-hearted girl would give him the slip out of pure perverseness and then later marry him in the fullness of love. She pitied him, pitied intensely a human being so deprived; though perhaps he was happy in some way unknown to her. She remembered once feeling deeply sorry for a pair of caged foxes at the Mankato zoo, thinking how weary and boring their narrowed lives must be; but then learning that the foxes were content, being well fed and secure. Yet this small man, whoever and whatever he was, did not look happy.

Martin Dyck was succeeded by one of Marlin's employees, who began telling tales about townspeople and their obstreperous cars brought in for impossible repairs. At one point, while everyone was laughing, Amanda leaned toward her husband and whispered, "Who's that little man at the back wall, near the lady in the gray hat?" He looked, frowned, shook his head slightly, and said in an undertone, "That's the Brauns—father's with MCC, sister works at the hospital . . . I think his name is Jake."

Jake. Jake Braun. The name sounded familiar. Had she encountered him before, somewhere? Years ago, it must have been. Grade school, maybe? High school? She could not remember.

The men's quartet bounded up to sing a fast-paced song. The audience applauded enthusiastically and then settled down to listen while an uncle began telling stories about Amanda's girls creeping into the cornfield to avoid washing dishes, and putting liniment in the cake instead of vanilla. Ellie and Trudy laughed and shook their heads.

The pastor of the Alliance church rose to make a few remarks. The children still at the tables (the younger ones had been let go to play outside) were visibly weary of the program by now and were amusing themselves by dipping moistened fingers into the sugar bowls and licking them, until told to stop, or kicking at each other under the table. The pastor began: "Way back when it was still a novelty and possibly a sin for young people to ride together in cars . . . ." At that precise moment a scene sprang into Amanda's mind, complete in all details.

A summer day when she was in high school. A tent meeting and picnic for young people had been announced for a certain day, to be held in the park near Heron Lake, twelve miles distant. Her cousin Abe was going in the family car with his girl Marian and had invited her to go along. "You can sit in back with Jake Braun," he told her. "I said I'd pick him up." He looked at her teasingly. "He'd like that. Okay with you?" Jake Braun was the little guy the others made fun of. He was pale, his hair fell in his eyes, and he never said the right things. While he never openly said he had to ask his mother, it was well known that she ran his life. Poor Jake. Amanda had told Abe with some fire that of course she would sit in back with him.

Just before starting off for Heron Lake, Abe and Marian had held a fierce whispered debate in the front seat. Finally Abe started the car and they drove off. Marian soon began complaining that if they picked up Jake they'd have to have him around the whole day and what a drag that would be. Amanda defended him, reminding Abe of his promise. She remembered driving lickety-split down a farm road past an orchard in a cloud of dust, a boy standing beside the road just ahead, Abe not slowing down but waving to the person as they fled past . . . it was Jake, she saw. He had been wearing a suit. Marian and Abe had been silent a moment, as if ashamed, but then they laughed. "Wearing a suit!—can you beat that?"Marion was saying. Amanda had thought it mean of them—he had been standing there, after all, waiting. "You should have stopped—you promised!" she protested. Still, later it had turned out for the best because the three of them had decided to go boating and there was room only for three—it would have been embarrassing to tell Jake he couldn't go, and too disappointing not to go at all because of him. She had had a wonderful time, had told herself it was no business of hers, and forgotten about it.

Amanda now knew with certainty that what Abe and Marian had done was thoughtless and cruel. Sometimes rebuffs, even small ones, hurt people for a long time. She looked with compassion at the small man crowded against the back wall. Then she collected her thoughts and turned away—this was not the time to be worrying about things that had happened so many years ago, she told herself severely; she should be paying attention to the speaker.

". . . home always open to anyone—the elderly, the poor, visitors from out of town," he was saying, and went on to describe Amanda's volunteer help at the German school and the church nursery. It was all true. She did all those things. Yet instead of joy at this moment, she felt a nagging worry. A wrong had not been righted. She glanced at Abe and Marian (married soon after, she a plump middle-aged woman by now) and wondered if perhaps they had apologized later. She thought it not too likely.

Marlin now stood up. He thanked his family, the committees and cooks and all others who had made this occasion so memorable. As for his brother Jonas, he said, he would deal with him privately later on (laughter), but let it be said that a woman you could catch the first time probably wasn't worth catching (much applause). He put an arm around Amanda to raise her to her feet. The audience applauded. She smiled at them all, kissed Marlin on the cheek. They sat down amid a general murmur of pleasure. Wonderful people, Amanda thought, happy in their goodwill, kindly friends all. She decided, at that moment, to speak to Jake afterwards, say a few friendly words to show she wished him well.

Then it was over. Everyone scraped benches back and stood up. The talking became twice as loud as before. Children escaped from parents and rushed wildly out of the auditorium. People crowded to the front to shake hands and wish the couple many happy years more. Amanda smiled graciously at them all. She congratulated Helena and Johann Jungas, who had rebuilt their burnt-out store and home above it. She thanked Rosie Pankratz for her committee's many visits to the widows and hospitalized, and the owner of the hat shop for her service to the women of the town. When Harry Harder came by she asked how his two boys were doing . . . his wife Katie had died some time earlier, of 'consumption' the family said vaguely, though the gossip was she had died broken-hearted over a betrayal in a love affair years ago. "Fine, fine," Harder said heavily, and turned away. Amanda was not offended—the man was still grieving.

All the while she was talking to the endless stream of well-wishers, Amanda kept an eye out for Jake. She glimpsed him once beside his mother, who was busy talking, then lost him in the crowd. Should she mention the incident, the only one that had, so far as she knew, connected their lives? He might have forgotten it, be embarrassed. If so, she would have to smooth it over somehow.

Goodbyes were being said, people were leaving, Ellie and Trudy had reclaimed their children, and still people were waiting to congratulate the honored couple. The crowd thinned out. Amanda was sure that Jake must be gone by now and that she had missed her chance, when she glimpsed him standing near by. As soon as she could excuse herself she walked over to him. "You're Jake Braun, I think?"

He looked up in astonishment at being so unexpectedly addressed. There was an awkward pause. "Yes . . . Jake Braun." He began nervously to adjust his tie, an old-fashioned one with broad red stripes.

Amanda, who always knew the right thing to say, now could

think of nothing, no reason to be talking to him after all. Her resolve seemed strange—what could she have been thinking? Then suddenly and simply, without the slightest hesitation, she put out her gloved hand and said, "Tonight I remembered something from a long time ago, when we were kids in high school—you've probably forgotten all about it. What happened is, my cousin Abe and Marian and I were supposed to pick you up to go to some meeting, and you were waiting at the road, but Abe didn't stop, just drove by . . . do you remember that? He was driving his new car. I was just a kid in high school, you probably didn't even know who I was."

She stopped, struck by the conscious misery in his face. He cleared his throat, looked down at the floor, pushed back the hair falling over his forehead with a nervous gesture, and finally stammered, "Yes . . . I, but you . . . ."

She put her hand lightly on his arm. "I'm so very sorry. We should never have done that, it was extremely rude. In fact I remember arguing with Abe about it. I thought he was going to stop. I don't know why he didn't. I hope—." She looked earnestly into his face, wanting to erase any pain they might have caused.

Jake glanced hurriedly at her, at the lovely woman in her wedding dress standing before him, her gloved hand touching his crumpled white shirt sleeve. Acutely embarrassed, he said, finally, "No, he . . . it was a long time ago, many years . . . ."

She saw that he remembered well enough. "Yes, long ago," she said, "but still—I hope you didn't mind too much, just put us down as a bunch of rude thoughtless teenagers."

He looked around nervously. "It was . . . I didn't expect . . . ." He looked up, hesitating, seaching for words. To save him further embarrassment, she smiled at him and turned away.

And that was all. She saw him walk away, not towards his mother as she expected, but straight out of the auditorium. Returning to Marlin's side to acknowledge a few final guests, she noticed Jake's mother looking around, walking stiffly off with the daughter, her face grim. Amanda hoped she had not caused Jake any trouble.

Not long after this celebration, rumors began to circulate about town that for some completely obscure reason which nobody could discover since he refused to talk about it, Jake Braun had begun building a house across the creek from the home place. He had already dug back the banks of the stream and laid planks to form a bridge of sorts and was driving over load after load of lumber on his truck. Ben, the construction man, was helping him. Mathilda of course was joking about it, but his mother was going about very tight-lipped. The town consensus, never openly stated but nevertheless known to all, was that it was about time Jake cut loose and acted for himself, like a man. If he brought home a wife to put in the house, so much the better . . . rumor had it that he was seeing a young woman who worked at the Red Rooster in Cloudy Lake. The town wondered, waited, and watched.

Amanda heard about it from Ellie and Trudy and rejoiced that this was taking place. It was a very nice spot to build a house, she said. She wondered if her conversation with Jake Braun had anything to do with this turn of events, but decided that probably it did not, that her apology had probably only embarrassed him. In her prayers she thanked God that Jake Braun was doing better in life, and turned her attention to other pressing matters.

EVA

A LITTLE GIRL ran up the wooden steps of the Bargen Church. She saw, just inside the doorway on the women's side, a tall woman straightening her head-kerchief before entering the meeting room. Her Bible teacher. Overflowing with joy, the child held up her arm to show a bracelet of sparkling blue stones. "My auntie gived me this!" she cried.

The woman looked down. "Which auntie?"

"My auntie Grace."

The woman's eyes narrowed slightly. Bending toward the child she smiled and said, "That's nice. But Jesus doesn't like bracelets in church. Maybe you should keep it in your drawer."

The child looked at her for a long moment. Then she slowly undid the clasp and slid the bracelet into her pocket.

The visiting preacher leaned over the pulpit, a long finger pointed at the audience, preaching in German. "Sisters, don't think to escape the Word. What does it say? Be modest, sober, especially in the Lord's house. Others have gone to worldly ways. Go into their homes, sisters, in this very town! What will you see? Carpets with patterns, fancy sofas, lamp shades with long fringes. Go, sisters, stand and watch as they step in their high heels into their churches. Hats with feathers, dresses of silk, bright colors—even red, flaming, the devil's color. They show their arms like harlots, they adorn their fingers with rings. What do you think, sisters? Is this fitting for the Lord's house? I hear that some of you are dissatisfied with the ways of our fathers. My sisters, our fathers were wise. They knew that worldly adornment tempts the spirit to stray. Our plain clothes and houses keep our minds sober, our hearts on heavenly things. Obey the teachings of the elders. God's judgment will fall upon the disobedient!" The preacher's dark eyes burned in his pale bearded face.

The women stirred uneasily and cast covert glances at each other. Little Eva, in a brown dress with high neck and long sleeves, sat dutifully beside her mother. Just ahead of her a small girl sat in her mother's lap playing with the mother's fingers, bright blue ribbons in her hair. Sitting upright without expression, Eva considered the preacher's stern gaze, the unease of the women around her, and the blue ribbons in the child's hair. Her gaze rested longest on the ribbons.

At the south end of town, where the houses straggled further and further apart and the cornfields began, the small Bargen Church stood in a half-acre of graveled yard bordered by weeds and rutted from the turning of many carriage wheels. The church was named for a local patriarch, one of a tightly knit and conservative group of church leaders who ruled a small cluster of churches in the Midwest. Members of the other churches in town tended to make fun of the Bargen congregation's old-fashioned ways, while the Bargen people held themselves to be God's hope of salvation for their heedless and sinful town.

Out in the country beyond the church yard, the cornfields sloped away toward the clear, quiet sky. Clumps of trees hid the farms; little clouds of dust rose behind farm implements moving in the fields . . . occasionally, if the harvest was urgent, even on the Lord's Day.

The small house in which Eva lived with her mother was beside the road out of town, only a few hundred yards from the church. Eva could see the church from their kitchen window: two rows of wooden steps with separate entrances for men and women, iron handrails down which little boys slid until someone stopped them, narrow tall windows, gray planks covering the ground-level entrance to the cellar. The church was as familiar to Eva as her own house. She and her mother walked there summer and winter, twice on Sundays and two or three times during the week. When her father was alive he used to carry her, she remembered—he would whisper in her ear and tickle her with his beard. But that was a dim memory from a long, long time ago. Always, at the sight of the church, a shadow fell over her. She would turn her eyes away, return to scrubbing the drain board.

Or she would run out into her garden behind the house. Only God could make flowers, her father had said. Blue bachelor buttons, brilliant red geraniums and frilled pink peonies dancing behind their shining dark green leaves. Wonderful, glorious colors. She would kneel down and run the warm earth, smelling of leaf mold, through her fingers. The God of the garden did not seem to be the same as the God in the church.

One Sunday morning Eva, hearing her mother come in from the garden, hung up the dishcloth and went to see if she needed help. Her mother had cut some gladiolas for the table. "It's going to be hot today," she said, slightly out of breath. White hair escaped from her kerchief to curl damply on the back of her neck.

Eva looked at her flushed face. "You shouldn't go out. Go lie down, there's time before church." She put the gladiolas in a glass jar.

"*Na nae*, we have to leave early, I don't want to walk so fast," her mother said, and went to change her dress.

On the way to church her mother complained of feeling hot in her obligatory long sleeves. She'll get another headache, Eva thought, but there was nothing to be done about it.

Her mother went to sit with the women, and Eva climbed the narrow steps to a small balcony, where the young people's Bible classes (the name Sunday School was not permitted) were taught, boys on one side, girls on the other, with a green curtain between. She sat down beside her friend Anita at the end of a bench, next to the curtain.

Scuffling and punching noises came from the other side, a loud "Ow!" followed by a thud, shrill laughter instantly stifled, sudden silence. The boys' teacher, Mr. Gingrich, must have come in. A pleasant masculine voice said in English, "Good morning, boys." The girls stopped whispering and looked toward the curtain—it was not Mr. Gingrich, but Charles Unrau!

"He's working on his dad's farm this summer," Anita informed the girls in a loud whisper. They looked at her with envy. Charles had wonderful dark wavy hair, nothing thin or straggly about him! Anita lived on the next farm and (according to her) saw Charles almost daily. She had earlier informed them that Charles played ball at his college: basketball, on a regular court, as part of a team. To go off to a college, and now to a seminary, most probably "liberal," was in itself next to a serious sin, but to be a ball player!

Two of the girls crept to the end of the curtain to get a look at Charles, but drew back instantly when they were seen and greeted with hoots of laughter. Anita got the girls' attention and told them that Charles had once secretly bought a small radio and hidden it in the hayloft. In the evenings after chores he would go up and listen. "Mr. Unrau found it, though. He took it awa-a-ay," imitating the older generation's drawl. The girls giggled.

"An elder found my brother's radio too," one of them said. "He found it in the barn and stomped on it! Lenny's going to buy another one and hide it in the basement under the potatoes . . . don't tell."

"Did you listen to it?" Eva asked, wondering how anyone dared to disobey the elders.

"*Jah,* sure, I like it," the girl said.

Steps thumped up the wooden stairs and Mrs. Froese came in, late as always. A stout woman, she was out of breath from the climb. She opened a lesson book. "Did you re-ead the lesson? Do you know the memory verse?" The girls were silent. She asked these questions every Sunday. Mrs. Froese frowned slightly. Switching to German, she began reading a lengthy passage having to do with Ahab and the wicked queen Jezebel.

On the other side of the curtain the boys were discussing the high school basketball game between Windamer and Dumfrey, speaking in English, eagerly but with hushed voices. The girls glanced at each other. It was a forbidden subject. The eager voices grew louder. An argument began about the unfairness of the umpire. Charles' pleasant voice said, "How do you know he wasn't fair? Did anyone see the game?" Silence. A small voice said, "The English boys told us." English . . . anyone not German. Charles said, "Umpires try to be fair, but they make mistakes just like the rest of us." Shrill voices. "Umpires got to be fair, they get paid." "My dad ain't fair, he makes me work all the time and he don't pay me, neither!" "God oughta be fair." "Teachers too." A drawling voice cut in: "If your teacher was fair you'd flunk every grade, Arn." Laughter. Charles said, "Most of us find ourselves in unfair situations sometimes. Take, well, the freedom to choose how to live your life. Some people have a lot of freedom, some very little, like people who have to obey a dictator or . . . ." "The elders," a voice muttered. Silence. Charles cleared his throat. "So, what do you think, why does God allow unfair situations?"

"Eva!" Eva started. Mrs. Froese was looking at her. "Pa-ay attention.

You're in the girls' cla-ass, not the boys'. Now girls, what can we learn from this scripture?" The girls said nothing. This was the third question she asked every Sunday. Frowning more deeply, Mrs. Froese began to comment on the passage.

A shrill voice asked, "Mr. Unrau, did God write every single word in the Bible?" "What do you think?" "I dunno—I guess so." The drawling voice said, "What about the *the's* and the *and's*?" Laughter. Charles said, "Well, all the books of the Bible were originally written in ancient languages—Hebrew, Greek . . . ." The shrill voice interrupted. "My grandpa, he said the Bible was wrote in German." Something like a stifled laugh. "No, Arn, nobody talked German in those days. German didn't exist until much later. In the days of the Old Testament, people spoke languages which aren't used any more, like Aramaic, Ugaritic." Giggles. "Never heard them words before, bet they ain't in no diction-a-ary."

Anita nudged Eva in the ribs—everybody was watching her. She must have been asked a question. Eva shook her head and looked at the floor. Mrs. Froese sighed audibly. "I do wish you girls would listen, you aren't learning much from the lesson." Beside her Anita muttered, "Who cares about this stuff anyway." The teacher cast a reproving glance at Anita and continued her explanation of the sins of Ahab and Jezebel.

The voices on the other side of the curtain could not be ignored. "I thought nobody could read in them old days." "Oh, yes, they had a written language. They wrote on pieces of clay. Archaeologists have dug up whole libraries of these clay tablets. I'll bring one next Sunday. Abraham—you know who he was? Yes, in Genesis. He lived four thousand years ago. He and possibly also his wife Sarah could read and write and do math, square roots even." "A square root?" Laughter. "That's a term in mathematics." A pause. A small voice asked, "Is the Bible edu-cated?" Another pause. Charles said, "Many books of the Bible were written by educated men, if that's what you mean. Moses went through the best schools of Egypt, and the Apostle Paul was a learned Pharisee. Other books were written by plain people like Amos, who was a shepherd. Sometimes they wrote on scrolls made of animal skin. What? No, the original scrolls don't exist any more, but we have copies in the museums. Yes, Arn? Well, scholars learn the ancient languages and translate the books of the Bible . . . they try very hard not to make mistakes, but some words are hard to figure out so they don't always agree. Next time . . . ."

A bell rang sharply. The girls filed down the narrow stairs, patted their hair into place before a tiny mirror on the ladies' side, darted laughing glances across at the boys lounging against the men's coat racks. Mrs. Froese walked heavily by, looking dispirited.

The congregation moved into the long benches in the church, men on one side, women on the other. Eva found her mother and sat down beside her. Apparently the headache had not come on.

During the long meeting Eva thought about the ancient writers, the clay tablets and the scrolls. She had immediately believed Charles when he told about ancient languages. The idea fascinated her. God must have known those languages to tell them what to write. But of course God must know all languages that had ever existed and would ever exist. Did God speak to them in a voice, or did he give them ideas and let them choose their own words? What if they made a mistake—if the translations were wrong? What if a tablet or a scroll got lost? Maybe there were other books that should be in the Bible but hadn't been found yet . . . nicer ones than that story about Jezebel. Quite probably she was sinning, thinking these things, but Charles Unrau had opened a door behind which many questions had been tightly shut away, and now it was impossible to stop them from crowding out.

After the final hymn she followed her mother outside, walking with bent head as was proper; but out of the corner of her eye she looked for Charles. He was talking with several older men out in the yard, hands shoved in his back pockets—an irreverent pose, to be sure. Anita and the other girls stood close by watching him. Girls were not allowed to talk with boys on the church yard.

Anita's mother caught up with Eva and her mother as they were leaving and handed them a small covered pail. "Eggs," she told them, "from yesterday; we had some left o-over." She waved off their thanks.

At home, eating cold chicken and fried potatoes with her mother, Eva was silent. At last she said, "Charles Unrau was teaching the boys' class today. He said interesting things. I wish he would teach our class maybe once or twice."

Her mother looked at her in great surprise. "Young men shouldn't teach girls, it wouldn't be good." She thought a moment, then added with a happy glance at her daughter, "He's a nice young man. We should invite the family over."

"No, we don't need to do that," Eva said hastily. "I just thought ... Mrs. Froese always reads from the lesson book."

"Mrs. Froese is a good woman," her mother said. "She tries her best to help you girls."

"I know," Eva said, and sighed. The women were good-hearted, kind, bringing eggs to help her mother out. They did the best they could.

Her mother reminded her that Elder Wiens and his wife were coming for coffee at four o'clock. Eva sent her mother to lie down while she washed the dishes. She wished the Wienses wouldn't come. She had been only five when that tall solemn woman had made her take off Aunt Grace's bracelet, but Eva still felt dull in her presence.

Later, rising from her nap with a start, her mother began rushing about, taking out dishes, spoons, napkins. "There's plenty of time," Eva said. "They aren't coming until four." They set the table, warmed up pie in the oven, cut bread, pressed butter from the crock into a glass dish, opened a jar of plum preserves. Maybe they'll forget to come, Eva thought.

They came at exactly four o'clock. Elder Wiens shook hands. He was short with a full graying beard. His wife's glossy black hair had broad streaks of white now; she wore it pulled severely back, as usual. Her face was more angular, her expression more dour than ever.

Fluttering nervously, Eva's mother invited them to the table. They sat formally, eating. Conversation, in German as always with the elders, was slow and ponderous. Finally Elder Wiens said, "I hear that Charles Unrau has come back for the summer. His father has need of him. A son's place is on the farm helping with the work, not running after foreign foolishness." He shook his head gravely at the foolishness of Charles Unrau.

Eva's mother brightened. "Eva says he was teaching the boys' class this morning."

Elder Wiens pursed his lips. "Very unwise. I was not in favor." He brushed crumbs from his beard. His wife sniffed and helped herself to the plum preserves.

Eva's mother talked serenely on. "Eva said he talked about interesting things. She would like to have him teach the girls' class."

Eva stared at her mother in dismay.

Elder Wiens stopped eating. "Well, what did he say then, Evangeline?"

Evangeline. Woman of the gospel. She looked down at her plate, her face burning. She did not want to answer, it was like a betrayal, but she knew she must.

"About the Bible. He said it was written in ancient languages . . . by Moses who was educated and Amos who was a plain person like us . . . ." She stopped.

Elder Wiens slapped his heavy hand flat on the table. "The Bible was written by the finger of God and no man! I warned Brother Unrau, once our young people enter strange schools they turn away, they fly around the barnyard like crazy cocks, next thing they're over the fence gone to hell. Yes, I told him that plainly."

"What did Brother Unrau say?" Eva's mother asked, always interested in everything.

"He said he could no longer govern Charles." Elder Wiens glared around at them all, then reached for the pickles.

Mrs. Wiens looked severely at Eva and her mother. "This practice of classes for young people . . . Mr. Wiens and I were opposed. When I was a girl we all learned together, old and young, in German." She turned to her husband. "How does it come that you were over-ruled and Charles is teaching a class?"

"Unrau himself did not oppose it," he answered, a little uncomfortably, Eva thought. It was true, Charles' father was an important man, a thriving farmer and shrewd, well respected. She wondered a little at Mrs. Wiens calling her husband to account. She could not remember her mother ever using that tone with her father.

Elder Wiens had turned his heavy gaze upon Eva. "When you hear such things as Charles Unrau may teach, close your ears. Remember that the first woman, with your name, lusted after knowledge and led the whole world into sin."

Eve. Betrayer of the human race. Eva studied her hands, hot all over. She remembered her wild rebellious thoughts in church . . . she had felt them to be her own thoughts, but with the Wienses here she began to doubt: perhaps the thoughts had been sent by that snake in the garden.

"Your mother is a fine woman," Elder Wiens told Eva, holding her with a stern gaze. "Learn from her. A woman's place is . . . ," he hesitated slightly. "Perhaps Mrs. Wiens will remind you."

"To obey their husbands, mind their homes, and rear obedient children," Mrs. Wiens said, as if quoting. She stood up. "We will go now. You are both coming to evening meeting?"

With dignity, Elder Wiens rose to follow his wife and they departed. There had been no offer of help from Mrs. Wiens to clear away the dishes.

"Fine people," her mother said. Eva listened in silence to her cheerful commentary on the visit, and sighed. Finally her mother stopped talking and looked at Eva. "You're so quiet today . . . you better take some medicine, maybe you're coming down sick.

Eva shook her head. "It was the Wienses, they always . . . ." She stopped.

"Don't you think they liked the lunch?" her mother asked anxiously. "The plum preserves were a little sour—."

"No, no, everything was fine," Eva said quickly.

Her mother smiled, reassured. "*Yoh*, a good visit. But you—lie down a bit, you look pale."

Eva went to her room. It was no use talking to her mother, who saw no difficulties; things were always fine the way they were. She leaned her elbows on the windowsill and looked out. Eve. Evangeline. Which was she? She did not know. She became confused, thinking about it, and finally took off her apron and combed her hair for evening meeting.

That Wednesday at prayer meeting, Eva glanced toward the men's side and saw, with a start of surprise and pleasure, that Charles Unrau was there. Maybe he would say something.

One of the elders began an exhortation on avoiding the evils of the community. Eva had heard it all many times before: women who used rouge, fathers who allowed their sons to listen to the radio, that great new glittering evil the motor car. "It is our duty, brothers, to witness against the worldliness of this town," the elder concluded vigorously, and sat down.

Charles stood up. "Friends. If we wish to be a witness to this town, I have a suggestion." He paused to survey the rows of men, farmers in long-sleeved shirts sitting with folded arms and watching him with impassive faces. "Yesterday I talked to Johann Jungas at the hardware store. Mr. Stoesz from the grocery was with him. Both men told me that of all the people in our community, the men of the Bargen Church are the hardest to do business with. We drive hard bargains. We want to sell expensive and buy cheap. Jungas told me that members of this church have hundreds of dollars on his books in debts, which he has tried for years to collect—patiently, as his manner is. Brethren! We are not so poor that we cannot pay our debts. Our farms are prosperous. We work hard, but so do these men. They run their businesses for the good of the town. Their profits are not large. They have families to support. We ought to pay our debts." He sat down.

The men sat in silence. A few looked at each other with raised eyebrows. Anita's father, in the back row, was nodding slightly. Eva leaned forward, watching them. Her heart beat rapidly. Was it true? How had Charles found courage to say these things! Such a speech was like lightning—thunder was sure to follow.

A man toward the back stood up. "Young man, we heard that in the boys' class last Sunday you talked about ball games. Is that true?"

"Yes," Charles said from his seat.

"What reason did you have to talk about worldly things when you were asked to teach the Scriptures? Was it the boys who wished to talk about such things, or you?"

Charles passed a hand over his face as if, Eva thought, he was trying not to smile. "I brought it up. I wanted to know who won Friday's game with Dumfrey."

The man spoke with greater emphasis. "So! I also heard from my son that you said the Bible was written in strange languages. And did you say that men, not God, wrote the words of the Bible? Young man, we do not need to hear accusations from you. Go and put your own house in order." The man sat down.

The men began murmuring to each other in low voices. Anita's father spoke quietly to Charles, leaning toward him across the bench. A few cast openly hostile glances at Charles. After a few minutes the elder asked, "Does anyone else wish to speak?" He waited, but no one stood. "If not, let us go to prayer."

With a rustle of clothes, men and women knelt at the long benches. Eva, stealing a glance from under her clasped hands, saw that Charles was kneeling with the other men; but stiffly, his shoulder jutting up at a sharp angle. He's angry, she thought. When they rose to be dismissed, his face bore two red marks where his knuckles had pressed against his temples. She wanted to shout to Charles across the aisle that he had said the right things, they should have been said long ago! If it was true about the debts.

The days passed slowly. Eva could scarcely contain her impatience to hear Charles teach the class the next Sunday, until it occurred to her that in all probability he would not be permitted to do so. The elders would see to that.

To her immense surprise, he was there. A great deal of commotion was taking place on the other side of the green curtain: Charles was showing them the clay tablet. "Looks like a chicken walked on it," a voice drawled. "Yeah, ain't nobody can read that." "Oh, yes, Arn, they can," Charles said. "This is Ugaritic, an ancient language. This tablet is a business agreement between a merchant and a cart driver to deliver certain goods. No, I didn't make that up. Scholars have learned to read Ugaritic. But listen, boys, we are supposed to stick to the lesson, so open your Bibles—I Kings 21, *auf Deutsch, bitte.*" A chorus of protest. "Who says?" "*Unsere Eltern.*"

The lesson today was about Elijah and the prophets of Baal. Eva tried to follow the discussion on the other side of the curtain, but Mrs. Froese asked her to come sit with a younger girl at the far end of the bench.

The usual long service followed. After church a knot of boys gathered around Charles, passing something from hand to hand. "Chicken writing!" they were saying, giggling. "That tablet is thousands of years old," Charles explained. "But listen, boys, haven't you seen the petroglyphs out at Red Rock Ridge? They were made hundreds of years ago, too, by Indians. Just a few miles from here.

Oh—careful there, boys, don't push—I have to bring this back to my seminary library."

Eva drifted toward them. She wanted desperately to get a glimpse of the tablet—that must be what they were looking at. Charles noticed her and walked over. "Here, take a look," he said, and put a small object into her hands. She looked at it, scarcely breathing: a small, hard piece of clay, reddish-brown, smooth, with marks on it—tiny scratches but clear and deep, arranged in neat rows. An ancient language.

Eva raised her head at last, her eyes shining. "You can read this?"

"Not yet," he replied seriously. "I'll be studying Ugaritic next spring." Catching her eye, he smiled. "Not many girls are interested in this sort of thing."

"I have so many questions." The words flew out before she could stop them.

"You too? Yes, so many questions. There are answers, but one has to look for them." He spoke thoughtfully.

Eva put the tablet carefully into his hand. "Thank you for showing me," she said. Seeing Elder Wiens walking toward them, she hastily turned away and went back to the girls. The boys scattered.

The following Wednesday night old Pastor Bargen, nearly eighty-five but still firmly in charge of his congregation, announced a matter of discipline: Charles Unrau and his class of boys had been seen playing ball out in the pastures beyond the creek, not once, but twice, and on the Lord's Day.

Eva gasped and looked over at Charles. He sat with arms folded, his face impassive. Beside him his father sat with downcast brooding dark eyes. Neither of them looked surprised. They knew about this, Eva thought.

Asked why he had so transgressed, Charles replied, "I figured they'd sit still better in evening church if they ran around a bit in the afternoon. Sunday is a long day for boys." The remark was considered unrepentant. Rev. Bargen read the church rules forbidding unseemly activity on the Lord's Day and ball games at any time. He issued Charles a stern reprimand.

Eva turned hot, restless, anxious for Charles. Why did he have to push things so far? Now they would make him stop teaching, that was certain. Glancing around, she observed Charles' mother, sitting one bench ahead. She was looking full at Rev. Bargen, head tilted to one side, frowning slightly, as if puzzling the matter over in her mind. Most women would be crying with shame. Women were not allowed to speak in church, but Charles' mother looked as if she might suddenly stand up and ask a question.

However the family—father, little Peter, mother, the girls, Charles—listened in silence. After the meeting they left at once. They're in disgrace, Eva thought, the whole family, because of Charles; but she did not want Charles to unsay a single thing he had said or undo a single thing he had done. Please please please make them leave him alone, she prayed silently, walking home beside her mother.

On the third Sunday Eva again sat next to the curtain, avoiding Mrs. Froese's eye. But when the teacher of the boys' class spoke, it was Mr. Gingrich. "Where's Charles? Why ain't he here? Is he sick?" Mr. Gingrich answered mildly, "No, boys, Charles is not sick, but he won't be teaching you after today." The outcry grew louder. "We like him. Why can't he teach us? He learned us good." Mr. Gingrich grew stern. "It's time for the lesson, boys. Get out your Bibles." A voice drawled, "I bet he got sacked for playing ball."

Eva was dismayed. She had known it would happen, yet she was outraged. While Mrs. Froese was reading about the sufferings of disobedient Israel, she suddenly jumped up and ran downstairs, ignoring the shocked silence behind her. She ran to the carriage shed, around to the far side, leaned against the sun-warmed wood, breathing hard. Out here the air was clear. A small breeze ruffled her kerchief. Birds flew noisily in and out of the huge tree at the back of the churchyard. The cornfields lay golden in the sunlight.

She watched a cat in the weeds at the edge of the yard—crouching, stalking a grasshopper. Suddenly the cat sprang, but the grasshopper whirred away. Eva smiled a little . . . you got away, she thought. Charles was right. It was good that the boys played ball in the pasture. They shouldn't have taken the class away from him. All their rules, their mountains of dark words. Out here in the warm sunshine the words and the rules seemed remote, irrelevant. She wondered if God was in the words, or out here. But of course that was a silly question. God was in the Bible, and the Bible was words. But I like words, she thought. I liked the words on the clay tablet.

She could not puzzle it out. But she must get back to class or Mrs. Froese would think she was ill. She walked back up the narrow dark stairs. Now it was the sunshine, the cornfield and the pouncing cat that seemed remote. Which was true? She did not know.

She glimpsed Charles a few more times at church, caught him looking at her with an intensity that startled her, and then he was gone back to Kansas. His voice was no longer there to encourage her. Or was it to tempt her toward forbidden knowledge. Maybe God is being kind, she thought; he knows I can't resist—I'd be gone flying over the fence in a minute, off to . . . she stopped. Hell could not be out there. If it was, Charles was in it, and that was impossible. It occurred to her that hell was perhaps farther off than Elder Wiens said.

Then the news raced through the small community that Hope Rielke, a young school teacher, a Bargen Church deacon's daughter, was going to marry a Canadian by the name of Jean L'Engle. Completely outside the church.

A few Sundays later the young woman was brought before the meeting. Rev. Bargen asked questions. Hope, a quiet girl with abundant brown hair, answered with composure. Jean had grown up

Catholic, she said, but they would be attending a Protestant church in Toronto. Not a Conservative church since there were none in that area. Her parents had met the young man, believed in his sincerity, were sorry her choice had fallen so far from home, but had told her she must do what she felt was right.

The consequences of marrying outside the church, Rev. Bargen told her bluntly, would be excommunication. Hope replied quietly that she was aware such an action would probably follow. She was sorry, but she could not agree with the stance of the church.

Rev. Bargen, standing to his full height, pronounced judgment: the day she married this English man, she could consider herself excommunicated. Hope smiled faintly. "He's French," she said, and sat down.

"That poor Taunte Rielke," Eva's mother said on the walk home. "Hope shouldn't go off like that . . . she could have married one of the boys at home."

Eva did not reply. She kept thinking of the quiet woman standing, defying the tradition—was she escaping into freedom, or a snare?

Her mother's sick headaches kept her in bed most of that month. Eva spent hours reading to her while thinking of other things: the clay tablet with its ancient language, the seminary where there was a library with books that had answers to questions, people like Charles and Hope Rielke who talked with astonishing freedom. Another world, unattainable. She sighed; and when her mother was asleep went out into the garden, which was dry now, a patch of bare earth littered with dry stalks, to sit under the trees in the corner.

Often, from her bedroom window upstairs, she watched the birds migrating south. Whole flocks of them wheeling in, settling briefly down, then rising to fly away. Idly she watched, thinking that birds didn't ask anything, they flew wherever they wished. They never worried about obedience, yet God loved them freely. It was only people who had to be obedient. She wished she had been born a bird . . . how she would fly, skim the tops of the corn stalks, wing over the trees, fly far away.

At church she tried obediently to follow the sermons but found herself mentally tracing the letters of the sign painted at the back of the stage, "*Weide meine Laemmer.*" Feed my lambs. A tender statement, lambs being fed. Where had it come from?

Three weeks before the school year was to begin—though Eva, having finished eighth grade, would be staying home or helping the little ones at the German School—her Aunt Grace, her father's youngest sister, returned from a journey to the East coast where she had been touring art galleries. She came over at once for a visit. "I've got something for you, Eva," she said, already talking as she walked in and took off her coat. She stopped and examined the girl closely. "What's the matter with you? So thin, no color in your face."

"*Joh*, she don't eat," her mother said. She turned worried eyes on her daughter.

"I'm all right," Eva replied.

Aunt Grace said no more, but took off her hat and laid it carefully on the couch. She wore a smart dark red dress with tiny black buttons. "Come on, let's have some supper—I'm starved, haven't had a chance to buy groceries yet. Sit still, Nina, Eva can help me."

In the kitchen Aunt Grace bustled about, looking for forks, setting out plates. "How old are you, Eva? Sixteen? Why are you dressed like an old lady?"

"I'm fifteen," Eva said.

"Do the Bargen Church girls all dress like that? Just some pie and brown bread, pickles if you have some—fine, that's enough. Do you still have the blue bracelet I gave you? I didn't suppose they'd let you wear it, but I wanted you to have it anyway. It's too small now, I'm sure."

"It's in my drawer," Eva said.

"Well, put on something bright once in a while. Now let's eat."

During supper Aunt Grace, observing her closely, asked questions. "You went to the German School, I suppose? Can you read English? Yes? Who taught you?"

"I taught myself," Eva answered.

"You what? Well, I should have guessed. You read German, of course. What about Russian? Too bad. Well, I can't read Russian very well either, any more. Here, have more pie, put a little fat on your bones. Studied any poetry? Goethe, Schiller? What on earth do they teach you at the German School? How about world history? Oh goodness." She talked on, now about Pennsylvania, then about losing her handbag on the train and finding it under somebody's overcoat.

They cleared the table. "All right now, Evangeline Amanda," her aunt said, "I'll bring in what I found for you in my cousin's attic. Sit tight, it's just outside the door. I wanted it to be a surprise." She went out and reappeared a moment later struggling with a large, evidently heavy box tied up with rope. "No, don't help me, I can manage it. Martin Dyck drove it over for me." She set it on the floor, untied the rope and pried off the lid. The box was full of books.

"There you are. Your grandpa's library, part of it, anyway. The rest are at my house."

Eva's mother looked at the box in astonishment. "Grandpa Brandt's books?" She picked up a heavy black volume and opened it. "*Na joh*, look, his name, written here."

"Grandpa's . . . what kind of books?"

"All kinds. For heaven's sake, don't just stand there, look at them. Here—history of Europe, world atlas . . . ." Aunt Grace was piling them on the table. "Goethe. Essays of some kind, studies on India, Russian grammar, stories of Dostoevsky, unfortunately in Russian. Oh yes, your grandfather was quite a scholar. Look at the notes he wrote in the margins. Can you read the handwriting? Didn't you say you learned German script?"

Eva had not moved. "An educated man—a scholar?" She spoke almost in a whisper.

"Oh, but yes, of course. You didn't know that? He went to the University of Heidelberg and was head of a teacher training institute in Molotschna. In fact, your dad was training to be a teacher there before he came to this country."

"But . . . my father was a carpenter," Eva said.

"Yes, over here, but he wanted to be a teacher. I thought you knew that. He was a smart one, Teilhard was! It made me mad. I always had to study hard, but he had it all in his head. After he moved here and married your mother he gave it up. The town needed builders so he learned carpentry. He built this house, you know."

Eva's mother put down the book to say happily, "*Joh,* when we were first married. He asked me how I wanted everything."

Eva sat stiffly, not touching the books. Why hadn't they told her? Her own grandfather a scholar. Her father, trained to be a teacher. She had scarcely known her father—she had been barely six when he died. She knew nothing of her grandfather. It occurred to her for the first time that perhaps . . . . "Which church did Grandpa belong to, in Russia?"

Her aunt glanced at her mother and said quietly, "General Conference Mennonite, like Parkside. Your father joined the Bargen Church because of your mother."

Stunned, her world turning rapidly upside down, great cracks appearing in its formidable walls, Eva sat staring at her aunt.

"Well, Eva," her aunt said impatiently, "aren't you going to look at the books? I was going to put them in my library, but then I thought they should really be yours."

Obediently, Eva picked up the books one by one with uncertain hands. On the flyleaf of each was written in faded ink, "Teilhard Brandt." Her grandfather. Little notes in tiny ornamental German script were scribbled in the margins of the yellowing pages. She tried to read one: "*Am 14 Sept. 1885 habe ich diese Stadt besucht.*" This city I visited . . . the note was beside a photograph of Strasbourg.

Relief, immense relief, relief so great she could hardly bear it, was washing over her in strong clean waves. The floor under her seemed to be floating. The leaden sky was rising, breaking into bits, drifting away. Her grandfather, a scholar who visited cities in Europe.

A sudden thought checked her. "Grandma Brandt? Was she educated too?"

Aunt Grace was busy piling more books on the table. "Of course, what do you think? Mother was the one who made us do our lessons properly—if we spelled a word wrong we had to do it over. The Molotschna women complained that she neglected her housework to read her husband's books. In fact she wrote some poems . . . I'm hoping to find them in here somewhere."

"She wasn't put out of the church?"

Aunt Grace stopped stacking books and looked at her. "So that's where the wind blows. No, dear, nobody was put out of church for reading books. The Brandts, also the Kopps—your grandma's family—they were teachers and leaders in the Mennonite colonies. You don't have to worry, Nina, these are all good books." She thought for a moment, cast a shrewd glance at Eva. "I can see you have your grandpa's mind, your dad's too, you don't belong to . . . ." She paused. "Now mind, these are your books. Nobody can stop you from reading them. Lucky they're mostly in German, not Russian."

Eva's mother was studying a photograph. "Look—Grandpa and Grandma Brandt in Russia, in front of their house." Eva looked at it: a dignified-looking gentleman in a dark suit, the woman wearing a light ruffled blouse and black trailing skirt, standing before a building with pillars. Their eyes—thoughtful, serious, confident, even a little proud. Her father's family.

Aunt Grace handed her a small notebook with a leather binding. "Your grandpa's journal. Can you read it?" The pages were covered with the same tiny German script. Eva read aloud: *"16 Mai. Heute ist Sonntag. Ich danke dem Herrn mit Freuden denn er hat alles schoen gemacht; die Erde singt vor Freude . . . ."* Today is Sunday. I thank God with joy because he has made all things lovely; the earth sings for joy.

"Good for you! I see your German School was good for something, anyway," Aunt Grace said. "Nina, where did you put my coat? I should go home."

Eva brought her aunt's coat and scarf. "Thank you," she whispered. "I'll read them." She paused, said suddenly, "I want to go to high school."

"Well, I should hope so!" Aunt Grace exclaimed. "What's to stop you? You finished grade eight? Well then. Doesn't your mother want you to go?"

Eva was staring at her aunt as if rooted to the floor. Where had this decision come from? It had come of itself, as if an interior self of which she had lost track had been making it all along and just now announced the fact. High school was frowned on at the Bargen Church, especially for girls.

"She never minds anything," Eva whispered, "but they might make trouble for her."

Aunt Grace was silent. "Still like that, are they?" she said at last. "Listen, Eva, I happen to know two or three others from your church are going to high school this fall, you wouldn't be the only one. If the elders want to make a fuss, let them." She laughed. "Actually, one of the boys starting high school is an elder's son, so they can't say too much. Yes, it's a good idea. I'll help you get registered next week."

It was as if a hurricane had struck. Eva stared at her in disbelief. "An elder's son? You're sure? But who . . . ." She stopped to think. "I'll have to tell them at German School—I was supposed to help with the children."

"Yes, do. Well, goodbye. Goodnight, Nina!" Aunt Grace walked briskly away.

"Take the books upstairs, Eva, we need the table cleared off," her mother said. She was still studying the photograph. "Just imagine. They look like fine people, don't you think, Eva?"

Eva carried the books upstairs. Under her grandfather's name on the flyleaf of each book she wrote, very carefully, "Evangeline A. Brandt." She put the best ones in a row on her dresser, the way she had seen them in people's houses sometimes, side by side, and propped them up with her heavy water pitcher on one side and an iron doorstop on the other. The rest of the books she arranged in the box and put them at the foot of the bed, where she could see them.

She sat down on her chair by the window. For the first time in years, it seemed to her, the air outside was light and playful. She could see things clearly, distinctly, as if their outlines were sharp, dark separated from light.

Her eyes returned to the books on the dresser. In the light from the setting sun the gilt bindings shone a bright red-gold, like the gates of heaven.

THE BAKER

"A BAKERY CAKE I will not have!" Helena snapped. "She schmears the icing on with a shovel. Always pink roses and yellow roses, all flat." She scraped fried potatoes onto her husband's plate, under his nose, and set the frying pan back on the stove with a bang.

Johann did not look up from his plate. "*Na yoh*, Helena, they're good enough." His voice was quiet. He broke off a piece of brown bread and sopped up the cream from the green beans.

"Twenty years the owner of the store, and that's all you want—a bakery cake that's nothing worth?" she cried. "If it was up to you, we would all go hoe in the garden all day, forget about celebrating."

Johann wiped his mouth and beard with his handkerchief and stood up. "Why not?" He smiled, glanced at her, and added quickly, "Do what you want. I'm going down."

"You should rest a little," she fretted. "You run up, swallow everything in five minutes, and run down. You'll wear out."

He looked up at the clock. At the same moment the distant whistle of a train floated in through the open kitchen window. "Almost 2:00," he said. "Waldemar has to go for lunch." He hurried toward the front staircase going down to the street. They lived on the second floor, above the hardware store.

"Wait!" she called, walking after him. "Gerty Stoesz told me about a lady near Dumfrey who makes cakes. I want Al should drive me out."

Johann stopped. "Al is unloading stoves." He thought a moment. "Maybe at four o'clock."

"You'll get leftovers for supper, then."

Johann nodded and ran down the stairs. She heard the door at the bottom of the stairs close.

What does he care about supper, Helena thought—he would eat whatever was on his plate, any old shred of sausage or dried-up pie, there wasn't any use making fine meals for such a man. She piled the dishes into a large tin pan, poured hot water over them from the kettle on the stove, added soap, and began to wash, setting the clean cups and plates upside down on a dishtowel spread out on the table. Such a man! Any old cake was good enough . . . he didn't even want a celebration. Wait until thirty years, he said. If we live so long. The finest hardware store in any town around, business even from Cloudy Lake and Mankato, and he runs in and out of his store like a brown mouse. Everybody else had their names in the paper—Mr. and Mrs. Stoesz entertain important guests from St. Paul, Mr. Emmet Sykora speaks to businessmen at Mankato hotel luncheon, things like that. But he stayed in the store all day and after supper worked in the garden. Well, she would show the town for once. He had started in this town as a clerk barely able to speak English, selling shoes for his uncle, and now here he was, twenty years the owner of Jungas Hardware. It was time to let the town know. She would see to it, let him complain.

She hung the wet dishtowel in the pantry, put the dishes away, and swept the linoleum. Thirty-five guests had been invited, maybe more. Business people, store owners from nearby towns, those high-and-mighty Janzen relatives who thought they owned Windamer. Friends too, of course—Klaas Dyck from the drug store across the street, the Dickmans, Rev. Schulte and his wife from Parkview where Johann taught Sunday School, though she still held a grudge against Schulte for passing over Johann when he was appointing deacons.

Forgiving, she had told her sister Lieze, was like burying a cat, only she always left the tail out in case she needed to pull the cat up again. Well, she would forgive Schulte later, on her way up to heaven.

She sat down in the dining room to rest her feet and looked around to see what needed to be done. Frieda could polish the furniture. It was an expensive set, bought after the store and home had been rebuilt. The dark mahogany table and buffet gleamed, the finely carved legs catching little curves of light. The seats of the chairs were made of dull red leather. She would put her black tapestry tablecloth from Russia on the table—the fringes hung almost to the floor. The design of blue flowers woven into the dark cloth looked very fine against the polished wood. Thus fitted out, her dining room was a joy to look at. The Stoeszes, she thought, might parade up and down and have their names in the paper, but their dining set was cheap pine, an ugly set she wouldn't have allowed in the house. Gerty didn't seem to care, though—her whole house was full of cheap stuff.

Himmel sei dank, Helena thought, still resting her feet, the new parlor furniture had come in time: dark gray plush with black tassels and a fine pattern on the cushions. But that man! A new parlor set, and where did he go with visitors to discuss business? To the small sitting room! He was there yesterday with some guy from Mankato sitting on the old wicker settee, the chintz already fading; but he liked to sit there, he said it was comfortable.

She surveyed her handsome rooms with satisfaction. She could hold her head as high as any of the guests now. The days were long gone when she had worked as a lowly maid for the Janzens, recently come from Russia with her old parents, immigrants looked down upon by the German business class of the town. And then, to their surprise, she had married Mr. Janzen's nephew!

Too bad none of the girls would be present. Anna had married the son of that black-haired, eagle-eyed preacher at the Mennonite Brethren Church—a huge wedding, downstairs in the newly rebuilt store before all the stoves and other stock had been moved in. Sorely against Helena's wishes, she had gone off to India with John, taking their tiny daughter along. The other girls were in Montana visiting their father Heinrich who, thank God, had finally pulled himself together and built up his homestead out there. At least her boys were here working in the store, Al and John, and Henry, the adopted one.

She eased herself up and telephoned Al. "Bring the car to the front, I'll come down at four."

At three o'clock Helena dressed carefully in her navy silk crepe with the frills at the wrist. The day was sultry and she would be hot, but the lady who made cakes was no doubt well off, and she did not want to appear at a disadvantage. She combed her hair higher than usual, making sure the hairpins were pushed in tight, and put on her best navy blue hat. She looked to see if the name and directions were still in her handbag: Mrs. Rena Funk, Dumfrey Road.

She remembered that she had not yet asked the Rohrs about serving. Johann would certainly invite them. The Mrs. cleaned stoves downstairs, and Mr. worked with freight. They were Bargen people. How God put up with that bunch, she didn't know. Mrs. Rohr wore her hair parted in the middle and combed tight to the sides, with a kerchief tied over, as was their custom. Her cheap cotton print skirts hung limp and uneven like a rag over her high shoes. And such watery eyes, as if she hadn't any spirit at all! Mr. Rohr looked like a goat with that silly red beard on his pointed chin. Franz's beard was full and dark, but this straggly thing! No, if they would consent to serve in the kitchen it would be much better. She would pay them something.

Al called up the stairs: the car was ready. Helena picked up her handbag. Before getting into the car, she stepped into the store to tell Johann to heat up the soup for his supper if they came home late; the bread was in the pantry.

Al drove without speaking along the road toward Dumfrey.

Beside him, Helena was thinking busily about many things. The silver had yet to be borrowed. She herself had service for twenty-four, an elegant set Johann had bought her, but she would need more. Perhaps Gerty Stoesz would lend hers. But where would she get enough glass plates?

Al turned off onto a small dirt road, raising a cloud of dust. The cornfields rustled with a dry papery sound. Grasshoppers whirred and hopped on either side of them, disturbed by the thin bumping wheels. Helena began reading the names on the mail boxes. Reimer. Junke. Tieszen. Next farm maybe. To the right, a set of tumbled buildings, gray and unpainted, showed above the corn. No name on the mailbox. Keep going. A quarter mile further on, an immense white gabled barn stood on a rise, near it the tidy black roofs of other farm buildings. Yes, this must be it. The name on the mailbox, however, was Dickson. They came to the county road, where the small road dead-ended. Helena frowned. "We must have missed it. Go back."

Al turned the car around. "It must be the one with no name."

"*Ach waut*! That junkpile? Maybe we got the wrong road." But when they stopped at the place, Al pointed to a small hand-painted sign tacked to the fence. Funk. He turned into the rutted driveway and jolted into the yard.

Helena clutched her bag. House, barn, chicken sheds, all built of weathered boards sagging off their nails. Chickens ran about pecking at the chickweed that grew everywhere. An untidy hedge straggled along behind the house—the garden must be back there, Helena thought, if there was such a thing in this forsaken place. "No, we go home. This isn't right!"

But Al had stopped the motor and said he would ask and see. He walked to the door and knocked. In a moment he was talking to a young girl through the screen door. He turned and nodded—yes, it was the right place.

Ferekjt! She wouldn't even get out of the car . . . mud, chicken droppings, dirty straw, there was hardly a spot to set one's foot. She beckoned to Al, they would go. But he was talking to the girl and paid no attention. At last she climbed down from the car and walked across the yard, stepping on clumps of chickweed to avoid the muck.

The girl let them in. "Ma's in the kitchen. Want to see the cats?" she said to Al, and the two went out, slamming the screen door.

It was hot in the kitchen. Helena smelled meat cooking, maybe pork. She glanced swiftly around. An enormous black wood stove took up one wall of the room. The meat was cooking in a cast-iron pot pushed to the back of the stove. In the corner a pile of split boards overflowed from a huge woodbox. An old-fashioned sink with a rusty hand-pump mounted to one side was beside her, near the door. A pail full of garden stuff stood in the sink.

On the other side of the room was a large table, behind which a woman sat sewing a piece of yellow cloth, her large arms lying flat on the oilcloth. Scissors and spools of thread were scattered about. The woman had raised her head and was looking at her. Helena said nothing. She could not imagine cakes being baked in this old farm kitchen, by this woman. She had imagined a clean modern place, a baker in a smart white apron wearing a cap.

"*Jo-oh*?" the woman said, making no move to rise. *Nae oba*, she talked flat, like the Bargen people. But her hair, instead of being combed neatly back under a kerchief, the way Bargen women wore theirs, was hanging loose in skimpy gray strings. Anyway, Bargen farms didn't look like this, they were hard-working people. Where had this woman come from?

The woman had stopped sewing. "Can I help you something?"

"You are the lady who makes cakes?" Best to ask, then make an excuse to leave.

"*Jo-oh*. Sit down." The woman nodded toward an old chair. Her cotton dress hung damply about her stout body. There were black speckles on the loose skin of her neck. Helena stood stiff and straight, clutching her handbag. No, this was surely a mistake.

The woman watched her, head slightly tilted. Under thick eyebrows her eyes were dark, observant, alert. Finally, with great dignity, Helena sat down on the chair, smoothing her dress.

"A ca-ake you want?" The woman turned and pulled out something from a small cupboard near her—a scribbler of the type used by school children, with a red cover frayed along the edges. She shoved aside her sewing and began to turn the pages. "What kind ca-ake?"

"For my husband, Johann Jungas." The thought of her respectable husband braced Helena's mind. She said with dignity, "My husband is twenty years the owner of Jungas Hardware in Windamer. We have a celebration, two weeks from Sunday."

The woman's expression did not change. She turned the book toward Helena, pointing at a drawing. "This one you like?" Helena looked at the drawing—a tower-like shape ornamented with loops and swirls, drawn with a carpenter's pencil, smudged with much handling. The woman watched her, turned pages to other drawings. Helena opened her mouth to say she had changed her mind, would not order today, but closed it again. She thought rapidly: they could order a small cake here and then stop at the Dumfrey bakery and get another one.

"Eight dollars, this one," the woman said, pointing to a drawing. "Very nice, all white with flowers." A reasonable price, certainly. But made in this kitchen? No, she could not. Helena noticed suddenly that the oilcloth covering the table, a bright blue, was clean and of good quality. Still, a wood stove! "Ba-aker charge ten, twelve." the woman said, watching her.

Al and the girl walked in, laughing. Their hair was blown and dusty—they must have been in the hayloft, Helena thought. The girl held a tiny squirming kitten to her cheek. Helena frowned. Cats in the house. There might be dogs, too, and cockroaches and who knew what else. No, she would on no account order anything.

The woman spoke up sharply. "Ruby, out with the cat."

Ruby protested. "Ma, Al wants to show it to his mother."

"Out!" The woman reached over with a long arm and slapped the girl on the rump. Ruby made a face and walked out. Al followed, grinning. The woman turned to Helena. "*Kaute, emma Kaute.* Alwa-ays cats. I tell her kitchen is for ba-aking, cats go in the ba-arn." She picked up the cake book. "I make this one for you."

She spoke as if the order was settled. Let be, then, order it and see what happened. It might be money wasted, but it couldn't be helped. "We will come for it on August 6," Helena said, and opening her purse, put the eight dollars on the table.

"*Yoh,*" the woman said. "I have it ready. I write the name. Jungas, yes?" She found a stub of pencil in her apron pocket and wrote on a back page of the notebook. A long list of names, Helena saw. Then she picked up her sewing and watched as Helena went to the door.

Al and the girl were by the car. He was cleaning grasshoppers off the radiator with the rag he always kept under the seat. She was watching the kitten run about in the chickweed. At a nod from his mother, Al got into the car, and they drove off.

On the way home Helena was silent, upset with herself that she had paid eight dollars for who knew what, though comforted slightly by the list of customers. Now she would have to spend nine or ten more for a cake at a bakery, the one in Dumfrey since everybody knew by heart what the cakes from the Windamer bakery looked like. She was disgusted with the woman for not combing her hair—did she bake with it hanging like that over the pans? And for not so much as standing up to greet her, such a way to treat a customer. And for the whole miserable-looking farm with its weeds and chickens. And besides all that, to slap a great grown girl on the behind, it was *unjescheit,* indecent. This was all Gerty Stoesz's doing—she had recommended this woman.

Helena remembered suddenly that years ago when she had been trying to learn English, Gerty had treated her poorly, had told her to say a word which in German meant something very bad. "Go on, say it, in English it's a good word," Gerty had urged, but Helena would not say it, and Gerty had laughed. Maybe this was another of her jokes. Well, let be, she could do without Gerty's silver set, she had other friends in town.

Al drove without haste, whistling through his teeth. He'd better stay away from that Ruby and her cats, Helena thought, though once a young man drove a car, there was no telling where he went. For his father's sake he should associate with the young people of a higher class, whose fathers ran businesses and were on the town boards. Not that Johann would care, she thought with some bitterness—he would probably take all the children out to the barn himself to see the cats.

Al parked in front of the hardware store, and Helena got out, stopping before she went upstairs to notice the display in the window: Rain King revolving sprinklers, a new kind of kitchen faucet, a large bright sign for Sherwin-Williams paint proclaiming "You can't paint a house with apple-sauce." People always laughed at that sign. A good display, all tidy and shiny and new. A good businessman, her Johann. He deserved a better cake . . . she hoped the Dumfrey bakery had something suitable.

Johann ran up for supper, ate, picked up two empty pails, saying quietly that he would help with the dishes when he got back; and hurried off to the garden. "Don't bring home too much," she called after him. A tidy well-kept garden, tomato plants tied neatly to stakes, all the flowers—bright tulips, tiger lilies, white and pink peonies. People walked by just to look at the garden. It was fine that he worked in the garden, only he always came back with pails of peas and cucumbers, and she had to clean it all. Well, it was better he go there than fool around in Quevli's, like her brother Heinrich.

She sighed. She would of course not leave the dishes until he came back. She was tired, but so was he. She would wash them quickly and then sit down with her crocheting. She had begun a centerpiece in fine white cotton for the round parlor table, with an unusually intricate pattern. But she had made a mistake quite far back. Though it was small, the mistake bothered her. If she unraveled it, she would never finish in time for the celebration. She decided, as she put the last pots away, to let it go; the mistake was tiny and nobody would ever see it. She sat down in her rocker and managed to crochet several rounds before Johann came home.

Later that evening Johann, sitting with her shelling peas, asked how it had gone with the cake. "I ordered it," she said shortly. She did not tell him about the woman or the farm. Let's see first what this cake looks like, she thought.

The next week Frieda came to help clean the house. "Lots of work," Helena told her, handing her a dust cloth.

"*Na yoh*, lots of work," Frieda answered, looking around with her bright curious eyes. "I use Gold Dust Twins. It works good. Taunte Wienscha, she told me at the dime store, her son in the Cities . . . ."

"Yes, yes, you can tell me later," Helena interrupted. "You need to dust the cabinets. Take all the things out of the shelves, shake out the doilies."

For three days the house was upside-down. Rugs were taken out, floors polished, furniture shined, curtains straightened. Mr. Rohr came up to wash the windows. Mrs. Rohr polished silver and scoured pans. Johann ran up twice a day for a bite to eat and ran down again.

"I invited the Rohrs," he told Helena one evening at supper.

"*Nae oba!* I was going to ask them to serve in the kitchen. She doesn't have a decent dress, not one I've ever seen." Helena looked stormy.

"Give her money to buy one, then," he said quietly, and hurried off downstairs.

With bad grace Helena gave Mrs. Rohr ten dollars. "You work hard," she said. "Maybe you could buy a dress for the celebration, if you want." Mrs. Rohr thanked her humbly and mumbled something about a black dress on sale at Franz's. Helena nodded. "The gray one would look nice too, or the brown, the one with the lace collar and little buttons in front," she suggested. Mrs. Rohr's watery eyes brightened, and Helena became bold. "Would you be allowed to wear a hat instead of your kerchief, just that day?" Mrs. Rohr looked doubtful, but said she would ask her husband.

Helena asked several friends to do the serving. Then, still upset with Johann about the Rohr business, she demanded that he buy a new suit and a different tie.

Johann looked at her in surprise. "I have a suit," he said. "It's plenty good enough."

"From Grandpa Janzen's funeral! No, maybe still from our wedding! Listen, go to Mankato, Henry can drive you. I heard about a store with fine suits for short men like you. You can take off one day! Look at Stoesz and Franz, what good suits they wear, and ties too."

Johann reluctantly promised to go to Mankato if he had business there. That was all she could get out of him. Such a man. Her own new gown had been hanging ready for weeks, a handsome printed silk with a wide tan neckband and loose ties hanging down either side in front, as the fashion was. But Johann—he would wear that old suit if the Czar of Russia came to visit!

Now the cooking began. Pies, *zwieback,* raisin bread, rye bread, *platz*, three kinds of *mooss*, sausage, ham. From her cellar below the store Helena brought up pickles of all kinds. The upstairs pantry shelves were full.

Johann did not go to Mankato to buy a suit. Helena hurried to Peterson's to buy a tie—Johann would wear at least something new!

On the sixth of August, the day before the celebration, Al drove out to the Funk farm to get the cake. The one from Dumfrey had already been delivered. Helena looked at it and made a face. The roses were even flatter than the Windamer ones, but at least they were a slightly different color. Well, there was plenty other stuff to eat. If the guests ignored the cake, she could bring what was left to the Old Folks Home.

She went down to buy tins of coffee from Stoesz's. When she returned, she found a large cardboard box on her sideboard. The cake. Now she would know. She set the coffee down and opened the box. The cake was swathed in layers of tissue paper and stood on a large glass plate. Very carefully she lifted it out of the box, set it on the sideboard, and removed the tissue paper.

She stood without moving, staring at the cake, still holding the paper in her hands. The cake was completely white. The ridges of pure icing were sharp and shapely, the flowers around the border crisp, each petal softly rounded, each chain and loop around the sides perfectly formed; the scallops around the bottom of the cake were like fine crochet work. It was like the park when snow had newly fallen and every twig was molded in white, each tiny thing had a clean bright shape. Beautiful, like lace, like music; like the white peonies in the garden, their petals clean and frilly at the edges. The cake stood in lovely grace on the dark polished wood.

Helena leaned against the sideboard and gazed at it for a long time. She was astonished and ashamed. She remembered the woman with black speckles on her neck and skimpy hair hanging down, she saw the torn covers of the cake book, the smudgy drawings with a carpenter's pencil, the woman's watching eyes. How could she have known? How could this beautiful thing have come from such a place? It was as if God had been walking around with a lily, looking for a place to plant it; and finding the dirty ground behind the store where they poured out the used oil, had planted it there, in the worst place.

She carried the other cake to the pantry; it would do if they ran out at the end. Then she covered the dining table with the black tapestry tablecloth and very carefully placed Mrs. Funk's cake in the center. Such a cake had not been seen in Windamer, unless perhaps at some wedding to which she had not been invited. With her silver coffee pot and cream pitcher gleaming beside it, even the Mankato guests would exclaim. Yet it was not the admiration of the guests that occupied her now, but the beauty of the cake itself. She sat down and studied it once more. How had that woman pictured such a cake in her mind, where had her fingers learned the skill?

It occurred to her that perhaps she should have invited Mrs. Funk to the celebration. Her heart sank. But no, it would not be expected. Helena could not imagine that woman in her house, mingling with her guests. Seeing the Rohrs walking about would be bad enough, though the new dress might help a little. But Mrs. Funk with her stringy hair and black speckles—everyone would whisper and stare.

Without warning an image floated into her mind: Tante Joht in her old coat and black hat, carrying a worn bag, trudging about town giving away fine vegetables. In those years she, Helena, had been a friend of the poor, having herself known hard times. What had happened? Had she, now that she was married to a prosperous husband looked up to in town, now that she owned a home with fine furniture, had she become like those other women, like Mrs. Janzen who looked down her nose at everybody?

Suddenly Helena became angry. That woman. She had made this perfect thing, she had a gift—why couldn't she get to work and smarten herself up too, a bit! Put Ruby to work, she was old enough! How many days now had she, Helena, and all the others slaved to get this house ready! Every rounded leg of the tables and chairs shone in the dark, the sun fell through clean windows on the silver and glass, on the flowers from Johann's carefully tended garden now in tall handsome vases! God might have given the gift, but people had to work . . . hard, too!

Seeing on a chair the white mound of her crocheting waiting for a last round, with the mistake still in it, Helena snatched it up crossly and threw it into a drawer, slammed the drawer shut, and walked into the kitchen, wondering how, where she would find the grace, white and lovely, perfect grace from heaven, to invite Mrs. Funk to the celebration.

GARDEN OF GRACE

THE HUMID AIR, thick and warm like air in a laundry, lay inert over the half-tamed wilderness that was Grace Krahn's garden. The long row of blue spruces shone blue-green in the sun. The tall grasses did not stir; small insects buzzed steadily among the weeds.

Mrs. Krahn, wearing a torn straw hat, dug energetically around the gooseberry bush. Throwing down the hoe, she knelt and pulled at the grass with her hands. It came out in bunches, black dirt falling from the roots. She reached for the dry grass farther underneath the bush, but the thorns scratched at her arms and she gave it up. Sweat ran down her back, though it was early in the day. The trouble was, she thought, one couldn't get away from that heavy air—she could drive out to a farm or the next town or the next state, it would make no difference. Only here under her trees and inside the house, where all the drapes were drawn, was it a little cooler.

Picking up a small rake, she swept the uprooted grass into a pile, then stood and looked around. Behind her the potatoes and tomatoes flourished in straight green rows. The raspberries had not yet been completely cleared; the new growth ran out in long runners through weeds and over the dirt clods. The currant bushes too were still tangled in tall grass. It would take another week to chop the grass away, and then she was going to quit.

Leaving hoe and rake on the ground, she followed a narrow path past the spruces to the back part of the garden, where the crooked trunks of old apple trees were half hidden by the undergrowth. The branches, long unpruned, met each other so that a gloom was cast over the area, even in mid-day. Here the air was even more oppressive. Nothing stirred. The leaves of peony bushes and lilacs, grown together in a tangle, hung motionless, drowned in deep shade.

She stood looking around. She supposed she should hire a man to clear under the trees. The neighbors were probably horrified at the mess her garden was in; but she didn't really care, let them look if they enjoyed it. She would rather spend her money on books.

A wire fence, barely visible through the weeds, ran along the back border of her garden. A wooden shed stood under the trees: Henry's tool shed. She saw that the door was hanging open—the children from the German School must have been playing there again. The fence was intended not only to mark the boundary of her garden but to keep the children out; however they climbed over it easily enough. The school was too close by. She would have to go there again and warn the teachers. She could have the shed torn down, but the real danger was the old well; she had covered it with heavy planks, but the children might try to move them.

She picked some mint growing wild along the fence and stuffed it in her pocket; closed the shed door, pushed a piece of wood against it; and walked back toward the house.

She stopped where the orange tiger lilies were in bright bloom above the weeds. Henry's flower beds. If she had time she would try to rescue the lilies, at least. She wished, as she had every day for twelve years, that Henry's grave were here instead of in the cemetery at the other end of town. That was an alien place, all those squared-off stones lined up in rows in a mowed lawn. Henry wasn't like that at all. No, he belonged here, under the trees in the shade near his flowers. He wouldn't have minded the weeds.

In the vegetable garden she picked up a clod of dirt. The dry gray earth crumbled in her hands. Everything needed rain. A good storm would clear the air nicely—thunder and lightning and lots of rain. "Well, come on then, get on with it!" she said, addressing the heavens.

Entering the screened-in back porch, she dropped her straw hat on the floor and went inside to the kitchen, where she made herself a bowl of cucumbers sliced into buttermilk with a sprinkling of dill. She dropped the mint leaves into a pot for tea. While she ate she read, for the third or fourth time, *Pride and Prejudice.* The precise language of Jane Austen pleased her; it seemed to impose order and charm on the sometimes insufferable rudeness of the world . . . of this town in particular. Rudeness was not quite the right word; paltriness maybe, pettiness, some word denoting narrowness of mind buttressed by stubbornness. She needed to know that somewhere people gave precise and intelligent thought to things.

After lunch she changed into a smart blue dress, put on white shoes and hat, added a silver brooch, and started to town.

At the post office she inquired after parcels and found that her books had arrived. She leaned over the counter. "Klassen, you tell your wife to stop by my house and have a look. These are art collections from the National Gallery in Washington. D.C., that is."

The postmaster, wearing a green eyeshade, glanced at the oversized parcel. "Wait till canning's over. She's elbow-deep in cucumbers and beans right now."

"Good gracious, hire your sister to do that and let her paint! She's got talent, that woman of yours!"

He laughed and shook his head and turned to the next customer. Mrs. Krahn walked out with her package. The earth would split in two before a woman could be released from canning in order to paint pictures. She walked toward Uncle Klaas's drug store, thinking that perhaps she could arrange for Mary Klassens' bright, child-like paintings of farm life to be shown in his store or maybe in the high school auditorium. If one or two sold for hard cash, Klassen would start singing a different tune.

Some of the Bargen people from south of town had come in, she noticed: two black buggies were standing by the park in the shade, the horses lazily switching their tails at flies. Exactly why they eschewed motor cars and clung to their horses and buggies, she did not understand. Black aprons, squabbles about attending ball games and the precise tying of kerchiefs struck her as an obnoxious perversion of life on earth rather than the life of heaven. She wished that her niece Eva were safely away from that crowd. The transformation that had begun when Eva started reading her grandfather's books must be secured. Thank goodness she was in the high school, at least.

In front of the bakery Mrs. Schroeder stopped her. "We're cleaning Butcher Dick's place tomorrow."

"Well—all right, I'll do the curtains again if I can take them home," Mrs. Krahn said without enthusiasm.

The lady nodded vigorously. "Good. It's been over a year. It's simply terrible, the mess his place is in. We ought to dump everything in the incinerator and be done with it. I keep telling old Dick he ought to get married, let his wife clean up after him, save us the trouble."

"I read once," Mrs. Krahn remarked, "that when Martin Luther was a bachelor he didn't change his bed for a year. They found his sheets full of mildew."

Mrs. Schroeder looked at her blankly. "Mildew's terrible to get out," she said after a pause. "But that's the way bachelors are, I guess." She hurried away.

She doesn't know Martin Luther from the town elevator, Mrs. Krahn thought, and there's a Lutheran church not two blocks from her house. She stopped at Stoesz's for a package of tea, then entered Klaas's store intending to ask him about her land deal; but he had gone to the Cities on business leaving his assistant, the young Block boy, in charge. Handsome kid, she thought, seems to know what he's doing. "Give my greetings to Mr. Dyck," she told him.

At the park she stopped to rest on a bench, glad to set down the heavy parcel. Idly she watched the goings-on across the street: people entering Ben Franklin's Five and Dime, Jasch Dickman tinkering with a plow outside his workshop, a few women walking to Mrs. Dehmler's hat shop, work going on at the auto repair place next to Marlin Junke's Ford dealership. Narrow wooden buildings, most of them, with high square false fronts. Like the people in this town, she thought—narrow, old-fashioned, careful to observe small-town codes, but (she wished to be fair) firm on their foundations, hard-working and practical. A few, like Marlin Junke and the Jungas clan, were willing to change as long as the innovations didn't disturb their beliefs too much.

She picked up her package and walked home. Turning the corner near her house, she saw a black buggy standing in front of her gate. On the high seat a man sat severely upright: black beard, black clothes, black hat. Beside him was a woman wearing a head scarf. Bargen Church people. She recognized them as the Unraus, Charles and little Peter's parents.

"*Guten Tag*," she greeted them formally, wondering if their business required that they come in.

"*Guten Tag*." Mr. Unrau descended from the buggy, followed by his wife. The horses stood quietly, smooth brown skin glistening under heavy leather straps. It was an official visit, it seemed. Mrs. Krahn invited them in.

She led the way to the parlor, hastily moved a pile of books off the couch and asked them to sit down. "The children's library is at my house," she explained. "I don't have enough shelves yet for all the books."

The couple sat side by side on the couch. Mr. Unrau removed his hat and held it on his knees. Mrs. Unrau was short and comfortably plump, her face round and rosy inside the kerchief. She surveyed the room with quick bright glances—the bookshelves filled to bursting with rows of books in shiny jackets, more books in stacks on the floor, a red box containing paper and pencils, the vase of tiger lilies on the round parlor table. In the citadel of their foes, Mrs. Krahn thought.

She sat opposite them in Henry's brown leather armchair. There was a long silence. At length Mrs. Krahn inquired, "Your crops look good?"

Mr. Unrau's brooding face relaxed slightly. "Good. A little dry."

"Soon is time for the corn . . . how you say?" Mrs. Unrau looked at her husband.

"Detassle."

"*Ja-ah*, the corn de-tassle." She repeated the word several times to herself.

"Didn't somebody from your church win the detassling contest last year?" Mrs. Krahn wondered how this woman endured those layers of dark clothes in summer, that black head scarf. What kind of monotonous life did she lead on the farm without many books or even a radio, which was forbidden? Those women spend their entire lives peeling potatoes, she thought.

"God is good to us," Mrs. Unrau said.

Surprised, Mrs. Krahn looked at her. The colors absent from the dark clothes glowed in the woman's face: pink cheeks, pleasant blue eyes—a flower in a dark frame. The mother of Charles and Peter.

"Your boys are well?" she inquired, wondering if this visit had to do with Peter's asking to come to her library. "Charles is doing well?" This was wicked, since Charles the renegade, now attending a seminary, was a forbidden subject in the Bargen Church, or so she had heard.

Mrs. Unrau darted a quick glance at her husband. He said quietly, "Charles is well. He studies now in Kansas."

"In August he comes!" Mrs. Unrau said, evidently understanding she had been given permission to speak of him. "He has now a ca-ar."

A car! A forbidden thing! Still, they're proud of him, Mrs. Krahn thought. She doesn't mind about the car or she wouldn't have said it so eagerly. Mr. Unrau probably did, though. Aloud she said, "Charles is a fine boy. Very bright. He used to come here to read, you know. Full of questions—he wanted to know everything." She laughed. "Once—he was just little— he asked if everybody walked backwards, would time go the other way. I told him to try it. He said he had, but it didn't work. Later he asked if the sun went around the earth clockwise or counter-clockwise."

Mr. Unrau gazed soberly at the floor; but his wife was considering the question thoughtfully, with attention. After a moment she asked, "Which way it goes?"

So she understood the question, Mrs.Unrau thought in some amazement. "It's clockwise if you look from the north, I believe. And Peter, how is he doing in school? And the girls?"

Mr. Unrau answered. "Peter is first in his class. The girls are finished already in the German school."

"I haven't met your girls," Mrs. Krahn said, thinking they would all look like their mother, round rosy faces in black kerchiefs.

"Peter, he makes always dra-awing," Mrs. Unrau volunteered. "He dra-aw our horses, the cows, the chickens, everything. He dra-aw in school books. The teacher is angry Peter is spoiling the books."

Why didn't they give the child some paper? "You will maybe let him take drawing classes, in the public school?" There were no drawing classes in the German School, she knew.

"Peter wa-ant . . ." Mrs. Unrau began, but her husband checked her with a quick move of his hand.

"Peter will not go to the public school," he said firmly. "Peter will not be disobedient like Charles. We will not speak of that now."

Mrs. Krahn was silent. The brightest children I ever had, one of the German School teachers had said. What spark of genius lay hidden in this family? "I will make coffee?" she offered, still unsure what business they had actually come about.

Mr. Unrau spoke in a formal tone. "There is no need. I come to ask about Mr. Krahn's land next to the German School."

"My land," Mrs. Krahn said.

He glanced at her sharply. "It is in your name now," he corrected himself. "One-quarter acre only, by the fence. We wish to build for our school three more classrooms."

They wanted her land. She should have guessed that. They were always buying land for some project of theirs, extending their farms, building barns. "It's all grown to weeds. I haven't had anybody clear it for three or four years."

He nodded. "Our men will clear it. We offer $75."

They were rich, these Bargen farmers! She was silent for a moment. Then she said, "You may know that I have offered my land—the back piece including part of my garden—to the town for a public library."

He lifted his eyebrows in quick surprise. "You are giving it to the town?"

"No, I'm selling it."

"How much they will give?"

"Oh, I don't know yet. They haven't decided about the library or the price."

"You could withdraw your offer?"

"It's not in writing," Mrs. Krahn said slowly, "but . . . no, I don't think I would do that. They may not want it, of course. They're meeting one of these days to talk about it."

He watched her with dark steady eyes. "We have four rooms only. The children have not enough room on the benches, the desks also are not enough. We wish to build three rooms more. Also we make a small place for playing."

Mrs. Unrau had ceased listening and was looking intently at a picture hung near the bookshelves. "Look, Pa!" she exclaimed suddenly. "Our Donneker's fa-arm!"

The painting was of a white square house, red barns and silo against a pale blue sky, trees, a fence. Mrs. Unrau pointed: "Donneker's house, ga-arden behind, the ba-arn."

He frowned. "We talk business," he reproved her. At once she sat back and placed her hands in her lap; but her eyes strayed to the picture.

"Mrs. Klassen—you know, the postmaster's wife? She painted that," Mrs. Krahn explained. "She paints very well. She has more pictures at her house. You could stop there and see them one day. Who knows, maybe she painted your farm!"

The woman's eyes widened and she started to say something, but recollected herself and was silent.

"We will wait for the word," Mr. Unrau announced. "Maybe the city will not buy all. Maybe one-quarter acre we could have." After a moment he added, "We can pay more."

Mrs. Krahn considered. At last she said, "It's not the money. Mr. Krahn was a teacher in the high school. It was his wish that the land be used for the good of the town. He talked about building a public library here. You can see, I have no room for the books. More are in boxes in the basement. I just got some new art books, there in that package. They should be in a special cabinet to keep out the damp. And we desperately need a reading room, with tables and lamps."

"You crowd books, we crowd children," he replied drily.

Well said! He's no dummy, she thought. She asked curiously, "What sort of books do you have in your German School? They say you use only the Bible and the hymn book."

He smiled a little. "We teach also arithmetic, spelling, history, geography."

"Singing," Mrs. Unrau put in. "Every day, all sing."

She could guess the type of songs the poor kids had to learn. "How about poetry? art?" Mrs. Krahn grabbed a book from the pile on the floor and turned the pages rapidly, stopping at a watercolor plate of a child flying a kite. "Look—these illustrations are by a German lady, Esther Ludwig. Look at the fine lines . . . the colors!"

"*Ja-ah*?" Mrs. Unrau studied the illustration with interest.

Her husband gave it a passing glance. "Drawings the children can make at home. It is for us to teach the life of obedience, not so?"

Mrs. Krahn faced him. "Literature, if it's good, attempts to tell the truth about life just as history does. Writers of history have their prejudices, they slant the truth—you can't believe everything they say either."

He replied calmly, "In a made-up story one can believe nothing. In history, at least something."

Mrs. Krahn took a deep breath. "What about science? Why don't you teach science? The study of God's works in the universe? It's fascinating, wonderful!"

Mrs. Unrau was listening closely. "It is good for children to learn many things, *ja-ah*?" She nodded as if answering some question of her own.

"Goodness, yes, why not?" Mrs. Krahn's face was flushed, her eyes bright. "Look at your own boys, they're brilliant, extremely gifted. They should be studying all sorts of things!"

"Our Peter reads here?" Mr. Unrau's dark accusing eyes swept over her.

She drew a sharp breath, then lifted her chin. "No." But he will, she thought stubbornly.

Mr. Unrau turned away. "He will not read here. Let others do as they wish. For us the path of obedience is plain."

Plain. Yes, very plain. She thought of Eva and grew angry. Should she mention Eva? Surely he knew about her and her grandfather's books. Never mind, Eva was not his business.

A long silence followed. Mrs. Unrau was again looking at the picture, frowning. She half-closed one eye and lifted her hand as if measuring something. Suddenly her eyes cleared. "It is *schrots*," she announced. "The ba-arn, it is crooked, not right." Getting up, she placed her hand along the barn, correcting a line. "This way."

Mrs. Krahn was astonished. Hardly anyone had detected the mistake. How had this unschooled woman . . . . "You're right, the perspective is wrong, just a bit. That was one of her first paintings." It's clear enough where the kids got their brains from, she thought; and the father is nobody's fool either. She looked over at his dark, brooding, upright face and felt the rebellion she always felt when some male leader laid down the law.

"Tell you what," she said brightly. "I'll sell you the quarter-acre if you hire Lottie Schultz to teach music in your school, and Martin Dyck to teach government—they're both wonderful teachers."

Mr. Unrau turned his clear gaze on her in reproof, but said only, "The Board would not agree, Mrs. Krahn." He stood up. His wife at once stood up also. "We will go now. When the Council has made a decision, you will tell me?"

He understood her joke all right, she thought, and didn't like it. On impulse she said to Mrs. Unrau, "Take the painting. I can buy another one."

Mrs. Unrau cast a sidelong glance at her husband and shook her head. "The crooked ba-arn, I would see it every day, *ja-ah*?"

Mrs. Krahn stood at the door and watched them climb into the buggy. He slapped the horse expertly with the reins; they started up and the buggy moved away. They'll go on like that until the end of time, she thought—Mr. Ford leading the world astray with his shiny motor cars. Including Charles.

Charles. She loved that boy. He had found his way. But Peter . . . what would happen to sensitive little Peter? The trouble about Charles would make it doubly hard for him. Hard to break free, even harder to stay. She badly wanted to shake some sense into those people.

At noon she ate rye bread and cheese, thinking about Mrs. Unrau. Somehow she was bypassing that husband of hers without disobeying him—a free bird choosing not to flutter out of the cage. How did she do it? Yet out of the cage, how glorious a bird she would have been!

A fresh wind had sprung up at last and the air smelled of approaching rain. She went about the house closing windows. For the next hour she studied her new books, spending a long time on Rembrandt's self-portrait, noting the finely drawn nose, the intelligent, eloquent eyes and elegant attire. Another time and place, another world. I belong there, not here in this town, she thought . . . a round peg in a square hole, always uncomfortable, I with them and they with me.

Today being Wednesday, her library was not open. She spent the rest of the afternoon mending books—Beatrix Potter, Andersen's fairy tales. Eva could be doing this, she thought. Eva would make a wonderful librarian in the new library. At the thought she sat back. That was it! Get Eva in here after school! She could help the kids choose books, check them out. That would force her to get acquainted with all these authors, read all the marvelous stories she had missed growing up. She would talk to Eva and her mother directly.

Before going to bed that night she read a chapter from Proverbs and prayed for her niece, for Peter and Charles and Mrs. Unrau, with hesitation for Mr. Unrau, and for God's guidance concerning her land.

During the night she awoke. Lightning was flashing in the drifting black clouds, followed by low thunder and sudden spatterings of rain. It didn't last long. The storm was passing to the east, as usual. She went back to sleep.

Next morning early she went out to look at the garden. Small birds flew in and out of the newly washed trees. The tiger lilies, still wet, glittered in the early sunlight, and along the far side of the garden her great blue spruces smelled deliciously of resin. How beautiful, she thought. She envisioned a stately white building rising beyond the evergreens, flanked by beds of asters and marigolds. She wished the Council would hurry up. She wanted to begin building immediately, now, today!

She decided she might as well go into town first thing and get Butcher Dick's curtains; then stop by Klaas's to see if he had any idea what the Council was thinking. By mid-morning the grass would be dry enough to finish digging, and in the afternoon the children would be coming to read.

Butcher Dick lived in a yellow frame house a block from the park. His shop in town, with its enormous three-legged chopping block, was fairly clean; but his house was not. Once a year a group of women went over to clean the place—not, Mrs. Krahn thought, because they loved Butcher Dick so much, but because they couldn't stand seeing dirt.

When Mrs. Krahn arrived at nine, half a dozen women were already busy with rags and buckets. "We need a couple more up here," someone shouted from upstairs.

"I came for the curtains," Mrs. Krahn said. "I can wash them at home."

"Take them and welcome." Mrs. Schroeder, in charge, was scrubbing frying pans in the old sink. "Maybe you could open the windows while you're at it, get some fresh air in here."

Mrs. Krahn pulled a chair to a window of the small living room, climbed up and tugged at the rods. The curtains fell in a dusty heap on the floor. She rolled them up and stuffed them into flour sacks found on the pantry floor; tried to push the window open, but it wouldn't budge—stuck, perhaps painted shut. She gave up and started on a second window.

A voice shrilled from the bedroom: "Ladies, come and see! Mice! Hundreds of them!" The others rushed up to look. A tall bony woman was holding up the bed quilt and pointing to a thick mass of gray dust rolls under the bed. The women burst out laughing.

"*Na,* Leppsche, I thought you really found something," one of them complained, taking a tentative poke at the dust rolls with her broom.

"Smells like a chicken coop in here," another said. She had opened a closet and was looking at the contents with distaste.

The women began bundling together sheets, bed covers, work shirts. "Soak the whole *schmear* in home-made soap with lye, it'll come out fine," one of them advised.

"*Joh*, soap with lye is good," a flat voice remarked. Turning, Mrs. Krahn saw Frieda. Too bad. By tonight everybody in town would know to the last dirty sock what they had found in Mr. Dick's closets. "Go help on the back porch," she said firmly to Frieda, who obediently walked out. Mrs. Krahn returned downstairs, shoved her sacks of curtains toward the door with her foot, and walked to the kitchen to announce that she was leaving.

Mrs. Schroeder had put a kettle of water on the stove and was cutting a pan of plum *platz* into squares. "Well, and what are you doing these days?" she asked Mrs. Krahn.

"Weeding my land," Mrs. Krahn said.

"Takes a man to do it," Mrs. Schroeder remarked, pouring cream from a syrup pail into a pitcher. "Them grass roots is long."

"Oh, I don't try to clear it all, just my front garden. Maybe I'll sell the rest." She refused *platz*. "Unrau from the German School was over yesterday. They want to buy the back lot."

"You don't say!" Mrs. Schroeder was setting out an array of broken cups from Mr. Dick's shelf. "Good school. Kids got to mind." She rinsed out the cups one by one and dried them with a dishtowel made from a flour sack.

"Sent all mine there," observed a plump lady, on her knees scrubbing furiously under the sink with a brush. "Learned a lot more than in public school, let me tell you. Memorized a pile of hymns and scriptures, you wouldn't believe." She wrung out a rag in a pail of water beside her and wiped off the area she had just scrubbed, got up, and went outside to empty the pail.

"What do they want your land for?" Mrs. Schroeder asked. She measured coffee grounds into a kettle of boiling water. The pleasant odor filled the room.

"They want to add on rooms, the school's crowded out." Mrs. Krahn laughed and added, "I told Unrau I'd sell the land if they'd hire Lottie Schultz and Martin Dyck to teach for them."

"Martin? Used to teach at the high school?" Mrs. Schroeder paused, looked at her in astonishment.

"Of course he'd never go there, Lottie either," Mrs. Krahn said hastily, seeing Mrs. Schroeder was taking her seriously. "I was just joking. Anyway the German School'd never ask them."

"I certainly wouldn't think so!" Mrs. Schroeder poured coffee into the cups. "Ladies—coffee!"

Mrs. Krahn looked at the bundles of curtains. "Could one of the men get these over to my house? I can't carry them. No, thank you, I don't want coffee—I'm going into town."

She left the house and walked to Klaas's drug store, thinking that her library was going to be a touch of class in this town. It would be an airy structure with polished floors, low round tables, a deep green rug in the reading room. Not a large building, but beautiful. She would make inquiries about an architect she had heard about in the Cities.

Klaas was waiting on customers, a young couple from out of town. When they left, he came from behind the counter and sat down on one of his old-fashioned chairs. "Been over to Butcher Dick's? How are they getting along?"

"Oh, cleaning their hearts out. I think they enjoy it." She took the chair opposite his.

"He's a lucky man," Klaas said, his old eyes smiling through gold-rimmed glasses. "All those women to take care of him."

"You're the lucky one and you know it," she retorted. "Marina keeps your place upstairs shining—it's more than you deserve! Listen, have you heard anything from the Council? I want to know about my land."

Klaas thought a moment. "I think they met two nights ago. Martin is over at Jungas Hardware—wait here, I'll get him."

He shuffled across the street, and returned shortly with his brother Martin. Though it was a work day Martin wore a white shirt and pressed gray trousers. "On my way to Gessel to check a contract for a grain elevator," Martin explained, "but I got a minute. What's on your mind?"

"You know perfectly well what's on my mind," Mrs. Krahn said. "I want to know what the Council's going to do about my land."

"Nobody called you yet?"

"No." Mrs. Krahn looked at him impatiently.

"How come you want to get rid of it?" Klaas complained. "It's a pity to pull down that orchard. Henry's dad planted it. We used to have fights throwing green apples. Henry's ma would run out with her broom and chase us off."

"It's all going to weeds," she said. "Well, did they decide anything?"

Martin considered her thoughtfully. "I'm not the one to tell you, but they're willing to pay $60 for the quarter-acre nearest the house. Tchetter wants the other quarter for a hatchery."

"*Liebe Zeit!* Absolutely not! A hatchery!"

"That's what I told them," he remarked, smiling. "I told them you wanted a nice green lawn with shade trees around a library with marble pillars."

"Did they agree about the library, though?"

"Well, they talked about it. They couldn't build for a while. First they want to construct a laundry for the Old Folks Home so they won't have to use the one at the hospital. And Klassen complains his post office needs repairs."

"Oh, stuff and nonsense!" she exclaimed angrily. "Next they'll want to pave the lake or some other *dommheit.* The post office looks fine to me!"

Martin grinned and went on. "They don't want any strings attached, either."

She looked up quickly. "What sort of strings?"

"They don't want it called the Krahn Library. They say if it's built with town money it should be the Windamer Public Library."

"Who said anything about a Krahn Library? All I want is donate one room and call it the Krahn Reading Room."

He shook his head. "No Krahn. They say it would bring up all the old trouble. People might not like it."

"What's the matter with them!" Her eyes blazed. "He's been gone twelve years."

"Twelve years in this town is as one day," Martin observed. After a pause he added, "And sometimes one day is as twelve years."

She looked him straight in the face. "Exactly what did they say?"

"The old things. Henry was modernistic, young people being led astray, that sort of thing. Same things they say about me."

"Pooh! The kids were crazy about him. Who's saying this, Bekker?"

Klaas, arranging bottles in his display window, remarked, "Henry taught them to think. What they wanted was—."

She interrupted. "What they wanted was somebody to lead the kids by the nose! Like Hubbart. The children hated him. But Hubbart's father was a deacon in the Parkside Church—they couldn't ignore a pious family like that!"

"Now, Grace," Martin reproved her. "Hubbart did the best he

could. Anyway the main objection to Henry was that business about Lottie."

Mrs. Krahn closed her eyes. "I don't believe it."

"In this town a principal should never, never take his female teachers out to lunch," Martin observed drily, "or talk to them in his office with the door shut."

"They were discussing the music for the Easter program, for Pete's sake!" she cried. "Go ask Lottie! The whole thing was completely silly!"

"Of course it was, everybody knew it. But when a man like Bekker has it in for somebody, he uses anything he can get his hands on. And of course Pfeil and a couple others are only too happy to go along with him. Not everybody—Johann Jungas stood up for you."

Mrs. Krahn rose. "I'm not arguing with those *glumskups*. I'm going straight home and sell my land to the German School. They'll give me a good price, cash!"

"The German School?" Martin exclaimed. "What are you talking about?"

"Unrau was by yesterday making an offer. Quite a bit more than what the city will pay, incidentally. I'll take their money and build a library, myself, where my garden is. Call it the Krahn Library!"

"Ask Helena Jungas to help you," Martin suggested. "She tars their roof every year, by herself."

"Joke if you want to," she retorted. "It's the women who get things done in this town. You men just sit around and squabble."

"The Council—they're mostly good men, trying to help the town," Klaas said mildly. "They just see things different from you."

"They can't see past their noses!" Mrs. Krahn snapped. "Don't you go sticking up for them, Klaas Dyck."

Martin interrupted. "But why sell to the German School? You really want them in your back yard?"

"I'd rather a lot of other things," she said, 'but they're offering good money. If the Council knows I've got another offer, maybe they'll wake up and do something."

Martin looked at her thoughtfully for a long moment. "Be careful what you give your land for, Grace," he said at last. "Whatever's built there is going to be there for a long time. It'll change the town, one way or another. Give us a few years, we'll put up a nice library."

"And where am I supposed to sleep in the meantime, in the potato bin? Books are stacked over half my bed."

'You can have my store," Klaas said. "I can move into Saathoff's shoe repair place. He wants to sell."

"Good! I'll move in tomorrow! Leave your candy behind—the kids can eat it while they read." She stomped out of the store, slamming the door ungraciously behind her, thoroughly upset by Martin's news.

On the way home she considered asking Johann and other store owners for private funds for a library, but decided it wouldn't work. The project was too big. Also, small-town businessmen had to be careful whom they endorsed, and if it was true that the nonsense about Lottie was still on people's minds, she would get nowhere.

The sacks of curtains were on the front step. She dragged them inside, pulled out the curtains and put them in the laundry tub to soak; prepared supper; and went upstairs to bed, still pondering the matter of her land.

She wondered whose side God was on. He might for some reason be on the side of the German School—it was inconceivable to her but one couldn't rule it out. Really, though, having that school built right up against her library would be like putting the Amalekites next to the Israelites, no love lost in either direction. It would change the town forever, as Martin had said. On the other hand, if God was on the side of the Council (excluding Bekker), she would have to be patient, believing in the good faith of the town fathers. She was not sure she was capable of this act of faith. And if perchance God was on her side, He had better do something, the sooner the better.

She knelt down intending to pray that her land would be a place of blessing, especially to the young people; but her mind wandered, and she found herself planning ways to lure Peter in to read without Unrau finding out.

Next morning she was awakened early by the ringing of the telephone. It was Lottie. Flustered, half-crying, she protested to Mrs. Krahn that nobody had asked her about teaching at the German School, and she would rather leave town than do it if they did ask.

"What? Wait a minute—what's all this?"

Didn't she know about it? Mrs. Reimer had told her last night that she had heard Grace Krahn was selling the German School her land for a building, and in return the school was going to hire Lottie and Martin Dyck as teachers. She didn't see how anybody could make such arrangements without asking her . . . that was the last place on earth she would . . . .

Mrs. Krahn interrupted. "Wait. Stop. Where did Mrs. Reimer hear this?"

From old Taunte Wiensche. It had been told to her, Lottie, as a fact. Lottie began to cry. She didn't want to give up her piano students to teach in that . . . .

"No, no, good gracious, they'd never ask you—they don't even allow pianos. Listen, I did say something like that but it was only a joke . . . yes, a joke, not true at all!" She promised to call Mrs. Reimer, Taunte Wiensche too, and explain the mistake. Lottie was not to worry, there was nothing in it. No, absolutely nothing. Yes, she was sure. Yes, she would call today, right now.

She hung up, much disturbed. Who in the world could have talked this around? Not Mrs. Schroeder, and she was the only one who had heard the joke. She telephoned Martin. The phone rang many times before Martin, breathless, answered—he had been out watering his cucumbers. Why had she called so early, had someone died?

"Not yet," she said sarcastically. "I just wanted to warn you to put on your black suit and hat, the German School board is coming over to ask you to teach for them." She explained the whole matter.

Martin was delighted with the joke and hoped it would get around, just to see what people would say.

"No, never! I don't care a bean about you, but Lottie's frightfully upset. Next thing they'll be bringing up that old stuff against her. If you hear anything, just say you know for a fact it isn't true."

Next she called up Mrs. Reimer, who stated that Taunte Wiensche had met her at prayer meeting with the surprising news. "I thought it was a good idea," Mrs. Reimer said. "It's about time they got some good teachers over there."

Taunte Wiensche, being deaf, could not understand what Mrs. Krahn was saying. She loved to talk on the phone, however. She told several stories about her childhood when she had boarded at a farm house for ten cents a week, asked about Mrs. Krahn's raspberries, gave her a recipe for garlic dill pickles, and finally mentioned seeing Frieda outside the grocery store yesterday. Frieda had told her the German School was hiring Lottie Schultz and also Martin Dyck, the teacher of evolution. She thought the school must be going downhill, they ought to be teaching the Bible.

"It's a mistake," Mrs. Krahn shouted into the phone. "Mis-take! Frieda had it wrong. No, that's right, they aren't going to . . . yes, a mistake. Martin's not going to teach there, he's working at the lumberyard . . . no, not Lottie either." Taunte Wiensche was very glad to hear it. She remembered Lottie had been in some trouble but had forgotten what it was.

Mrs. Krahn hung up. Frieda. If Frieda had heard . . . but how? Finally she recalled that Frieda had been working out on the back porch just beyond the kitchen. She might have, must have, overheard her talking to Mrs. Schroeder. Well, there was no hope, then. Whatever Frieda got hold of might as well be broadcast from the rooftops. It was going to be a lively day. She made her morning coffee and waited for the phone to ring.

At nine-thirty a call came from Bekker. He was extremely angry. He accused Mrs. Krahn, speaking in rapid shrill Low German, of dealing behind the Council's back, of scheming for a better price while pretending to make a generous offer to the town. She told him that she had heard of no Council decision at the time Mr. Unrau talked to her. It didn't matter, he said, she could have asked. They weren't going to be fooled by her tricks, they couldn't afford a cent more. If it came to that, they could buy Olaf Tollefson's land north of town for much less.

Much good may it do you, that swamp! she thought. She explained as calmly as she could that a mistake had been made. There was absolutely no agreement with the German School. Her offer to the town stood firm, providing a library would be built there.

But Bekker wasn't finished. Her land, he said, was very suitable for Tchetter's hatchery—the man was ready to build, had the money, and what the town needed was business expansion and not a library, which would likely be the ruination of the youth with all them worldly books.

"I'm not selling for a hatchery!" she shouted, and slammed down the phone, muttering a fervent wish that Bekker would go back to South Dakota to live among his hard-headed brethren. She got out scissors and began to cut with violent slashes a cardboard box into squares for library cards.

The phone rang. It was her cousin's son, a carpenter from near Windrow. He professed to be deeply hurt that she would sell property to the very group, the German School, that had publicly denounced Henry years ago.

"I haven't made a land deal of any kind," she told him crossly. She did not like the young man.

He was deeply hurt anyhow. He felt that if she was selling land she might have notified him—he was thinking of building a couple of small rentals, possibly in Windamer.

"I don't want a bunch of renters next to me, buy somewhere else—buy Tollefson's swamp!" she told him, and hung up.

Half an hour later a knock sounded at the front door. She found a delegation from the Bargen Church waiting: Mr. Unrau and Elder Wiens. She invited them in.

They took off their black hats and sat down. Elder Wiens surveyed the shelves of books, frowning severely, both feet planted firmly in front of him. He inquired about the rumor they had heard just that morning. She explained everything carefully, apologizing for her levity. The misfortune was that Frieda had overheard her foolish remark. They knew Frieda? Yes. Well, there it was.

Mr. Unrau said nothing. Elder Wiens was not satisfied. He pointed out that any rumor that people like Lottie Schultz and Martin Dyck would be hired by the German School would give the school a very bad name. Something must be done.

Mrs. Krahn suggested that she write up a statement confirming her offer of land to the town and print it in the next *Herald.* For their part, the school board could print an official list of their teachers for the fall. As for the rumor, the less said, the better.

The men agreed, after some discussion, that this was the best that could be done. "No more jokes, Mrs. Krahn!" cried Elder Wiens, wagging a long finger under her nose. "You see what the devil does with joking!"

"I certainly do, in this town anyway!" she replied tartly. Mr. Unrau cast a dark glance at her . . . he got my meaning all right, she thought.

As a parting shot Elder Wiens pointed to her brightly colored books. "Such things lead children astray, like iniquitous Eve they forsake obedience and are smitten of God, who . . . ."

"Unlike you, I prefer to look freely upon all of God's good

creation," she interrupted in quiet fury. "Now, if you please, I have work to do." Rant away, she thought fiercely, I'm a match for you!

The Elder fumed at this rebuke from a woman, glared at her, drew himself up to full height; but Mr. Unrau grasped him firmly by the elbow and, wishing Mrs. Krahn a good day, piloted his companion out the door.

She stood stiff and straight until they were gone, then shut the door hard. She walked about, distracted, picking up books and putting them down again. Never, not if God himself commanded it, could she tolerate people like Wiens. Even Unrau saw what a pest the man was. But it was Unrau she would have to reckon with in the end. He was as inexorable as stone when it came to his beliefs; yet he was an intelligent, just man. She wondered who would win in the battle over little Peter. For battle there would certainly be.

Seeing the curtains still soaking in the tub in the back porch, she dumped them in the washing machine, ran hot water into it, added quantities of soap, and started it going.

It occurred to her that Frieda had possibly done her a favor. From all points of view it was now inadvisable to sell her land to the German School, at least for a long time. That temptation had been removed. Maybe the school would move somewhere else altogether—a solution, she thought, altogether to be desired. In the end she might have to bless Frieda who, in God's idea of a joke, might have been the answer to her prayer for guidance.

In the afternoon the children came. For two hours she took in books, answered questions, mended torn pages, put new books into eager hands, wrote down names, smiled, encouraged, patted heads. Norah's little Carly always came. Two or three were from the German School, from less dogmatic families apparently. The children skipped out, their treasures tucked under their arms: Peter Rabbit, alphabet books, books about engines and whales and the North Pole.

Peter, of course, had not come, nor would he, not until all this blew over, maybe not until next year when he was older and more able to decide things for himself. She would have to bide her time.

Just before supper the phone rang again. It was Martin, not joking this time. Bekker had come into the hardware store in the afternoon and stirred up a row, saying that the town needed a revival (actually, a hatchery, Mrs. Krahn thought), not a library, which was worldly etc. etc. Johann had tried to shut him up, but Bekker never shut up as long as he had an audience.

"Who listens to him!" she exclaimed.

She shouldn't underestimate the problem, Martin warned. Bekker had a following, a minority it was true, but strongly vocal. They could swing the conservatives their way, at least enough to do damage.

She was silent. At last she said, "What can I do?"

"We'll have to wait it out," he said. "Bekker will be off the Council in two years."

"I can't wait forever!" she cried out. "I'm sixty-three!"

"My grandchildren will have to do some of the things I've wanted to do," he said. "We should have been born later."

"I know what I'm going to do," she told him. "I'm going to tell Frieda something nasty about Bekker to start things going the other way for a change!"

She heard him snicker. "By the way, he was bragging that God sent him an inch of rain the other night. How much did you get?"

"Exactly as much as you got—six drops per square inch!" she retorted, and slammed down the receiver.

She went outside to look at her garden. The late afternoon sun lit up the blue spruces and the tops of the apple trees. Bushes and trees stood solid and silent, exactly the way she had seen them hundreds of times. The land doesn't care what's built on it, she thought moodily, or if anything is built at all—it can sit here and wait, five years, twenty years . . . but I haven't got twenty years.

She knelt and began tearing at the sharp-edged grass around the raspberries, yanking it out by the roots in sliding handfuls. She worked furiously for almost an hour. Only when she noticed that she was breaking off some of the young vines did she sit back on her heels, breathing hard. The joke was on her, it seemed. Her flippant remark had started an avalanche. For once in her life she should have been *fromm,* proper.

She crumbled a clod of dirt in her hands . . . too dry. The whole garden needed a good soaking rain, the inch Bekker got. She flung the bits of dirt away. "All right, rain on Bekker if you want to," she cried, addressing the heavens, "just keep him away from me! Wiens too!"

It occurred to her that this place was, after all, still hers . . . an island, a refuge, a safe place where unwanted persons could not intrude. She could hang her walls full of paintings, stack books everywhere. A mercy left to her by Henry, under God, whose good creation the land was. As for the garden, it would rain sooner or later.

She rose stiffly from her knees and walked to the house. At the steps she looked back: the raspberry vines, freed of encumbrance, swung in pale green arcs over the tumbled black earth.

She went in, washed her hands, and, remembering her agreement with Unrau, scribbled a note to the *Windamer Herald.* Then she called her cousin's son on the telephone and told him crossly to get out as soon as he could to build her more book shelves.

A FAREWELL FOR AGANETHA

IT WAS A Saturday afternoon funeral.

That was the reason, the people explained afterwards, feeling ashamed, that so few had showed up. Saturday was the day the farmers reserved for business in town. At home the women were elbow-deep in baking and cleaning, preparing for Sunday. Furthermore, it was the last day of the annual missions conference of the Parkview Church—the sessions had finished late, after one o'clock, and their hosts were busy serving lunch to the delegates.

No, it was not a good day for the funeral. Also it had been miserably hot that week, and the Valley Church was not a cool place. Morning services in summer were bad enough; everyone fanned with the cardboard fans provided by Grogan's Elevator Co., kept in the hymnal racks, and endured until the benediction. But fans would not help very much on a stifling afternoon when the sun beat down on the western windows.

Besides all that, there had been a rash of funerals lately. First, Taunte Wiens at the good old age of 81. Then Uncle Berg. Then, shocking the town, Katie Harder, who had been ill but should have recovered given her natural youthful strength, but apparently she had had no will to live, had simply turned her face to the wall and died. Her funeral at Parkview was crowded out, of course, banks upon banks of flowers, the richest of caskets from Minneapolis. But the people's tolerance for funerals was wearing thin. Nettie should have waited a little.

Whatever the reason, only a few mourners sat scattered here and there in the dim sanctuary of the Valley Church on the afternoon of Nettie's funeral. The casket stood in front below the low wine-colored curtain that curved around the stage on a brass rail. Near it were arranged a few sprays of flowers—red, gaudy yellow, blue, standing stiffly above white ribbons embossed with the names of the senders.

The people sat quietly in the varnished pews, waiting. Up in the balcony the flies buzzed loudly against the hot panes of small windows. The people paid no attention; they were accustomed to the summer buzzing of flies. Long shafts of light shone through the west windows and made hot bright patches on the floor. The people fanned themselves and whispered, waiting for the pianist to start playing. She should have been here by now.

Tante Lieze, sitting midway down the rows of pews, hands folded in her lap, studied the casket. A decent plain gray. Whoever picked it out had understood that unnecessary expense must be avoided. Nettie wouldn't have minded. She would, in fact, have been surprised at the quilted satin inside and the wreath of lilies on top—for that matter, that anybody at all was attending her funeral. "My, my, so very nice, you are all so very busy!"

Two women she did not know sat just in front of her. They plied their fans vigorously, whispering at first, then speaking aloud as no pianist had arrived. "Worked her to death and that's a fact!" The speaker wore a large straw hat trimmed with a cascade of crimson and mauve flowers. Altogether too fancy for a funeral, Tante Lieze thought. The lady went on talking. "That steamy hot kitchen ain't no place for an old person like her. Them big cooking pots is heavy as cream cans. She wore herself right out lifting them around. In this heat, too."

Her companion nodded. She was decently dressed in black, with a small dark hat. She murmured, "I worked at the Home once for four days, but I couldn't take it. My feet gave out. I felt sorry for the cooks, being canning time with all those vegetables to put up, but my feet were swelled up so bad I had to quit."

The first woman sniffed angrily. "They expect too much at that Old Folks place. It's the Board's fault. All they worry about is money, they're scared a penny will roll loose somewheres. That old Pfeil is stubborn as a pile of rocks." She opened her purse and pulled out a handkerchief to wipe her forehead. "Late starting, wish they'd hurry up."

"I heard they had trouble finding anybody for the piano, singers too," the other observed. "Not that Nettie doesn't deserve better, poor thing, but . . . ." She broke off—someone near by had broken out in a fit of coughing.

The old people from the Home sat across the aisle. They had probably been there half an hour already, Tante Liesze thought; they always came early for lack of anything else to do. They sat bowed by age and infirmity, stared vaguely at the front of the church or fidgeted with purses and hats. It was Uncle Toews coughing.

They'll miss Nettie, those old folks, Tante Liesze thought, and not know what they're missing. Nettie had always been there, but they never paid much attention to her because she never scolded or bossed them around. Whatever they said, she agreed . . . yes, yes, the soup was certainly too salty, she would tell the cook . . . oh my no, they should never put wax on the floor, anybody could slip and break a hip. The women in the kitchen used to joke about it. If they told her the cooking pots needed scouring, she would agree vigorously that yes, they should have been scoured long ago, and start hauling them to the sink. If they instead said the pots were good enough, she would agree that a little black on the bottom never hurt anyone, and put them back on the shelf. Well, the old people would miss her; but they would soon settle down again and forget what it was they were missing.

The woman in the flowered hat was talking again. "Trouble with Nettie was, she couldn't say no. If it was me, I'd tell 'em straight out, so much and no more. But not her. She'd work till she dropped and apologize for dropping. No, you got to complain when it's too much." This lady would complain no matter what, Tante Lieze thought, her eyes on the fancy hat.

A small commotion at the back of the church denoted the arrival of the pallbearers, who filed in and sat in a stiff row in a front pew, looking uncomfortable in their dark formal suits. The pianist still had not come in.

". . . worked like a hired hand at her brother's farm, on her day off, can you imagine? They made her candle eggs." The woman spoke indignantly, the flowers on the hat quivering.

Her companion spoke up suddenly. "With six children and all those chickens, Leona couldn't keep up. She told me she was always tired."

"Why couldn't them kids help more? 'Nettie, help me fix these stockings, Nettie, help me with the weeding,' Nettie do this, Nettie do that. Them kids was worse than anybody."

"She doted on the kids . . . only family she had."

Their conversation came to an abrupt end when a door to the stage opened and a young girl hurried in, set up her music and began to play.

A stir at the back door: the family were coming in. Silently, in single file, they walked down the aisle to a front pew: Nettie's brother Pete from the farm, his wife Leona and their brood of children; a cousin from Oklahoma; a few relatives from other towns. Leona sat bowed with her hands in her lap. The older boys fidgeted in tight collars. The smaller girls looked shyly around, proud in Sunday dresses and new hair ribbons.

The lady in the flowered hat was leaning forward, looking eagerly toward the family. It was not considered proper to show grief in public, but there were always tell-tale signs: red eyes, noses being blown into handkerchiefs. The family sat subdued and silent; they were doing very well.

The audience was hushed now, listening to hymns being played on the piano. Tante Lieze smelled the faint perfume of flowers. It seemed strange to her to think of Nettie lying there on the satin, still as a stone, the busy hands motionless on her breast.

Yes, the Old Folks Home would miss her, she thought. Nettie's long scraggy arms and bony fingers had worked with amazing speed. She did the distasteful jobs—wiped out ovens when pies ran over, washed grease splatters off the walls, shelled bushels of peas some farmer donated, washed the kitchen floor by hand every night, late, before going apologetically to bed. If there wasn't anybody up to apologize to, she probably apologized to the kitchen clock, Tante Lieze thought. Nettie always wore an apron, always smelled like soap and kitchen fat. Who would they find to take her place? The younger people refused to work like that any more.

The minister and a trio of ladies walked in and sat down. An embarrassed latecomer, a young woman with a girl of nine or ten, slid into the pew next to Tante Lieze. The child took from her mother's handbag a large tablet and a box of crayons and began to draw.

The minister made his opening remarks and read the obituary. Aganetha Fast ... born ... confessed her Savior at age eleven, baptized into the Valley Church ... because of hardship in the home left school at an early age to help her parents ... known as a quiet, kind and hard-working woman ... twenty-four years in the Old Folks Home ... fell ill twelve days ago, died at the local hospital at the age of sixty-four years five months and thirteen days ... survived by her brother and his family, cousins and other relatives, friends, who mourned her untimely passing. He read a selection of scripture passages. "I go to prepare a place for you . . . will receive you unto myself, that where I am, there ye may be also." He closed the Bible. "Our dear sister has gone to the place prepared for her, a glorious place, to her rest and reward."

Something was going on among the old people: one of the elderly women was grumbling audibly while Rempel, the attendant, rummaged hastily in an ancient black handbag. At last the attendant pulled out a pair of glasses and handed them to the woman, who put them on and quieted down.

Tante Lieze smiled to herself, remembering something that had happened at the Home. Nettie had been upstairs washing the hair of the second-floor ladies, as was usual on Friday. But at supper time one of the women had refused to come down, had sat in her room in a tiff, scolding at the top of her voice that she couldn't see, her eyes were burning, Nettie had gotten soap in her eyes, she would never let Nettie wash her hair again, and on and on. Nobody could calm her down. Soon another old lady had begun the same complaint—she couldn't see either because of soap in her eyes. The two of them fussed so loudly that the whole second floor was in turmoil. The attendants ran for ointments and soothing eye-washes, but nothing helped. Nettie, beside herself with distress, had wanted to run for a doctor—she had been so careful not to get soap in their eyes, she said. At last the supervisor had come upstairs to examine the women's eyes but found not even a redness. Remembering that the women took off their glasses before hair-washing and put them on a small table, she had finally put two and two together, switched the two women's glasses; and sure enough, both ladies found they could see perfectly well. Nettie had fallen all over herself apologizing though it wasn't her fault. The women in the kitchen, laughing heartily, had told Tante Lieze the story.

The minister was describing the glories of the place prepared by God, a place of no pain, no tears, a shining city of gold. The people listened with reverence. The old folks held their purses and canes, looking toward the front, except Uncle Funk who had gone to sleep. Nobody paid any attention to him; Uncle Funk always slept during services; he would wake up at the benediction.

The little girl was poking her mother, wanting to show what she had drawn. Tante Lieze glanced over: a scribbled blue sky, tall yellow towers or gates, a small brown stick figure floating in clouds . . . Nettie entering heaven, probably. The mother looked down briefly, smiled, and resumed listening.

The ladies' trio sang "Does Jesus Care?" Fortunately only two verses—it was too hot to listen properly. "Haven't practiced much," the woman in the flowered hat whispered. Her neighbor nodded slightly.

". . . realize that even the lowliest among us is of great worth in the sight of God. Our dear sister . . . ." The minister was speaking with great sincerity as if to make up for the poor singing. Certainly Nettie had been the humblest, the most insignificant figure in the community, Tante Lieze thought, someone to joke affectionally about if she was mentioned at all. Few people spoke to Nettie even at the Home. She was always busy in the kitchen or scuttling down the hall with a mop, her thin hair straggling about her ears and the bib of her apron sagging. If someone did stop her to say hello, her face would light up, her eyes blink rapidly behind the thick glasses, and she would stammer hurried remarks, agreeing with whatever the visitor was saying, anxious to please. "Oh yes, it is so nice you came to see Uncle Regehr, you are so very busy, he will be so happy for a visit, room 5, just go in." Even at the hospital when Tante Lieze went to see her, she had apologized: "It's so nice you came, oh my yes, it's so very hot outside."

The little girl had placed her tablet on the bench and gone to sleep with her head on her mother's lap. To the drawing she had added several figures that looked like angels, and what looked like sun-rays around windows with purple and red panes. Tante Lieze recalled the stained-glass windows of the cathedral in the Cities she had once seen, together with Dietrich, before Frieda was born.

She wondered who the young woman beside her was. A relative of one of the old people? Old Mrs. Haasla's niece, perhaps? She recalled the day Nettie had brought up a supper tray to cantankerous, bed-ridden Mrs. Haasla, whose mind was wandering. The old lady had taken one look at the tray—a bowl of sweet milk soup and a square of bread without butter—and said haughtily, "That stinking stuff I did not order!" She had grabbed the bread and thrown it into a corner. Nettie had hastily snatched the tray to get the soup out of her reach, saying, "No, no, maybe this isn't your tray, I'll go and see," and begun to walk out. At once the woman roared, "Where are you taking my tray?" Confused, Nettie hurried back. "Where's my bread, don't they even give bread any more?" Mrs. Haasla shouted. Nettie had picked it up, dusted it off, and put in the plate, whereupon Mrs. Haasla smiled as if nothing had happened and said, "Thank you, you may go now." The attendants had laughed about that one all week, Nettie along with them, delighted at the joke.

With an effort Tante Lieze turned her attention back to the service. It was hot, her eyes wanted to close.

The minister was reaching the end of his sermon. "Let us be faithful, each in the place God in his wisdom has put us, however humble." The audience listened quietly. Up in the balcony the flies buzzed loudly. The shafts of hot sunlight crept across the floor.

The minister's voice faded. The hush grew more and more intense. Now, with an indescribable mingling of light, along the sides of the great aisle, people were gathering, rank upon rank, a multitude, the walls receding . . . Old Uncle Tieszen from the Home was there, she saw with surprise, others long gone. They stood with bright faces, expectant. Overhead the high vaults of the ceiling soared upward, fanning out at a height so great the topmost panels vanished into the deep blue of heaven. A fragrance, clean and cool and fresh from the

Tree of Life, filled the immense space. A radiance shone from the great throne of gold at the far end of the hall, and from Him who sat upon it. A trumpet sounded, its brilliant tones circling, echoing high above. The people turned, not toward the King, but toward the towering pillars guarding the entrance. White-winged angels swung open, slowly, the massive doors. A small bent figure entered, alone, wearing an apron; paused, bewildered, gazed awestruck at the multitude, caught sight of the King. He had risen and was standing with right hand outstretched. With hesitant step and brightening face she walked toward him, unaware of her worn shoes, her sagging apron, between the ranks of rejoicing friends. The rustling of their white robes filled the hall . . . .

. . . the congregation was rising. They would file by the casket, row by row, to view for the last time Nettie's plain face, remote now in death. The young woman wakened the girl and the two hurried out, the child clutching her picture. The old people from the Home shuffled slowly along, bent over their canes. Uncle Funk walked briskly by, looking around as if to prove he was wide awake. "At least there'll be a breeze in the cemetery," the woman in the flowered hat said. "You going?" The other shook her head and murmured something about her husband waiting at Stoesz's. They moved out of the pew. The minister came down to say a few words to the family before they took their last farewell look at the deceased.

Tante Lieze did not rise. Holding her handbag, she sat with bowed head. Long after the family had gone, after the casket had been closed and carried out by the pall-bearers, after the funeral director had removed the flowers from the stands and gone out, closing the door softly behind him, she sat on, astonished.

GUIDE TO LOW GERMAN TERMS AND PRONUNCIATION

PRONUNCIATION

ae = ay: *nae* = nay

a = ah: *danke* = dahnke, *na* = nah

au = ow: *Taunte* = Townteh, *Kaut* = kowt

ch at the end of a word = soft sound as in Bach

e at the end of a word = eh: *Taunte* = Townteh, *Lentye* = Leyntyeh, *de* = dey

eu = oy: *heute* = hoyte, *Freude* = Froydeh

j = y: *joh* = yoh, *et jeit* = et yeht, *Taunte Joht* = Townteh Yoht, *fejaete* = feyehteh

kj = k + soft sound like the "y" in "yes": *ekj* = ekye

o = oh: *schrots* = schrohts

oe = ay: *schoen* = shayn

s at the beginning of a word = z: *so es et* = zo es et

sch = sh: *schnapps* = shnahps

w = v: *waut* = vout

DEFINITIONS of Low German terms (High German words are marked HG)

ach du lehva!: oh my goodness!
ach waut!: oh, what!
Alpenkraeuter: a herbal tonic
auf Deutsch, bitte (HG): in German, please
borscht: soup made of cabbage, dill, etc.
danke: thanks
dankeschoen: thank you
daut es schrotz: it's crooked
daut meint aula nuscht: all that means nothing
de: he, that person
de es nuscht: he is nothing
de es schwack: he is weak
Diese Stadt habe ich 14 Sept 1885 besucht: (HG) I visited this city on September 14, 1885
domma Lied: foolish people
dommheit: foolishness
dommkopf: dummy, idiot, fool
dommsta: foolish person
du Kaut!: you cat!
ekj kaun den nich fejaewe: I can't forgive them
emma Kaute: always cats
ekj brocht die waut: I brought you something
et jeit: it goes, it's okay
fael mol dank schoen: thank you very much
ferekjt: crazy
fromm: pious, proper
gauns schoen: very pretty
glumskup: cheesehead
goondach: good day (HG, *guten Tag*)

Grosser Gott, Wir Loben Dich (HG): Great God, We Praise You (a hymn)
Heute ist Sonntag (HG): today is Sunday

Hier unter dem Baum	(HG)	Here under the tree
dank ich dem Herrn mit Freude		I thank God with joy
denn er hat alles so schoen gemacht,		because he has made everything so lovely
die Erde singt von Freude.		the earth sings for joy

Himmel sei dank (HG): thank heavens, heaven be thanked
joh: yes (HG *jah*)
Jugendverein: young people's meeting
Kaut, Kaute: cat, cats
kommt nen: come in
Leewe Tiet!: good grief! (HG *Liebe Zeit!)*
Mooss: a sweet fruit soup
na: well, oh, well
na joh: well, yes
nae: no (HG, *nein*)
na nae: but no!
nae oba: you don't say!
nein, danke (HG): no, thank you
nuscht fejaete, nuscht fejaewa: forget nothing, forgive nothing
pirozhky: pastries made of fruit wrapped in a square of dough and baked
platz: dessert made of a dough layer with fruit on top, baked
plaupamuel: blabbermouth
schlopbenkj: sleep-bench
schmear: smear, spread on sloppily
schnapps: brandy, liquor
schoen: pretty
schrotz: crooked
she or *je* ending to a name: familiar form of the name, e.g. Wiensche = Mrs. Wiens
so es et: that's how it is

Taunte: aunt (HG, *Tante*)
Tweeback: bun made of two balls of dough, one on top of the other (HG, *Zwieback*)
ungescheit: improper
unsere Eltern: our parents
waut du sagst: what are you saying
waut deist?: what are you doing?
Weide Meine Laemmer (HG): Feed My Sheep

Note: exclamations like *Leewe Tiet!* are not translated literally (love+time!) but given an equivalent in English (good grief!).

CPSIA information can be obtained at www.ICGtesting.com
Printed in the USA
...0743280313

BV00002B/5/P